LipService

OTHER TITLES AVAILABLE BY JESS WELLS

The Price of Passion, an erotic novel

Lesbians Raising Sons, an anthology

AfterShocks, a novel

Two Willow Chairs, short stories

The Dress, The Cry, and a Shirt With No Seams,
   short stories and erotica

The Sharda Stories, prose

The Herstory of Prostitution in Western Europe,
   essays

Run, prose

LipService

alluring new lesbian erotica

edited by Jess Wells

alyson books
los angeles | new york

MANUFACTURED IN THE UNITED STATES OF AMERICA.
COVER DESIGN BY CHRISTOPHER HARRITY.

THIS TRADE PAPERBACK ORIGINAL IS PUBLISHED BY
ALYSON PUBLICATIONS,
P.O. BOX 4371, LOS ANGELES, CALIFORNIA 90078-4371.
DISTRIBUTION IN THE UNITED KINGDOM BY
TURNAROUND PUBLISHER SERVICES LTD.,
UNIT 3 OLYMPIA TRADING ESTATE, COBURG ROAD, WOOD GREEN,
LONDON N22 6TZ ENGLAND.

FIRST EDITION: OCTOBER 1999

99 00 01 02 03 **a** 10 9 8 7 6 5 4 3 2 1

ISBN 1-55583-503-1

LIBRARY OF CONGRESS CATALOGING-IN-PUBLICATION DATA
    LIP SERVICE : ALLURING NEW LESBIAN EROTICA / EDITED BY JESS
    WELLS.—1ST ED.
        ISBN 1-55583-503-1
        1. LESBIANS—SEXUAL BEHAVIOR—FICTION. 2. SHORT STORIES,
    AMERICAN—WOMEN AUTHORS. 3. LESBIANS' WRITINGS, AMERICAN.
    4. EROTIC STORIES, AMERICAN. I. WELLS, JESS.
    PS648.L47L57 1999
    813'.01083538'086643—DC21   99-34648 CIP

CREDITS
• "THIS IS THE FAMOUS BATH SCENE FROM DIRTY ALICE—REVISED" FIRST AP-
PEARED IN *THE LEADING EDGE*. EDITED BY LADY WINSTON, LACE PUBLICA-
TIONS, 1987. THE STORY IS EXCERPTED FROM *DIRTY ALICE* BY MERRIL HAR-
RIS, OLYMPIA PRESS, 1970.
• COVER PHOTOGRAPH BY PHYLLIS CHRISTOPHER.

Contents

Introduction

Lips ripe with lust, moist and parted. Lips grazing your earlobe, tracing your rib cage, pressing into your knuckles in supplication, or whispering orders you long to follow. Lips introducing themselves to the inside of your thigh, ushering a tongue to the place where you live.

Thirty authors offer you lip service of the finest kind—tantalizing stories of lesbian sex. Sex in fantasy, in public, with delicious "Blood Hunger" by Ginger Simon, or with Xena—make that Jeena—in "A Real-life Superhero" by Kate Dominic. Sex with the postal delivery person in Anne Seale's "Rural Free Delivery" or the rock-and-roll star in Wendy Caster's "The Sacred Sex Tour." Imagine sex with the minister of a Norwegian small town in "God Blessed Eva" by Randi Oklevik Solberg or with the woman of your dreams, the woman you've lived with for years. Savor stories "Of Human Bondage" by Danya Ruttenberg and "Love Play" by Myra LaVenue. Relish tales of sex in the long-term relationship or the adored sought and conquered. And then there are funny stories such as Rhonda Jackson's "The Perfect Gift" and magical stories such as "Chosen" by Renette Toliver, who leads us through the dark streets of New Orleans.

We offer you a variety of writing styles—dense prose in

"Deo Gratias" by Connie Fox, conversational ease in "Marisol" by Carla Díaz, and the poetic wonders of Sarah Van Arsdale and Juliet Crichton. There are lots of fresh voices here— unique angles by veteran writers as well as first-time authors; stories from England, such as "Thank You, Jackie James" by Caitlyn Marie Poland, who gives us a unique view of school in Britain. M.N. Schoeman from South Africa teaches us about racial healing, and Canadian Karen X. Tulchinsky shows us the heat of baby making. Here are stories of butches, stories of femmes, yarns from all over the United States, tales by women of color—the new twist on the tryst, longing, and satisfaction for all sorts of proclivities.

From our lips to your ears, we offer you our fantasies of lesbian lust.

Jess Wells
Editor

How I Ended Up on My Back

Amie M. Evans

Our lips are as close as they can be without actually touching. All the muscles in our bodies are tense, tight, controlled.
My lips, dark with deep burgundy lipstick, are at rest, slightly apart. I can feel her breath on my face as she exhales. I know
she can smell my lipstick and perfume as she inhales. We are
sitting on the sofa next to each other, our bodies turned toward each other. Her hands are on my elbows. My hands are
in the crocks of her bent arms, my palms resting on the bottom of the slight bulge of her upper-arm muscles, my fingers
wrapping around the side of her arms. I use my arms as a brace
to maintain this distance between us. My arms are not a
weight-bearing structure; if she applies pressure to the backs
of my arms, my brace would collapse, and I would tumble into
her, unable to resist her embrace.

I brush my resting lips against hers, transferring lipstick,
gently teasing her mouth. I let the tip of my tongue run along
the inside of her lips; her mouth opens wider, beckoning my
tongue to enter it. I plunge my tongue into her mouth, probing her tongue as it responds to mine. I close my eyes. I keep
our lips from touching as long as I can. I squeeze my fingers
into her arms. She pulls me toward her. Our bodies collapse
against each other. She kisses me deeply, pushing her lips hard

1

against mine; our tongues invade each other's mouths. The taste of lipstick, cigarettes, scotch, and a hint of sweetness from the sugar in the soda mingle with the soft, fleshy taste of the mouth and is transferred in saliva from my mouth to hers, hers to mine.

I grab the back of her head and clasp my fingers into her hair, pushing her lips harder against mine. She wraps her arm over my shoulder and around the back of my neck. She grabs the front of my neck. My moan is absorbed into her mouth. Her other arm wraps around my waist and pulls my body harder against hers as if she is trying to assimilate my flesh. I pull away, biting her lip as I create a pocket of air between our bodies, separating us. My breath is coming in faster surges. I want her to fuck me. I know if I said, "Fuck me, now," she would. I know she wants to fuck me.

I straddle her, putting one leg on either side of her lap, resting my weight on my knees. The full skirt of my dress fluffs out and covers my bent legs, her lap, and part of her stomach. I kneel over her. Only the inner parts of my knees and calves touch her. Her hands clasp my ass. She can feel through my skirt that I have no panties on. Her fingers search for the straps of my garter belt. She finds and gently snaps it. She rests her head, arched upward, against the back of the sofa. A small puff of air, a slight moan, escapes her like someone tired from a long day of work. But her work hasn't begun yet.

She pulls me closer toward her. Her fingers squeeze my ass. I grind my pubic bone against her, moving my hips, then bending at the thigh, spreading my legs. I put the weight of my body on her lap, rubbing my bare cunt against the cold metal of her belt buckle and then against her crotch. I wiggle and squirm using her body as a point of friction for my erect nipples and lusty clit. I rub my breasts against her, licking and biting her neck and ears. I pinch her nipple through her T-shirt. I plunge my tongue into her mouth; my lips press hard against her flesh. Her hands move under my skirt, clasping my sensitive ass. I move my hips, pushing my wet cunt against her. *Fuck me,* I scream in my mind. *Fuck me now.*

I pull away, dismount, and position myself in the other corner of the sofa, fixing my skirt, smoothing my hair. She takes my hand and leads me to the bedroom. I see gleaming, twinkling, burning want in her eyes. My cunt is wet. My clit is warm, and a fire rages deep inside me. My nipples throb to be touched, pulled, bitten. I arrange myself diagonally on the bed, pulling my dress over my knees, crossing my legs at the ankles, leaning up on my elbows, as she lights a few candles and dims the overhead lights. If I had refused to get off of the sofa—I wonder as I wait for her, watching her tight, small ass as she bends or walks—would she have taken me there, or would she have dragged me into the bedroom? The second answer appeals to me, and I toy with the image of her pulling me from the sofa, grabbing my hair, locking my neck in a wrestling hold, and dragging me, stumbling into the bedroom. The film in my head skips, and I imagine her throwing me over her shoulder, my ass in the air, my legs kicking. Hmm. She stands in front of me, mischief in her eyes, looking at me. I examine her as if she were a prize-winning animal: her slim body, slight hips, and tight little ass encased in a second skin of black leather pants; her firm, small breasts, the curve of her shoulders, and the bulge of the muscles of her upper arms accented by a white tank top and the straps of her leather suspenders; her feet slightly apart in black biker boots with chain mail. I separate my lips as my eyes feast on her. Bold butchness oozes from her. I wonder if she can lift me onto her shoulder. I store the fantasy away for future use.

She lies next to me, slipping her arms under and around me. I collapse into her embrace as she kisses me. Submissive. Ready to be taken. Wanting, needing, and in heat. We move our hips against each other. Our tongues plunge roughly into each other's mouths. Her hand slides up my stockinged leg and under my skirt to my bare upper thigh. I clamp my hand around her wrist, stopping its progress. Her hand pushes to move forward; I do not yield. It concedes and allows me to guide it back to the outside of my dress, where I rest it on my waist and release it. We begin again. She nuzzles my breast and bites at the nipple through the material. I moan and grind my hips against the air. I want to feel her mouth on the bare flesh of my breast. I want her to pull on my nipple rings and bite them as if she were removing the tips.

Her hand moves faster this time, pulling my skirt up and heading directly for my cunt. "No," I say sternly as I clasp her wrist, pressing with all my strength against her resistant arm. I am stronger than she thinks, but she is still stronger than me. She could easily overpower me. *Is she aware of this?* Again she concedes, allowing me to lead her hand from my wet cunt and to my upper body. I release her and begin to pull my skirt down. She firmly grabs my wrist, stopping me. I concede. I turn to her, grab the back of her head, pull it hard against my mouth, and kiss her deeply. I rub my exposed cunt, wet from want, against her leg and push hard so she can feel my pubic bone through her pants. I squirm against her, rubbing my breast, nipples erect, against her body. She cups my ass in her hands, pulling the cheeks up and slightly apart; her fingers dig into the bare flesh. She licks and bites my neck. Groaning, growling. Her hips push hard against mine. My hips move against hers as I clasp and squeeze her butt cheeks. We simulate fucking, imitating the movement of penetration. I moan in want. I bite her neck, dig my nails into the naked flesh of her arms, untuck her shirt, and run my nails up her back— first slowly and lightly, then increasingly faster and harder. Her arms clamp around my back, pulling me hard, pinning my body against hers. My body says, "Fuck me. I want you." I do anything I can to make her want to touch my wet cunt, to make her unable to control her want. Her hands are weak-willed; they plunge between my legs. This time I let her feel my wetness. I let her slip one finger deep inside me. She groans as her finger penetrates my flesh, separates the folds that cover my wet hole, and enters my cunt. I echo the groan as my cunt lips open and yield to her invasion. The wet, warm flesh of my pussy engulfs her finger. She prods, stroking the walls of my cunt as my hips move to meet her. My senses slip from me. I cannot hear the music I know is playing.

This is dangerous. I am ultimately weak, and my cunt is greedy. My cunt wants nothing more than to be finger-fucked. Sex doesn't only happen to my clit and cunt. Sex happens to my whole body. Sex consumes me. My flesh turns into one hot, pulsating cunt dripping wet with want. Sex happens in my head. My mind shifts as her lips, tongue, and teeth connect with my neck, mouth, or hand. Sex floods over me. My body fills with excitement, but my mind changes. It slips, falls, and crashes into a state of willing sexual accessibility. I go into heat like an animal. I will do anything for her to touch me, stroke me, fondle me, lick me, fuck me. Anything to make her not stop fucking me. My mind and cunt are constantly at war. My cunt lives for the moment, the very instant of orgasm, and my mind wants prolonged gratification, the rough, hard slow hourlong screw. My cunt usually wins each battle, my mind the war.

I try to pull myself away from the submissive, fuckable state of mind she forces me into with each thrust of her finger. I know she'll put another finger in me soon, and then I'll belong to her. I must momentarily maintain control. I try to focus on the music before she completely consumes me with her skilled strokes. I grab her wrist. This time she refuses, using her greater strength and her position on top of me. She prevents me from removing her fingers. She thrusts harder, deeper, using two, maybe three fingers, but I have other ways of stopping her. I slide my body up, using her shoulders for leverage, and unimpale myself from her hand. I squirm to get my legs out from under her before she regains control of my body.

Her eyes flicker a little, like a child robbed of candy. I have taken something from her she believes she has a right to possess. I meet her eyes—the lust in them makes my inner strength melt. I want her to have me; I want her. "Fuck me," my cunt screams, and it echoes through my whole body, causing a ripple of sensation that threatens to overwhelm me. I've paused momentarily in my escape, caught in my own desire to be overcome and forcibly fucked by her. She smells blood and jumps on me like a panther on wounded prey. Her fingers press into my leg and arm as she twists my limbs to regain access to my cunt. I squirm, twist, and struggle to get away. She kneels by my feet, her body extended over me. Angry at myself for losing concentration, excited by the struggle, a wave of panic fills me. I put my foot against the knee she is resting her weight on, pushing it from under her, forcing her to let go of me to regain her balance. I grab a handful of her hair, jerking her head back as I pull my body out from under her. She catches my ankles as I slither off the edge of the bed, pulling me back, pinning me on my stomach with the weight of her body across me. Her hands grasp my wrist and pin them to the bed. I buck against her, kick my feet frantically in the air between her legs, push against her upper body, and try to lift my pinned arms.

She bites the back of my neck and licks up to my ears. Her confidence in her ability to keep me pinned infuriates me and makes me wetter. As I struggle, she fondles my neck with her mouth. I cannot free myself—she knows this. I shriek in frustration. She whispers in my ear, "Why do you fight me? You are so wet; you want me to fuck you." Her words make my cunt hot. For a second I almost give in to her. My muscles start to relax, and my body says, "Fuck me, take me, use my body as if you own me, consume all of me."

Bitch, I say to myself, *how dare you confront me with my own lust, make me look it in the eye, point to my desire to have your fingers deep inside me, your mouth on my clit. That top's trick may make me hot and weak, but it won't get you inside me.* I fight against my deep desire to submit to her touch; I push with all my strength, lifting us both up—perhaps an inch—then collapse into the mattress.

She maneuvers my body, handling me like a feral cat. I allow my muscles to go limp for her to move me as she will, arrange me to be fucked. I wait for the opportunity, for the moment she carelessly grasps a leg to move it, the moment she reaches for a shackle, or the moment she shifts her body weight, leaving her momentarily off-guard, off-balance. I quickly bring my free leg around, planting my platform fuck-me shoe between her breasts, tumbling her back, forcing her to release my body. The toe of my shoe makes contact with her chin; the force from my release slams her mouth shut. I squirm to my knees and prepare to jump off the bed, dash into the other room, and maneuver a piece of furniture between us.

She is sitting on her ass, her legs bent at the knees and spread, her feet on the mattress. She runs the back of her hand across her mouth and looks at her own blood on her hand. Only her eyes move toward me. They lock on mine. Her normally blue eyes, soft and gentle, rage with fire, desire, need. They crackle, mesmerizing me. I am frozen. Hypnotized like a snake before a charmer, I cannot look away. I feel the panic and fear rising inside my chest. Her eyes say, "Now I will fuck you, penetrate you, slam you. Now I will have what I want from you. I will take it with force, and then you will beg me to give it to you again. You are mine, bitch." Her eyes cause my clit to stir, and a wave of warm arousal mixes with fear.

Without taking her eyes off mine, she licks the blood from her hand, and in a moment outside of time, she lunges, grabs a fistful of my hair, pins me with her body, and forces my right arm into a leather cuff with a large silver buckle. I mouth the words, "No. Please," as I watch the small drops of blood fall from her lips to my chest. I struggle as she cuffs the other wrist and attaches me to the O-ring mounted over the bed. I struggle in vain—the chain prevents me from going anywhere. She savagely pries my legs apart and plunges two fingers inside me. I moan; my hips thrust. I am as wet as if I had already come. She retreats, leaving me on my back.

Perhaps she will fist me, forcing my cunt to accept her whole hand; perhaps she will tease me until I beg her to make me come; or perhaps she'll fuck me with the dildo, plunging and slamming into me. It is beyond my control now. Whatever she does will fill the empty space inside me that started as a small yearning and has grown into a loud, insatiable demand that must be satiated. She must overcome, subdue, master, and fill my consuming hunger.

It is beyond my control. It threatens to consume us both.

The hunger grows, spreads from my body and reaches toward her, its teeth exposed to rip into her flesh. I push through it, and as she comes near me, her hand extending to grab my breast or neck, I flip onto my stomach and attempt to get on my knees. I will undo the chains from the O-ring and free myself. My upper body hits the mattress hard, face down. My arms extend in front of me, my weight on my knees, my ass in the air. I feel my dress slide up and expose my bare ass. She licks between the crack and pushes hard with her tongue. The palm of her hand impacts my bare ass. I tighten the muscles at the second blow. I clasp my hands around the chains. The stinging begins. Her hand comes down again and again against my ass. Her other arm is around my hips, preventing me from sinking onto my stomach, forcing my exposed, quickly reddening ass to remain in the air, accessible and vulnerable. She stops. My ass stings, my cunt throbs, and my resistance has been consumed and replaced by the hunger. Every part of me will submit to her touch. There is no resistance, no desire, except for the desire to be molded by her hands and tongue. The cells of my flesh will yield to her touch and transform themselves into whatever she desires as long as she touches them, touches me.

I feel pressure against my cunt lips. My own wetness has spilled out of me, basting my lips, betraying my desire. She does not use her other hand to separate and open me, there is pressure—intense and concentrated—against the lips of my cunt and a cool slippery moisture that doesn't belong to me. I feel the head of the dildo slip forward and slightly enter me, forcing my cunt to accept its size. It is too big. I feel the stretching and pulling of my hole as the pressure continues. I moan as I feel a twinge of fear that I might rip. I feel an intense stab of pain as she pushes the head in and the slightly smaller shaft plunges in afterward. My cunt is full; my body rises in an arch as the surge of pleasure rushes through me. She moves her hips slowly, working the shaft in and out of me. My cunt relaxes, submits to her invasion. The pain blends with the satisfaction of the fullness. I slide into The Fuck. After a few full strokes where the cock's shaft is consumed entirely by my cunt, her hips skip the steady climb and go from slow probing to slamming. Hard, fast, she plunges into me. Pounding away. Nailing me. Her sweat and the juices from my cunt are all over us like baptismal water. The nerves in the soft flesh of my vagina ache with sensation. Her front thighs slap against my back thighs; her hand clutches my red ass as she slides hard and fast in and out of me. I am on my knees; my face is against the mattress, and my arms are pulled tight. She pulls my ass toward her with each thrust.

I feel a popping sensation, followed by a severe emptiness, deep inside my cunt. My body is outraged; my hips stretch to follow her cock, but it isn't there. I groan with displeasure as she flips me onto my back, pushing my legs apart with her knees. There is no resistance in my muscles. Her hand pushes down on my pelvic bone. She reenters me with one strong, full stroke. There is no resistance in my cunt. She fills the empty void. I am on my back, my legs are in the air, and my arms are chained over my head to the wall. I can see the top of her head, white-blonde spikes dipped in black, sagging under the weight of her own sweat. Her face is pressed into my chest. I see my own legs in black, silk stockings; my six-inch fuck-me shoes bounce on either side of her ass as she rams into me. She clamps her teeth on my nipple, pulling on the ring, biting into the flesh. I reach for her upper arms, but the chains stop my arms and prevent me from touching her. I want desperately to touch her arms, sink my nails into her flesh, draw the blood to the surface, free it as she frees me. The chains clank against each other. She thrusts into me deeper.

I dig my heels into the flesh of her sides. She is a horse I am riding. I want her to fuck me harder. I want her to fuck me so hard that her cock breaks through my organs, tears through the muscles, and rips through the soft tissue of my belly, popping out in a bloody fountain. And still she would not stop ramming into me.

I know she can do it. I have faith in her ability to fuck, and I have felt the pure, raw animal in her. I believe that what drives her at this moment is our raw animal lust. Her sexual desire is fused to my sexual need. She wants to make me relinquish my mind to her. She will do anything to push me into that blue, bottom space, to push me to the edge, to make me give her my orgasm.

"Harder," I gasp.

And she responds as if the idea had been her own. Perhaps it was. I am not sure where either of us ends or begins. Right now it doesn't matter. At this moment all that drives us is The Fuck. All that exists is The Fuck. I look into her face, her eyes closed, her arms tense and fully extended holding her upper body above me. *Fuck me. Own me. I am yours to do with as you wish. Possess me. Consume me. Desecrate my body. Stab me there in that soft, sacred place, over and over. I will not resist you now. I will not refuse your request, any order, any demand, any desire.*

We are not two lesbians exploring each other's bodies; we are not two individuals. We are The Fuck, one consuming mound of carnal desires, impulses, raw primitive animal urges. Perhaps the desire to fuck harder, to plow deeper inside my wet, greedy cunt was hers, and I am merely the vessel that gives voice to her need. *Harder.* Perhaps the want to be fucked harder, deeper, faster was mine, and the word never crossed my lips; it just issued from deep inside my snatch to her mind or muscles. I want her to fuck me, fill my whole body with her cock. Plow into my liver, kidneys, stomach. Push her cock through my uterus into the lungs. I want her to fill my whole body with the length and thickness of her cock, to spread the aching, throbbing pleasure that she is creating in my cunt throughout my body with each stroke into me. I want her to pierce my heart and impale it on her cock, matching the rhythm of her fuck to the beats of my heart. I want her to fuck me until my eyes pop out and blood runs freely from my ears, nose, and mouth.

In one motion her arms press my shoulders as she grabs me for more leverage, and her next downward stroke into my open cunt is harder than I had imagined possible. Her hips smack against the back of my upper thighs; her cock slides roughly in and out of me. The fake, stiff balls bump against my asshole, stirring a new emptiness, a new need inside me, a new hole demanding to be filled. I clamp my legs around her, locking my ankles across her back. I shall never let go. My cunt and clit throb. My asshole stirs, demanding to be included. I want her to make me come, but I am a greedy slut. I don't want her to stop ramming her cock into me. I want to stay here, used and possessed by her hunger, locked together. I want to come before the fucking makes my clit explode, my mind implode. I cannot choose which I want—coming or prolonged possession. I cannot decide because I want and need both now. I want her to fuck me until I break, fuck me through the come, and not stop fucking me. Fuck me until I die; fuck me until there is nothing left of me but a shell.

She makes the decision for me, removing the dildo from its ring, fucking me with it in her hand, as her mouth engulfs my clit. Her tongue licks the engorged mass, flicking, pulling, putting pressure directly on it. I come, clamping her head between my legs, her mouth on my clit, her cock still slamming inside my cunt; she doesn't stop until the last spasm passes. My cunt and clit fuse. All that I am is condensed to that one single point. She creates the moment of my consumption, erasing me completely. This is the moment she unravels me, undoes me, releases me. This is the moment I exist for; this moment is the only reason I am alive. This orgasm she has ripped from me—she owns it as much as I do. At this moment I do not exist. I am a nerve ending, an extension of her sexual desire. I am one large cunt and clit. She has forced this orgasm from me; she has created it from my resistance. She has reached deep inside me, letting my blood cover her hands as she tore through my liver, stomach, heart and grasped my want, my sex, my power and pulled it to the surface—freeing it, freeing me. Even in this moment my mind wonders what we will uncover inside me, what is to come in the future, and what intense methods will be required for her to cut through my flesh, dig in my organs, unearth the rest of me, release the rest of my power, and give me her power. For this moment is small, these acts merely touching the surface of the dark we are standing next to. I know there is much trapped inside me.

She collapses on top of me, sweating, breathing heavily. I gasp, trying to regulate my breathing, pulling myself out of the euphoric mist she has plunged me into. We lie there with our individuality returned to us—each marked by the moment before, changed, however slightly, by our exchange of sexual energies. I know she is wet under her harness, wet from possessing me, fucking me. What little top there is in me yearns to engulf her cunt in my mouth, taste her wetness, plunge my fingers into her hole. I lie still on my back, waiting for her to undo my shackles as she kisses my neck. Even now as I lie in her arms, both of us collapsed from exhaustion, my cunt is freed. It thinks about the next time. Next time I'll scream so loud she'll have to gag me. Next time I'll be stronger, hold out longer. Next time she'll have to whip me into submission. Next time I'll keep myself from distraction. Next time—she nuzzles her face into my chest, squeezing me slightly, then kisses my cheek—I'll be as weak as I was this time.

Pearls

Jeannie Sullivan

That Saturday started out like most other days we had to ourselves. Karen and I woke up and had a cup of coffee together, then showered and got ready for the day. But after I dressed, things took a turn toward the more interesting.

I entered the living room to find Karen working at the computer. Picking up the paper, I started to settle into the recliner to read the local headlines.

"Don't sit down," she said without facing me.

"Why not?"

"Because." She swiveled around in the chair and locked her gaze with mine. "I said not to." Her expression was loving as always, but her tone was firm. Her blue eyes held that sultry look I know so well and love so much.

I was going to spend my day completely in her control, at her mercy. My clit twinged with anticipation, but I was aware it would be a long time before she would allow me release.

"Take off your clothes," Karen ordered. "Slowly."

I dropped the paper into the recliner and began unbuttoning my shirt.

She watched my hands intently.

I slipped the blouse off my shoulders and started for the snap on my jeans.

"No," she said. "The bra first."

I did as ordered and reached behind to unfasten the hooks. The satin undergarment slid down my arms and dropped to the floor, freeing my breasts. What was left of the morning chill in the house touched my skin, and my nipples began to stiffen.

Karen smiled. "Keep going, baby."

I unsnapped my waistband, opened the fly, and started to push the denim down my hips.

"Do this part real slow," she interrupted. "I want to watch your tits hang down when you bend over."

I moved tentatively, not wanting to go too fast and displease her. As I leaned forward I felt the increasing weight of my breasts being pulled down by gravity.

"Ooh, yes," Karen said in a low whisper.

My nipples grew harder from both her admiration and the pressure behind them. My pussy felt warm in the cool air. I stepped out of my jeans and straightened. I stood before her fully exposed, self-conscious under her probing eyes.

Her gaze roamed freely over my body, stopping for a long moment on my breasts, my stomach, the dark triangle between my legs.

I squirmed slightly under her perusal as her stare heated my flesh. Moisture collected in my slit.

"Come here." Karen's voice broke the silence. She patted her thighs. "Come here and straddle my lap. I want to play with your pussy."

Her words evoked a soft groan from me. Stepping up to her, I eased myself down, my aroused nipples almost level with her mouth.

She spread her legs, forcing my pussy wide open over the

empty space that had been her lap.

My cunt lips parted. My clit hung unveiled, vulnerable to her whims.

Grasping my waist, Karen coaxed me to her, taking one of my hardening nipples between her lips. She held it there while she flicked the tip of her warm tongue across the point.

My nipple heated. My clit tightened in response. I moaned.

She took my nipple deeper in her mouth, running full circles around it with her tongue. Then, with a sudden rush, she sucked it in hard.

I gasped and arched toward her.

She sucked and licked the nub until it stood hard and erect, then moved her mouth to the other one and started over. She continued the attention on the first with her fingers, rolling and pinching until both nipples ached with the fear of never getting enough.

My breath came shallow, fast. Groaning, I wiggled on her lap, trying to get some kind of contact with my swelling clit. But there was nothing around it, not even the soft labia that normally cushioned and caressed it. My cunt was hot and needed to be touched.

Finally, her mouth still on my breast, Karen slipped her hand underneath me and trailed a finger up my slit and over my clit.

I cried out and grabbed her shoulders, clinging to her for support.

She pulled her mouth from my nipple and looked up into my face. "Get your feet off the floor," she ordered. "I want you balanced on my fingers." She flicked a fingertip over my clit several times, then squeezed gently.

I whimpered and lifted my feet. All my weight rested on

my thighs where they crossed hers. The rough denim of her jeans rubbed against my smooth flesh. I gripped the arms of the desk chair and rotated my hips to rub my clit against her hand.

She quickly pulled it away. "Not yet, baby." She smiled. "You have to want it more than that." Returning her attention to my nipples, she left my pussy wet and wanting.

As she sucked, licked, and occasionally grazed her teeth over the engorged tips of flesh, I wiggled and squirmed and humped forward, whimpering and moaning from both satisfaction and frustration. Then I felt it—the feather-light flick on my clit.

I went wild. A loud moan escaped my lips. I lunged forward, trying to feel more.

A finger slipped into my hole, a thumb onto my clit.

I cried out and tried to tighten my thighs around Karen's hand to keep it there. But my cunt remained open wide.

"Oh, baby," she whispered. "You're so wet." She slid her finger out, then shoved two back in.

I gasped.

"Can you feel how wet you are?" She rubbed my clit.

"Oh, God, yes," I answered through a moan.

Her mouth found my nipple again, and she sucked it in. Her fingers worked my cunt, simultaneously fucking and stroking me. I felt my own juices covering the full length of my slit; I heard the slick noise of Karen's hand sliding in them.

"Your clit's so big and round, baby." She squeezed it and kneaded it between her fingers. "It's so hard. I'll bet you'd like me to suck it, wouldn't you?"

The thought set me on fire. "Yes, oh, please, yes." I pumped my hips faster.

"Well, I have some other plans for the day first. But maybe when we get home." Her breath was hot as she looked into my face. Her fingers still worked my pussy.

I couldn't think about what she was saying.

Suddenly she stood up, setting my feet to the floor.

Weak-kneed, I could barely stand. "Please, make me come," I begged, rubbing my mound against her thigh.

Stepping back, she scooped up my clothes from the floor.

"Oh, not now, sweetheart," she said with a sympathetic smile. "I want to take you shopping."

A desperate whimper slipped out of me. "Please."

"No." Karen's voice was more firm now. "Come on. I'll help you dress." Taking my hand, she led me into the bedroom.

Every step tortured my clit.

When we reached our room, Karen released me. "Lie down on the bed and spread your legs for me."

My heart leapt. She must have changed her mind. I quickly obeyed and lay there waiting. But instead of kneeling at my open cunt like I needed her to do so badly, she walked to our toy drawer and pulled out a long string of pearls.

My clit surged. Oh, God. How I love the pearls.

Karen stepped up to the foot of the bed and sat between my parted thighs. "I don't want you to get bored on our shopping trip," she said as she ran one end of the strand over my clit. "So you're going to wear these while we're out."

I stared. "You mean, out of the house?" I asked, partly in horror, partly in excitement. She'd never made—or let—me wear them out of the house before.

She grinned. Before I could protest, she looped several of the beads over a finger and pushed them deep into my hole.

My gasp replaced any words I might have planned.

Karen repeated this motion until she pushed almost the entire string of pearls inside me. I was accustomed to the feeling; I loved the feeling. Only four beads dangled from my wet cunt.

"There," Karen said with satisfaction. "You look so pretty."

My pussy clamped on its treasure.

She retrieved a pair of satin panties from my drawer and slipped them on me. The motion of raising my hips drew a low moan from my lips.

"Now get up and put on a very tight pair of jeans and a loose shirt, no bra," She walked out of the room. "And no touching yourself in any way," she called back.

I dressed in the ordered attire, but as I started to pull up my jeans, Karen returned and stopped me.

"I forgot something." She laughed. "It's just a little thing." Stretching down the waistband of my panties, she grabbed the beads dangling from my pussy and pulled slowly. As they slid from my hole, she guided them over my swollen clit.

I lost all balance. My knees gave out. I grabbed onto her.

She kept pulling. One at a time, the pearls slid over the hard, aching bud, torturing it with pure pleasure.

I quivered, my moan jerking with each new bead.

When she stopped, a six to eight inch tail of pearls extended from my pussy. Karen replaced my panties so that the end of the string stuck out the top of the undergarment. "There we are. Now, pull up your pants, but make sure I can still get to my little handle."

The tight jeans closed in around my mound, pressing my pussy lips snugly around both the beads and my clit— an incredible sensation. I flinched with arousal as I zipped the fly shut.

When I was dressed and ready to go, Karen reached under my shirt and tugged firmly on the beads protruding from the top of my pants.

The strand jerked against my clit. The sensation nearly brought me to my knees.

Karen smiled, then tossed a hairbrush onto the floor. "Pick it up," she demanded.

I bent down. The beads worked my clit and slit like an experienced lover. I moaned and squeezed my thighs around them.

"Pick it up, baby," Karen repeated, reminding me why I was bent over.

I grasped the brush and straightened, this motion almost as exquisite as the first. I groaned as I handed the brush to Karen.

"I think shopping is going to be so much fun today," she said. "Let's go."

As I got into the car, the beads massaged my clit. When I sat with my full weight on them, they rolled in my pussy. When I reached down to adjust them slightly, they tickled and caressed my cunt. Everything I did evoked a moan or a gasp. A puddle of cream developed in my panties.

Karen smiled the whole way to the mall.

She parked in the row farthest from the mall entrance. The walk was long and excruciatingly pleasurable, as the pearls caressed my pussy with every step. My shirt rubbed against the engorged peaks of my nipples, making them obvious to anyone interested. Inside we walked from one end of the mall to the other while Karen decided which store would be best to find the item she was searching for. We went into one shop where she bumped into a display table and knocked a bottle of lotion onto the floor.

"Pick that up for me, will you, baby?"

Carefully I bent down, trying not to let my moan escape. Straightening again with equal difficulty, I set the container back in its place.

Karen turned and knocked it off again. "Oh, I'm so clumsy today." She looked at me, her order in her eyes.

I bent over again. This time I couldn't hold it in: A soft moan drifted past my lips. I stifled it as I stood.

A man walking by glanced at me. A blush heated my cheeks.

"I think what we want is upstairs," Karen announced. She led us to the escalator and motioned for me to go first.

I did.

She scooted up behind me and whispered in my ear, "Walk up. All the way to the top."

I lifted a foot to the next step. The sensation overwhelmed me. It was all I could think of. My pussy became the whole world. I took another step. God, when could I come? Then another. By the time we reached the top, my clit throbbed. I stepped off the escalator with my pussy clamped tight.

"Was that nice?" Karen asked

"Ooh, yes." The words came out as a groan.

"You'd better start telling me about it, then. I want to know how good it feels."

"Ooh, it feels so good. I want to come so bad," I whispered. "Take me home and make me come. Please?"

She considered me for a long moment. "Well, you know, if it's that bad..." She grasped my arm, turned me around, and led me to the back corner of the lingerie department. There, amongst the panties, bras, and slips, she lifted my shirt and grabbed the beads. "I think you've waited long enough. And you've been such a good girl. I guess I could make you come right here."

A woman walked past in the next aisle.

Panic overcame me. "No, you can't," I said in a desperate rush.

Defiance flashed in Karen's eyes, and she raised an eyebrow. "I can't?" She tugged on the beads, and one slipped over my aching clit.

I gasped.

She tugged again.

Another jolt ripped through my pussy. I gripped her wrist for control.

"No." I panted. "I mean...please...please don't." My cunt was working against me.

"But you said you wanted to come." She pulled another bead over my hard nub, this time sliding the lower part of the strand up my slick slit. Several pearls slipped from my hole.

"Oh, God, don't," I pleaded. "I can't hold it. I can't be quiet."

"You'll have to, won't you?" She jerked again.

I let out a soft cry. "Please."

"Please what? Please let you come?"

"No, please don't." My limbs shook.

"Oh? Now you don't want to come?"

"No, not here. Please, not here."

Karen shook her head in mock disapproval. "What a fickle little thing you are. But if you're sure now..."

I started to relax a little as I glanced around us. The woman who had walked by was gone, and no one was close enough to have noticed any of what had transpired. My pussy still throbbed, but Karen seemed to be coming to her senses.

"I just can't help but wonder, though," she continued, "what would've happened if I'd done *this*." With a sudden jerk she pulled the strand of pearls and yanked about four inches worth right through my slit and over my clit.

Gasping, I stood up on my toes and grabbed for her shoulders to steady myself. Each bead rolling over my clit brought a loud whimper from my throat. I clamped my mouth shut, trying to keep quiet. When the pulsations finally eased, Karen grinned down at me. "So close and yet so far, huh, baby?"

Karen led us to a little boutique at the other end of the mall. She quickly found a display of intimate apparel and took down a garter belt. She held it up to my crotch.

Without thinking, I pushed her hand away. "Don't do that," I said, before I could catch myself.

She eyed me. "You're telling me I can't touch my property? There'll be a price for that."

I dreaded what she meant by that, but in a tantalizing sort of way.

She took three garter belts from the display and headed to a fitting room. She went to one toward the back surrounded by empty rooms. Inside, she locked the door and turned.

I waited for instructions.

"Try them on. Show me how nasty you can look."

I took off my pants and underwear and slipped on the first belt. Black lace, it looked incredibly decadent, especially with the strand of pearls dangling from my pussy.

"Mmm, very nice." Karen reached down and jiggled the beads. "Try the other, but I think I like this one."

I did as told, but Karen seemed to have already made up her mind. She fumbled around in her backpack as if looking for something. She barely glanced at the third belt before turning her back to me and placing her bag on the small shelf near the door. "Take it off and hang them all back on their hangers."

As I did, I smelled a faint, familiar fragrance, a perfume, or—no, it was the oil we used at home. Placing the last hanger on a hook, I turned to see what my lover was doing.

She faced me holding the large dildo we normally used in the strap-on harness.

My mouth fell open. "What are you doing with that?"

"It's not what I'm doing with it, it's what you're going to do with it. I brought it along just in case you couldn't behave yourself." Reaching behind her, she grabbed the bottle of lube and handed it to me. "Get it as slick as you need it to go all the way inside you."

My heart pounded. Part of me couldn't believe any of this; part of me burned with excitement. Voices sounded down the hall. "What if someone comes in?"

"Just do it."

I quickly rubbed the fragrant liquid over the dildo and handed the bottle back to Karen.

"Pull your beads out, slowly."

I obeyed, the sensation sending quivers through my pussy.

She took the pearls and, holding them beneath her nose, inhaled deeply. Her tongue flicked out from between her lips. She licked one bead, then another. "Mmm, you taste so good."

My clit ached as I watched her savor my juices.

"Come here," she said finally. She slipped the pearls into her front pocket. I stepped close to her, and she took the dildo from me. "Spread your legs and open up for me."

I did, knowing what was coming. I gripped her shoulders.

Lowering the rubber cock, she pressed the head against my

opening and pushed upward. It slid in easily from my thick juices and the lube. She pushed it all the way up until the fake balls at the base hit the bottom of my ass.

I released a shuddering sigh. It was so big, almost too big for me, but this was such a turn-on.

"One last thing before you get dressed."

Get dressed? I stared in astonishment.

But she was intent on her task. She twisted the dildo around inside me so the balls now pressed against my cunt lips. With her fingers she parted my labia and adjusted the balls so they pushed directly on my clit.

All thoughts of astonishment vanished. I moaned as she worked the balls against my cunt.

"Close your legs and get dressed," she ordered. "I'm going to go pay for this. I'll meet you out front." With that, she disappeared out into the fitting room corridor.

Stunned, I stood there in a public dressing room with a huge dong in my pussy, the feeling a mixture of terror and excitement. I bent down to get my pants and immediately winced. I had to be careful how I moved. With some effort, I got my clothes on. My underwear and jeans held the dildo snugly in place. It was difficult to walk completely normally, but I managed to get to where Karen waited without attracting any attention.

Karen smiled when she saw me. My stilted movements gave her great pleasure.

I blushed. She knew what was buried deep between my legs in the middle of a store.

Before I even reached her, she started down the mall at a brisk pace. "Come on," she called over her shoulder. "Don't dawdle. We have things to do."

Things to do? More things? I wondered. But with my pussy spread around my invasive companion, I almost dreaded the answer. All I wanted was to go home and come, but obediently I quickened my pace to keep up with Karen.

The dildo rammed into me with every step, fucking my wet pussy as I hurried after her down the mall. The firm rubber balls that pressed into my slit massaged and stroked my hard clit and stretched lips. A moan emerged as I felt my long-denied orgasm building. The rubber dick slid up and down inside me, rocked back and forth against me. I groaned, letting my eyes partially close as I struggled to follow Karen.

Suddenly she stopped. She grabbed my arms, bringing me to a halt in front of her. "You're not going to come, are you?" she snapped. Her voice was low but unmistakably demanding.

I squeezed my thighs tight and rocked my hips. Another moan eluded my control.

"Get your feet apart." Her voice was a harsh hiss in my ear. Her grip on my arm tightened. "Now."

With great effort I opened my legs, releasing some of the pressure on my clit. It ached for release. "Please," I whispered, hoping no one passing would hear. "Please, take me home."

Karen watched me, a slow smile shaping her features. "Come on, baby. You just have to make it a little farther now." Turning, she walked to the nearby exit.

Grateful, at least to be out of the mall, I tried to hurry after her. Had I heard her correctly? Were we going home?

My gait was shaky, my body slightly bent at the waist in an attempt to relieve the pressure in my slit. Each step made my legs quiver and sent shudders through my soaked pussy. I moved carefully, trying to avoid any further stimulation, but my entire cunt was raw nerves. My clit felt huge. Hard. It grew larger, more sensitized with every movement. My moans deepened with every footfall.

Finally Karen stopped.

I glanced up. We stood beside the car. Relief flooded me. "Oh, thank you," I breathed.

She smiled and opened the driver's door.

I waited on the passenger's side as patiently as I could. The afternoon sun beat warm on my already heated body. I watched her move my seat forward, adjust the back, fiddle with the position. God, what was she doing? I just wanted to go home.

After what seemed like an eternity, she reached across and unlocked my door.

Eagerly I lowered myself into the seat. As I pulled my legs in after me, I instantly realized what she had been doing. My knees pressed tightly against the glove compartment, and my ass was forced far back into the bucket seat.

"Spread your legs wide apart for me, baby," Karen said as she put the key into the ignition. "And sit up tall so all your weight is on that nice big dildo."

Parting my thighs as far as I could in the confines of the car, I eased upward and forward. I gasped as the fake dick sank even deeper into my pussy. My clit was pressed gloriously tight against the balls. I whimpered with agonizing pleasure.

"Now, don't move," Karen said with a wicked smirk. "Don't wiggle. Don't squirm. Don't even shift. You just sit there and enjoy the ride home."

I squeezed my eyes shut. The torture was exquisite. My pussy and clit were in a perfect position for the body-racking orgasm I'd been aching for all day, but I couldn't move. I knew better unless I wanted to spend the next week in this condition. My clit pulsed under the strain; my vaginal muscles clamped down on the dildo, but with every shred of effort I had, I sat perfectly still.

Karen pushed the gearshift into reverse.

The subtle jerk of the car ripped through my entire body.

A small whimper trembled past my lips.

"Don't worry." Karen laughed. "I'll get you home quickly. My pussy's awfully wet for your tongue."

The Sacred Sex Tour

Wendy Caster

You wake up and watch the sunlight throw rainbows through the crystal heart in the window. You get up, humming, and slip on your white fuzzy bathrobe. Then it hits you again, as it has every day for six months: Ex isn't there. After five years of living together, your Ex isn't there. And She'll never be there again.

You smile ruefully, proud that you didn't think about Her for a whole minute when you woke up.

Then you remember: You might see Her tonight. Ex and Her skinny new girlfriend The Poet will probably join every other lesbian in town to see Kall-ee B. and the Goddess Grrrlz on their Sacred Sex Tour.

Your stomach aches all day.

Of course you can't decide what to wear, so you settle on a short black skirt and a clinging black T-shirt. You lost 18 pounds on the grief diet after She left, and you want Her to notice.

After 20 minutes of fussing with your hair to get it just right, you're ready to go. At the last minute you decide it's time for your annual wearing of the spike heels.

As you walk to the theater, Oletta, your ex-lover before your ex-lover before Ex, says, "You know, if you're not ready…" but you tell her it's been half a year, and you're not going to miss Kall-ee B. and the Goddess Grrrlz. Not on their Sacred Sex Tour. Not when you've got first-row seats.

The sidewalks are thick with lesbians. A woman with the same haircut as Ex passes by, and you almost faint.

The usher, Vivienne, is the woman you had an affair with right after you broke up with Oletta. She tells you she finally got her social work license. You feel a tap on your shoulder. It's Ex, and she's sitting right behind you, and, yes, she's with Ms. Skinny Poet. You'd run screaming from the theater, but that would give them too much satisfaction.

You gasp "Hi." Oletta takes over the conversation. She and Ex chat about Kall-ee and the Goddess Grrrlz's past incarnations as aliens, pirates, leopards, and volcanoes, and they ponder what Kall-ee will do tonight.

You and Oletta sit down, and she squeezes your arm in sympathy. You focus on not turning around.

Gradually the auditorium floods with fog. When the air clears a little, there's Kall-ee, barefoot in white leggings. Her long dreads and deep brown skin contrast vividly with her loose white blouse. The audience is screaming. Kall-ee bows, and the screams get louder. The drummer yells, "Five, six, seven, eight," and they burst into last year's big hit, "Without You, I'm Everything."

Kall-ee struts across the stage as she sings. Every once in a while she stops center stage and stares at you.

No. It's probably just a trick of the light. But it sure looks like she's staring. At you.

Oletta leans over and says, "She keeps looking right at you!" You hope Ex noticed too.

During intermission, Vivienne says, "If Kall-ee checked me

out like that, I'd wait for her at the stage door with nothing on." A woman in a three-piece suit says, "Was that you? Wow!"

You're pleased. If they saw Kall-ee checking you out, then Ex saw Kall-ee checking you out.

During the second half, Kall-ee seems to be constantly watching you from the corner of her eye. During the final song, "Lovely Lady," Kall-ee smiles right at you, then leaves the stage to thunderous applause. The first encore, as always, is "Twat-a-Lot," with its sing-along chorus. When the song ends, Kall-ee bows deeply and heads stage left. But she stops, looks right into your eyes, and then points at you, as if to say, "I pick that one." You blush as she walks off stage.

The audience cheers and screams for another encore. The curtain goes down, and you figure the show is over, but the house lights don't come up. The theater stays dark for a long time.

You gradually become aware of the hairs standing on your arms, and an incredibly sexy bass line caresses you. Incense fills the air. The curtain rises slowly, revealing a dark stage with rows of candles on risers on the left and right. One light eases on, gradually revealing Kall-ee barefoot in black leggings, her arms and legs like an athlete's. She's staring right at you.

The audience is silent, mesmerized by Kall-ee's appearance and the rhythmic bass line. In a whisper the band starts chanting, "Sex is holy / sex is sacred / sex is how we're consecrated," over and over. They're also dressed in black, and they're barely visible in the candles and the spill from the light on Kall-ee. Slowly, almost imperceptibly, Kall-ee's right hand rises from her side until she's reaching out to you.

You can't believe what you're seeing, so you look to your left and right, but everyone's gaping at you. Kall-ee's still beckoning to you, but you're too thrilled to move. The band continues chanting, and the drummer adds a cymbal shiver to the relentless bass line. Out of the corner of your eye, you see that Ex has Her arms crossed. Her face is screwed up in that familiar I-can't-believe-you're-doing-this expression. You smile and stand up, reaching for Kall-ee's hand. In a single smooth movement, Kall-ee lifts you to the stage. You land lightly in her arms. You're very glad you wore the spike heels tonight.

You expect the audience to hoot and holler. You expect Kall-ee to kid around with you or just dance a little. But there's something in the air, and everybody knows it. The bass line and chanting and incense and candles have turned the theater into a place of worship, and the way Kall-ee is looking at you is not a performance.

As you stand, wondering what will happen next, a backup singer with long blonde curls and a flowing black dress moves you away from Kall-ee, then dabs your neck and wrists with musk. Never taking her eyes off of you, Kall-ee sings, "Sex is Freya, sex is Hera / sex is lady day and Gaia." The backup singer anoints your forehead, then the spots where your nipples push through your T-shirt. She paints a circle in the air just over your skirt between your thighs. She stands back and bows to you, then turns to Kall-ee and gives her a kiss you can feel three feet away.

Kall-ee comes closer to you and strokes the air around you, only millimeters from touching you. You imagine you can see sparks between her hands and your body. The band is still chanting.

Kall-ee leans over and kisses you. Your knees almost buckle. You moan gently, but your mouth is near the small microphone on her tank top, so your "ooh" echoes around the theater. The women in the audience respond with moans of their own, and you think you hear Ex muttering angrily, but the bass line is getting louder and more insistent, so it's hard to tell.

Kall-ee reaches for your hand, then pulls you to her. Her eyes are deep and practically black, and although you know that 2,000 women are watching—1,999 women and Ex—you feel a ring of privacy inside Kall-ee's eyes. Kall-ee looks at you quizzically, asking permission. Part of you wants to run, but a bigger part of you wants to stay. You nod yes.

You wrap your arms around Kall-ee's strong body, and she kisses you, breasts against breasts, and again your noises fill the theater. She pulls away slightly and starts murmuring in your ear—and into the mike.

The Grrrlz are still chanting, and the bass line is sure and steady. The lead guitar screams out a song of desire as Kall-ee kisses your shoulders and your breasts through your T-shirt. It's frightening to know all those women are watching you, but it's incredibly sexy too. As Kall-ee gently nibbles on your nipples, you feel the audience out there, sharing your experience.

Kall-ee strokes your hair and your face, then your shoulders and arms, then your back and your sides, taking her time and touching every part of you. You feel she wants you to stay still and receive her attention, and anyway, you're not sure you could move if you wanted to. As she caresses you she hums under her breath, a purring the microphone turns into vibrations up and down your spine. She strokes your breasts and your belly, your legs and your thighs. Each movement is careful and measured; she is sculpting your desire.

Kall-ee kneels to caress your calves and ankles, then kisses the top of your feet reverently. You feel blessed. As she rises she takes your hands. Then she looks deep into your eyes. A circuit of electricity goes from her eyes into you and out your hands back into her. You feel absolutely connected and alone with Kall-ee, and you bask in your feelings as she sings to you.

You're reminded it's a public event when Kall-ee says, "Will you be our gift to the goddess tonight?" You feel the tiniest bit silly—you don't actually believe in "the goddess"— but you whisper, "Yes." The mike picks up only the breath of the word, but the women in the audience fill it in, crying, "Yes, yes, yes."

Kall-ee turns to her backup singers and nods, and they walk to you. Two stand at your sides, holding your arms gently but firmly behind you. The third stands in back of you. Just as you glance at Ex, who is leaning forward in her seat and glaring, lips grimly set, the woman in back of you holds her hands over your eyes. You can feel her breasts against your back. The backup singers' voices are in your ears, quiet and hot, and also amplified and echoing.

For what seems like a long time, you just stand there, held in place and unable to see. You're very turned on but also nervous. You want to move your hands, but you don't. You're not sure whether you're scared that the three women won't let you move or that they will.

You feel warmth against your mouth, and you realize Kall-ee is leaning toward you, about to kiss you. She barely brushes her lips against yours, and you gasp. Then she kisses you hard, her tongue exploring you. You want to put your arms around her, but the women don't let you. It's scary to be held back—but very, very sexy too.

Kall-ee pulls her mouth away from yours, and you try to follow, but the women hold you in place. You want to know where Kall-ee is, you want to know what she will do next, but you accept remaining motionless, and you silently listen to the chanting and the bass guitar.

You think you feel Kall-ee touching your breast or your arm.

No.

Wasn't that her hair brushing your shoulder?

No.

Then you feel her hand, for sure, on the inside of your thigh just above your knee. You're throbbing all over, and you're grateful the backup singers are holding you so you won't fall over. You think you hear women in the audience murmuring, "Oh, my goddess," and "I wish that was me," and sounds that aren't words. Then the bass line gets louder and louder, until you feel it in your muscles and bones. The backup singers chant until their voices thunder through the theater. The lead guitar is frenzied. But Kall-ee moves deliberately, stroking you slowly, touching every inch of your thighs as she moves higher and higher.

Kall-ee stands in front of you, one hand on the small of your back, and strokes between your legs lightly, almost in passing, and you groan with astonishment and passion. She moves your underwear aside and strokes your hair and inner lips. You feel hypnotized and calm, like the odd quiet just before the tornado hits. She strokes you again and again. You want to suck her inside you.

Even though you're waiting and wanting as Kall-ee teases

you with long slow strokes, you're still shocked when her fingers slip into you. You gasp, and the noise bounces through the auditorium. Women moan and gasp in return, and you feel incredibly powerful.

Kall-ee slowly moves her fingers in and out of you, holding the palm of her hand against your clit. You can barely stand up. She chants, "Sex is the goddess, the goddess is sex." The audience chants too, almost in a whisper. Kall-ee moves faster and faster, fucking you and rubbing your clit. The chanting grows faster and faster, keeping pace with Kall-ee's movements. "Sex is the goddess, the goddess is sex. Sex is the goddess, the goddess is sex."

You're exquisitely turned on, but you're still feeling a bit like an impostor because you don't believe in the goddess. Then Kall-ee changes the angle of her fingers just a little bit, thrilling you to your breasts and shoulders and thighs, and you sigh to yourself, only half ironically, *I believe, I believe!*

The bass line speeds up, and the chanting follows. You no longer control your body as it follows the voices and guitar and Kall-ee's fingers. The lead guitar screeches out your passion, and you vibrate all over. Over the chant, Kall-ee wails wordlessly. Her voice travels down your spine, and the bass comes up through your toes until they meet at her fingers, and you feel pure pleasure. Kall-ee whispers in your ear—just to you—"Give yourself to the goddess. Please. Give yourself to the goddess."

You lose your thoughts and your self-consciousness as Kall-ee kisses you and fucks you and kisses you and fucks you. You know your body must be glowing white with sensation. And she fucks you. You see light behind your eyelids. And she fucks you. Your muscles turn to melted butter. And she fucks you.

Then you know you're going to let go, and Kall-ee must feel it too, because you both have orgasms that are pure music. Everyone in the theater seems to be coming, or maybe you and Kall-ee are coming for everyone.

The backup singers let your arms go, and you hang onto Kall-ee. Under the noise of the audience moaning and cheering, you hear and feel her sighing against you, and it's the sweetest moment, like turning a corner in a dirty city and glimpsing a hummingbird sipping at a pink flower. You are laughing, maybe crying a little too.

"Oh, goddess!" Kall-ee moans, and you whisper back, "Oh, goddess."

The moans and cries of the audience quiet to whimpers, and the chant and bass line tail off as you and Kall-ee kiss one last long kiss. She leads you back into your seat, then bows and kisses your hand. You sigh and mouth, "Thank you." She grins at you, then puts her fingers in her mouth—the fingers that were in you—and licks them one by one. When she's done, she holds her arms out so that her body makes a T and stays that way for a moment. The audience is silent. Then she snaps her fingers, and the stage goes completely black and the curtain comes down.

Oletta leans over and gives you a long hug, then the woman sitting on the other side of you hugs you too. You see that women all over the audience are tenderly touching each other.

You can't help it: You turn to check out Ex's reaction. She's halfway out of the row, dragging Ms. Poet along and bitching about how some people have no sense of privacy.

Leaving the theater takes a long time. No one wants to let the feeling go, and many women want to hug you personally. You decide maybe there is a goddess, and you thank her for whatever happened tonight—and for your body and your heart and your very, very wet underpants.

When you finally get home, you fall asleep happy, and you know that when you wake tomorrow, you will have better things to think about than Ex.

A Real-life Superhero

Kate Dominic

I want to be Xena.

Actually, I don't want to be Xena—except in my fantasies. Maintaining a body like hers would be way too much work. I just want to be a strong, sexy, all-muscle-no-fat warrior woman with royal connections—someone everybody knows will save the world, every time.

In other words, I want to be a real-life superhero, one named Jeena.

And I want to have a sidekick lusting after me. Not Gabrielle. She's taken. I want one who's all mine and who changes week to week to meet my latest fantasies.

I've decided my sidekick will be Arielle. She still has long blond hair and is very feminine—voluptuous, even—in a muscular, superhero sidekick-ish sort of way. Good with swords, a worthy companion, someone I can always trust to protect my back and fight at my side. We're totally in love, of course, touching each other whenever we want, even in broad daylight, in the middle of a village. Nobody minds. After all, we're their heroes, their defenders. We can do no wrong.

In one of our first adventures, Arielle and I are perusing a stand of ripe fruit in a typical medieval village's typical open marketplace. As we walk along, I run my hands along the smooth bare flesh below the silk short top that struggles to contain my lover's full breasts. Yes, I know silk doesn't travel as well as leather, but I like the way silk feels, and it's my fantasy. So Arielle's top is silk! Anyway, as I'm looking at the apples, I reach up under her short leather skirt and caress the curve of her luscious bottom. Her skin is round and smooth, and I like to bite it. Arielle never wears underwear. She wants to keep herself available for me. A good thing, because I'd demand it anyway. Being able to reach up under my lover's skirt and fondle her ass in public really turns me on. The villagers laugh encouragingly when I slip my fingers into Arielle's slick folds and draw out fingers dripping with her sex honey. I bark an order at the baker. She hands me a loaf of hot, fresh bread. I smear the sticky juices on it. I take a bite, then share it with Arielle. She licks my fingers appreciatively, spreading her legs wide for me to prepare another slice.

The women in the village nod and look knowingly at their girlfriends—some even at their husbands. "That's the way you're supposed to do things. Like Jeena does!" they say. Then there's a rush on the baker's cart, followed by the rustle of skirts being lifted and the contented moans of women being fingered. Then the sounds of people chewing as everybody has a mid-afternoon snack. Afternoon snack becomes a new tradition in the village—and they prosper forever after because everyone is so happy and energized.

We have several adventures in that country. In another of my other favorites, I teach the local nobility the proper way to negotiate a peace treaty. The meeting takes place in the castle of one of the feuding overlords. The combatants are a mixed crowd, some women, some men, most of them highly impressed with their titles and armies—and not so sure they

41

want to listen to the warrior woman their thoroughly disgruntled king has sent them.

As I enter the room, the assemblage rises from their seats at
the great table—the women aloof in their satin dresses and
silken veils, the men prim and proper in their velvet clothes.
There's a collective gasp as I saunter over to my chair, wearing
nothing but my boots, weapon harnesses, and my jewelry.
Arielle walks at my side—barefoot, shoulders erect, naked. As
I sit down, Arielle kneels beside me, resting her staff against
the back of the chair. While the others are still reeling in
shock, she licks my breasts, and I start to speak.

"We'll get nothing accomplished if our minds stay focused
on our anger and our differences. So I'm going to insist everyone remove their clothing and get comfortable. That will put
us all on equal footing." I shiver as Arielle licks a particularly
delicious spot. "Then we're going to settle this matter once
and for all. You're laying waste to the countryside, and it's
going to stop. Now strip!"

No one resists Jeena's orders. Pretty soon veils and shifts
and tunics are dropped on the floor. An army of servants suddenly appears to salvage the clothing before it needs to be
laundered, and since my second in command is servicing me,
nothing less will do for the others. Soon their sidekicks kneel
quietly at their sides, waiting to see what I'll say next.

"A properly negotiated treaty will be in everyone's best in-
terests." As I speak, I let everyone see how much Arielle's
ministrations are turning me on. My nipples are hard and
erect, dark with desire, glistening with my lover's saliva.
There's another collective gasp, followed by a loud murmur of
stunned disbelief as Arielle moves between my legs and licks
her way downward. When her hot, probing tongue slides be-

tween my labia, I hold up my hand for silence.

"Excuse me a moment," I say, purposefully letting my voice quiver with pleasure. "My sidekick's tongue is quite delicious. I must indulge myself for a moment before I can concentrate on business." With that, I open my legs wider and slide farther down in the chair.

I shudder visibly, then take a deep breath, looking pointedly at the other sidekicks. "I said get comfortable! Everyone will negotiate much more effectively that way." I rest my hand on the back of Arielle's head. "If you don't know how, watch Arielle. Pay particular attention to how she's sucking my clit while she fingers her own." With that, I close my eyes and lift my boots up to rest on the edge of the table, snuggling comfortably into my chair as Arielle settles herself between my wide open legs.

I watch surreptitiously from the corners of my eyes as shocked murmurs give rise to appraising glances. Then one of the overladies leans back in her chair, followed by another, then another. Pretty soon all the former combatants are comfortably ensconced, their seconds in command between their legs, studiously following Arielle's sterling example. Before long, the hot smells of good sex and the general sound of contented slurping fill the room. I close my eyes all the way and enjoy as Arielle's hot tongue teases an orgasm from me.

When my breath settles I start speaking again, motioning those who haven't yet climaxed to continue and participate as they're ready. "This is how we're going to do business."

The conference lasts all day. I don't keep track of the number of times I climax. Sometimes I take breaks, lifting Arielle onto the table in front of me so I can bury my face in the honeyed feast between her legs. Later on I eat my lunch off her belly, feeding her with my fingers as I address yet another point in the negotiations. I savor her pussy, then give her mine for dessert. As the negotiations draw to a close, I lift Arielle to her feet and kiss her soundly. She picks up her staff and stands behind me-sturdy, proud, her face glistening with my juices and flushed from her many climaxes. She's every bit a true superhero sidekick—one who's been instrumental in the development of a lasting peace treaty. She blushes even deeper as the sated negotiators thank her with a round of thunderous applause.

Of course, not all our adventures are as trouble free as that. After all, Arielle is a sidekick, so she sometimes doesn't follow orders. She'll go off on her own path, which—as is always the case in superhero tales—creates problems. So I have to punish her. Arielle expects no less of me, and my justice is always swift and fair. One day she wakes up grouchy and in a fit of pique spills the breakfast she's cooking. Superheros are big on courtesy, and we don't tolerate tantrums. So I sit down on a log, pull her over my knee, and spank her bare bottom until my incredibly strong superhero hand finally gets sore. By then her backside is bright red and hot, and she's crying and kicking and promising to be good. So I let her up and go off to sharpen my sword, ignoring her sniffles as she recooks breakfast and tends to the horses. Eventually she sets a plate of steaming pancakes next to me, lays her head in my lap, and whispers, "I'm sorry, Jeena. Please forgive me." So, of course, I do. After all, she's my sidekick…and I like spanking her.

Another time, Arielle is rude to me in front of a shopkeeper. As a wise superhero, I've made friends with the local craftsmen, giving them the tools and technology they need to fashion superior quality sex toys. I'm shopping in one of my favorite establishments when Arielle makes a snide comment that one of my choices must be for me because it's definitely too large for her petite derriere. Arielle knows better than to pull a sassy sidekick stunt like that in public. So I buy the plug, making a point of telling the shopkeeper Arielle will be wearing it before we leave the store. The shopkeeper is very matronly. As Arielle pouts, the shopkeeper pats her hand and says, "There now, dearie. Be glad you have a woman who knows how to pleasure your bottom. It took my girlfriend years to learn."

Arielle blushes. She blushes more as I set our purchases out on the counter. I bend her over the display case, lift her skirt, and nudge her legs apart with my boot. Then I pick up the new jar of cream, lube a smooth string of large duotone balls, and slide them firmly up her pussy.

"Jeena," she whispers. Just my name. "That feels so good. I'm sorry I was sassy."

"Apology accepted," I say pleasantly.

I put a large glob of cream on my finger. She jumps, yelping, as I touch it to the puckered pink hole between her cheeks.

"Now take your punishment as befits a sidekick."

Arielle whimpers and moans as I work the lube into her anus—slowly, lovingly, and very deliberately stretching her tight little sphincter open. Soon her pungent pussy juices trickle out around the bead string. Other women come into the shop as I minister to my young sidekick. We discuss the latest news, ignoring Arielle's groans of pleasure as we share our opinions with the shopkeeper. Within ten minutes, every toy similar to the ones I've bought has been sold out. Superheros have impeccable taste.

When Arielle's anus is finally relaxed, I pick up the new plug, slather it with cream, and touch it to her pucker. As she moans my name, I start working it slowly into her. It takes a while. The toy is bigger than anything she's used to. I wiggle it around, pulling it in and out as she gasps, as she gradually loosens. She yelps when, with one final, tiny push, I slide the plug in the rest of the way and her anus snugs up around the neck.

The room erupts in applause, and I pull Arielle to her feet.

"Does that feel good?" I ask, pinching her nipples.

"Yes, ma'am," she whispers, blushing as she smiles at the appreciative group around us.

"Is it too big for your 'petite derriere,' as you were so certain it would be?"

"Oh, no, ma'am." She shivers, clenching her butt cheeks as she thinks about the size of the plug up her bottom. "Um, I think it fits just right, just like you said it would."

The shopkeeper chuckles, and Arielle blushes again.

"Good," I laugh. "Then we will leave immediately for Argentown." As Arielle's eyes widen in shock, I say sternly, "Don't even think of taking those toys out. You asked for this. I want you ready and willing for me tonight."

Her hushed "yes, ma'am" is lost in another round of appreciative giggles as I take my other hand, lube up a second set of beads, and slide them up my own pussy. Then I grease a respectably sized plug and, squatting comfortably back, slide it up my own behind.

"I have plans for us tonight, Arielle. Don't screw them up."

To a round of thunderous applause, I wash my hands, then march my bemused sidekick out of the store. I toss her up on her horse, then carefully mount my own mare, setting off at a vigorous trot so Arielle will have no illusions about how the trip is going to go.

I stop a couple miles out of town. Arielle's flush lets me know she's miserably turned on. While I want to teach her a lesson, her little display doesn't warrant a true punishment. I pull my horse over to her. Her green eyes are shiny with un-shed tears.

"What's the matter, love?" I ask, brushing her hair back from her face.

"I want to come," she says softly, leaning into my hand. "I need to so badly I can hardly breathe. The motion of the horses is almost more than my pussy can stand. Please, Jeena, please, may I come?"

"Certainly, love," I whisper. I reach over and untie her top. She shivers as her soft breast falls into my hand. I lean over and lick. "Touch your clit, sweetheart."

Her horse whinnies, shuffling a bit as Arielle squirms to my biting. "Quiet," I command. The horse obeys, breathing heav-ily but maintaining her position as I suck my lover's nipple. All animals obey Jeena. Using just my knees, I nudge our mounts forward, very slowly, my lips locked on my prize, my pussy quivering as the toys rock inside me at the rolling gait of the horses.

Arielle whimpers, shivering. I can see her butt muscles clenching as she responds to the unrelenting stimulation of the plug in her anus.

"Make yourself come, Arielle." With one hand steadying Arielle's horse, I hold my own reins in my other hand, the thin leather straps tickling my thighs as my fingers rub my mons. "Come for your superhero lover, the way a good sidekick should."

Arielle lifts the front of her skirt, her fingers moving in a frenzy as she fingers her clit. She moans, shuddering, crying out softly as she comes. My own pussy answers. As my breathing steadies, another climax already starting to build, I sit up, tweak my lover's nipple, and move my horse away. Arielle smiles sheepishly.

"Is that better?" I laugh.

"Yes, Jeena," she blushes, still panting softly. "That felt really good."

"I knew it would. You have my permission to come as many times as you want between now and when we arrive at the outskirts of Argentown."

"Oh, thank you," she purrs, closing her eyes as her fingers start moving again.

"Superheros get to have super sex," I say crisply. "Now, close up your top and listen to my plan for dealing with the burghers tomorrow." I gasp, shivering deliciously as I climax again. This time Arielle's laugh rings through the clearing. I urge my horse forward, setting us off at a good pace to cover some ground.

We sleep soundly that night, wrapped in each other's arms. The next day, however, Arielle's self-confidence from a day of pleasure apparently overcomes her good judgment. She deliberately disobeys my direct orders, the negotiations collapse, and we end up having to defend ourselves and the good townspeople in one of those smoke-filled battles that really only look good on TV. With the city finally in good hands, we beat a hasty retreat, still pursued by angry bands from the factions whose coup I've foiled despite my sidekick's antics. I'm furious. And scared. Arielle has nearly been killed a dozen times during the day.

I've only really whipped Arielle a few times. In each instance I've done it because she's openly defied me, thereby causing problems that took me a whole episode to correct. While I like saving the day, I get really pissed drawing my sword and using my gymnastics for stupid stuff.

We escape with the 20 noblewomen hostages we've rescued, riding hard until we're certain we're safe. As night falls we make camp. I don't even wait for dinner. I take off my sword belt, double it over, and march Arielle off to the stump that holds my saddle. Arielle's face is already wet with tears of remorse and trepidation.

"Take off your clothes," I order as the women gather around to witness.

"Yes, ma'am," she whispers. She doesn't try to argue. She knows she's earned her punishment. She lays down her weapons. Then she unties her top, her firm, heavy young breasts falling out as she shrugs the smooth silk over her shoulders. When she hesitates, I nod peremptorily and snap the belt. She's sniffling loudly now. Arielle unties her belt. Her skirt falls open and drops to her feet. Then she leans over and unlaces and pulls off her boots. When she's naked, she slowly hauls her gorgeous, sorry butt to the saddle and bends over.

Arielle stays in position, yelling and wiggling and dancing on her tiptoes as I very methodically set her ass on fire with my belt. None of this holding back because she's a lady crap. Arielle's a superhero's sidekick, so she gets one helluva strapping. Every crack of that belt kissing her skin echoes through the forest, almost as loudly as Arielle's howls. I make sure she really learns her lesson. I strap her bottom until it glows hot red in the setting sun, and I see the other women watching reach back to rub their own behinds in sympathy.

Afterward, Arielle is properly remorseful. She is a very trustworthy sidekick. I lie down in my sleeping blankets and draw her into my arms. She snuggles against me, trying to get her blazing sore bottom comfortable under the scratchy wool. When she wiggles too much, I swat her.

"Owwie!" Her tears are still close to the surface.

"Settle down," I say sternly. "Your backside's supposed to hurt. That's why it's called a punishment." As she tucks tearfully up against me, I tug my top open for her. Her lips nuzzle around for a nipple—licking, sucking, kissing. When she's settled in against me, when her mouth and tongue are comfortably suckling, I stroke her hair with one hand and finger myself to a raging orgasm with the other. Our misadventure has really scared me, so I take a very long time, letting the sweet tug of her mouth awaken the need deep inside me before I let myself come. Then we go to sleep. Arielle knows better than to ask to come when she's being punished.

The next morning, since everyone in camp is female, I make Arielle go around naked, wearing only her nipple ring and bracelets—and a lightly pressured clamp on her clit. Since I really want to draw attention to her flaming rear, I hang weights from the clamp, so she has to walk with her legs wide open. The weights swing back and forth, tugging mercilessly on her clit, making her juices run down her leg as her hips roll with each step. I invite the women to inspect her rear. After all, they were also endangered by her behavior. And I want them all very aware of what happens to anyone who disobeys me. However, since Arielle has paid for her sins, I also invite them to admire her body. After all, she is beautiful, and she likes showing off. She's strong and sexy and worthy of being a superhero's sidekick. And she loves having people finger her nipples and clit and the smooth, naked folds of her vulva.

By the way, Arielle keeps her pussy shaved for me—except for the rare occasions in winter when I'm cold and in the mood to kiss soft, fur-covered lips.

After she kneels and apologizes to each of the women in turn, they show her their forgiveness by lifting her carefully into a sturdy leather sling they've hung on a nearby tree. They cluster around her and lay their hands and mouths and bodies on her in blessing. Arielle moans as the clamps are removed first from one breast—a blue satin glove reaches out and sharply twists the oversensitized nipple, working it hard as the feeling surges back into it. Arielle's groans die to whimpers as the pain passes and the sore flesh is sucked tenderly into a hot, wet, waiting mouth. Then the other nipple is released, then the weights on her clit—one at a time so she feels each rush of blood in exquisite detail. Finally the clamp itself is removed—quickly. Strong lips immediately suck hard on her pulsing clit, working the awakening hood back and forth over the swollen nub beneath. Arielle yells, thrashing, her arms held tightly, lovingly, by other women. Fingers, too many to count, some gloved, some naked, slide over her folds, exploring her outer lips, her inner ones, moving deep into her cunt. Some of the wisest curl up inside her, pressing hard until she begs for release. Others, coated with butter, cup and massage her sore, well-punished butt cheeks, sliding up and down her crack, teasing her open, then sliding up inside.

I love hearing Arielle's continuous cries of pleasure as she submits to each respectfully questing touch.

"Jeena!" she begs. "Please! Please—I want you!!"

Arielle is now almost insane with lust, filled with the warm, loving, passionate absolution bestowed by the strong hands that restrain her. I pull off my warrior's clothes until only the leather straps of my sword harness cover my body. Then, facing the minions I straddle my lover's face, groaning in pleasure as Arielle's hot tongue licks my slit. I shiver as her cry vibrates against me, as I share in what I know is only one of many orgasms sweeping through her.

Arielle knows just where to press, where to suck and lick, to make my juices flow onto her face. Women all around me follow my lead, taking off their flowing silk and satin gowns, helping each other from velvet robes—pleasuring each other with touch as they bare their skin. A young woman with short red hair steps to my side, runs her fingers up my arm, kisses me as I grind against Arielle's face. The young woman kisses her way down my neck, over my shoulders, licking hotly, tantalizingly, over the curve of my breast. She rubs her cheek against my nipple, teasing a response from my already hard nub. Then she looks up at me, her dark brown eyes laughing, and slowly sucks the tip, then the entire areola into her mouth. And she keeps it there, suckling as I gasp with pleasure. I spread my legs wider, feel Arielle's tongue snake up inside me, licking deep into my cunt. Naked women take turns at each of Arielle's pleasure sites, kissing each other as they fondle her cunt and ass, fingering each other's vulva as they suck her breasts and clit. Someone new—I see only luxurious swirls of golden blond hair falling from an errant comb— reaches up and slides her fingers between the legs of the woman at my breast. The red-haired woman shudders, sucking harder, just as Arielle again sucks my clit. I yell as an orgasm resonates through my body.

My cry sets off a frenzy of motion. Another woman is at my other breast. I feel a hand trace my buttocks, then the hot lick of a tongue sliding into my crack. I squat over Arielle's face, quivering as the tongue slides over my sphincter, then licks determinedly, relaxing me, working its way in. A finger teases next to Arielle's lips. I shiver as my lover moves up, concentrating mercilessly on my clit. The finger slides into my cunt. Farther and farther. Pressing deep, curling forward, teasing the core spot deep inside me that sings with my most heart-stopping orgasms. Arielle's climaxes are almost constant now, her cries continuous. I look down to see her chest heaving as she gasps for enough oxygen to feed the fire of her passion, to meet the need devouring her. She arches to meet the questing mouths pulling her passion from her.

Suddenly Arielle shudders hard beneath me. In response, the women at my breasts suckle deep and long, as if they are drawing nourishment from the strength of my body. The tongue between my nether cheeks pokes in hard, fucking me with ardent, ladylike glee as I shiver deliciously. The finger in my cunt presses relentlessly, stroking the fluid source of my sex. Finally Arielle shrieks, licking once more, then she takes my clit fully in her lips and sucks, mercilessly working the hood of my clit over the nub beneath.

I scream out my war cry. My whole body shudders as my cunt contracts, my whoop of release deafening. Arielle howls against my cunt, arching up hard against me, convulsing as if her body is exploding with pleasure. My ears ring with the cries of joyfully shared orgasms all around me.

I lift Arielle from the sling and into my arms. We kiss each other and slowly collapse onto the sweet grass beneath us. The smell of well-licked, well-serviced cunts fills the clearing as the rest of the women join us and the morning sun rises higher into the trees.

We nap together, all of us, our faces resting between each other's legs and against each other's well-suckled breasts. Arielle and I especially sleep soundly. After all, another superhero adventure will be upon us when we wake up. We need to be ready.

Broken Moratoriums

Nancy Ferreyra

Carly squinted, trying to identify the gender of the person on the side of the highway. She slowed her sporty minivan, pulling over to the gravel shoulder, and watched in her rearview mirror as the tall, lean figure rose from the shaded rock and swaggered toward her. The person wore faded jeans, a sleeveless black T-shirt, and a red bandanna tied tightly over the head. Carly took off her sunglasses, her eyes stinging from the glare of the mid-afternoon sun reflecting off the white hood of her van. She rolled down the window and turned around, recognizing that unmistakable gait, created by the swing of a peg leg.

"Oh, my God, it's Adam!" Carly exclaimed.

Adam peered into the open window. "Hey, Carly!" she grinned. "What are you doin' out here?" Adam sounded nonchalant, as if they had just bumped into each other in the old Mission neighborhood, not on some two-lane highway in the middle of the Utah desert.

"Just taking the scenic route," Carly hedged. "What happened? Did your bike break down?"

"Yeah, flat tire." Adam leaned her dusty forearm on the car door and ducked her head, scowling in the general direction of her motorcycle.

"Want a lift somewhere?"

"Sure," her grin returned. "How far you goin'?"

"Moab."

At first they were stumped about getting the motorcycle in the van. Then Carly noticed the portable ramps she'd been lugging around since last month when she and Joan were house hunting. While Adam unfolded the aluminum channel, Carly slid into her wheelchair and stacked her cooler, gym bag, and gardening tools in a pile to make room. She held the ramp steady while Adam pushed the motorcycle up, happily distracted by her perfectly sculpted shoulders and her tattooed, flexing biceps.

Adam joked about bargaining with scorpions for leads to water, seemingly unruffled by the last five hours spent in more than 100-degree heat. Then she explained to Carly how she ended up stranded. Two days ago she had gotten word that her grandmother had been in an accident. Wanting to get to Denver before there was any further trouble, she had packed a few essentials and hopped on her bike that very afternoon. Tired of dodging the trucks on the crowded interstate, she had veered onto a back road. Ironically, she had run over a metal shard that had broken off a truck, puncturing her tire straight through to the tube. She had tried to patch it, but the air leaked out at the same rate she pumped it in.

"I just spent a good part of the afternoon sitting on that rock, wondering why this was happening to me. I was sure there must be a reason." She took a series of long gulps from her water bottle, freshly filled from Carly's supply. "And then you showed up. Out of nowhere. Unbelievable."

Feeling Adam's eyes on her, Carly glanced over, shyly returning her grin. "Yeah, pretty amazing," she murmured.

"Thank God for miracles," Adam said. "Yeah, looks like my luck has changed." Adam directed the air-conditioning vent to blow against her neck. "So what are you doin' out here?" she asked Carly again.

Carly busied herself with setting the cruise control while she contemplated her response. They drove through a deep canyon built of red, rocky walls—a majestic maze. "I just needed to get away for a while." She wasn't sure what Adam would think if she knew Carly had just not gone home one night, had decided to pass the freeway exit to her home, and had driven east over 1,000 miles.

The day Carly had taken off, she had felt a childhood craving for attention. As a child she would get attention by hiding, pretending to be lost. She had always been a "good kid" and couldn't bear her mother being mad or annoyed with her. So instead of misbehaving, she would hide—in between aisles in a store or in the bushes at the park—so her mother would look for her, only to be relieved and happy to find her, showering her with love and concern.

When Carly had reached Winnemucca, Nevada, two days ago, she realized that she not so much wanted to be found as to be seen for who she was. She felt invisible, her identity smothered by Joan, her lover who had her own image of Carly. Joan saw Carly as a fragile femme, to be treated delicately— inside and outside the bedroom. Joan held this image even though Carly ran her own flower stand and was captain of the local women's wheelchair basketball team. This weekend Carly was supposed to be moving in with Joan, but as the week had progressed, Carly had felt a noose tighten around her neck. She had arranged for someone to cover the flower shop while she prepared for the move, freeing her up to just take off. By the time Carly had driven into Salt Lake City, she had decided to break up with Joan. She had checked into a hotel and had written Joan a letter explaining she needed to be alone—and single—for a while. After she had dropped the letter at the post office, she decided to visit a friend in southeast Utah before heading home. This would give the letter time to reach Joan and give herself time to regroup.

Upon mailing the letter Carly had felt as if she had woken up from a dream, peeled off an old layer of skin. She had looked into people's faces, noticed the colors of their clothes. With a fresh vigor, she bounced as she transferred from her wheelchair to the driver's seat, her muscles stretching as she swung the van door shut. Wanting to feel the sun on her back and shoulders, she had changed into shorts and a skimpy tank top before she hit the road. Suddenly her trip had turned into an adventure, inspiring her to turn off the interstate onto a two-lane road. But after Carly had driven for an hour on the deserted highway, anxiety began to seep into her newfound liberation. What if she never had another lover? What if Joan were the last woman who would ever want her? Hooking up with Adam pushed those questions to the back of her mind. Adam's familiar presence soothed Carly. Everything about Adam felt easy—her tone even and light, her manner calm.

As they rode in the van, Carly steered the conversation to the condition of Adam's bike and what it would take to get it fixed. Adam was certain any garage would have the tube size she needed.

Talking in the van, Carly was keenly aware of Adam's brown, muscular body in the passenger's seat next to her. She kept her eyes on the curving road but pictured Adam's face, her finely sculpted features, a wide nose accentuating high cheekbones. About a year ago Adam had taken her out for a sushi lunch to plan a fund-raiser. Adam had wanted Carly's basketball team to play the staff of the women's community health clinic where Adam worked as a nurse practitioner. Watching Adam park her bike, Carly saw that she carried herself with typical butch demeanor, sauntering down the sidewalk in her leather jacket, swinging her peg leg, then stomping in a steel-toed boot. The choice of a wooden peg leg had struck Carly as odd, but she admired the defiance of it. As Adam approached Carly's table, an easy grin and gentle, lingering handshake contradicted the tough stance. As they talked, Adam's hazel eyes, light under black lashes, mesmerized Carly. Set against Adam's dark skin, they looked almost golden, especially when Adam grinned. When Adam flirted with Carly, Adam's eyes pulsated with her raised eyebrows. The texture of Adam's black hair seemed to vary depending on the length. That day Adam had it cut short, and tight curls bobbed around her high forehead. Carly watched her slender fingers gracefully handle a pair of chopsticks as she pinched pink hunks of raw fish and popped them into her mouth. Carly couldn't keep her eyes off Adam's mouth; her tongue was involved in each word she spoke, her fleshy lips parted as if she were nibbling everything Carly said.

At the benefit Adam had joined her coworkers and gotten into a wheelchair to play the pros. As always, Carly played aggressively, yelling orders at her teammates while she set a pick on the toughest player. Adam chose to guard Carly, sidling up beside her in hopes of intercepting the ball. But Carly out maneuvered Adam every time, twirling around out of Adam's reach and tearing off down the court. Adam raced after her, her long, loose curls flying about, but by the time Adam caught up with her Carly was tossing in a two-point shot. Adam had no hope of catching up, for each time Carly stole a glimpse of the strong, handsome woman chasing her down the court, she was driven to push even faster. During the second half, Adam, determined to get Carly's attention, groped Carly's chest and arms, trying to snatch the ball from her grasp, her long fingers grazing Carly's breasts. Excited by Adam's persistence, Carly loosened up and returned Adam's playful moves, holding the ball just long enough for Adam to lunge for it before passing it to another player.

After the game, Adam had followed Carly across the parking lot, where Joan was waiting in her truck. When Carly had introduced Joan as her girlfriend, Adam smiled broadly and shook Joan's hand, murmuring, "Oh, that's too bad."

Within a few weeks Carly agreed it was too bad. While her teammates shared stories of exciting, illicit exploits, Carly listened attentively, taking mental notes of what she was missing. Her silence was interpreted as collusion, the assumption that Carly was getting hot, satisfying sex on a regular basis from Joan, a staunch, hard-core butch. But the truth was that Joan was a clumsy, unadventurous lover who seemed relieved to discover Carly couldn't have orgasms. Their lovemaking consisted of a few kisses, brief breast fondling, then Joan climbing onto Carly and fucking her with a few fingers while she got herself off by humping against her wrist. Many nights Carly lay beside a conked-out Joan, constructing detailed fantasies in which she would get her needs met. Many featured other women, although some involved Joan. Lately her most satisfying scenario had been tying Joan up and fucking her, deeply and roughly, showing her how Carly liked it. This fantasy was doubly taboo because

Joan had never allowed Carly to touch her below the waist.

Carly gripped the steering wheel. Remembering the stifling weight of Joan's body draped over hers, she heard Joan's
grunts in her ear. She shuddered.

"Is the air-conditioning too much?" Adam asked.

"No," Carly said. "On second thought, could we roll the
windows down?" Although the air was dry and hot, Carly
filled her lungs with it, turning her cheek to feel the force of
it on her face.

They chattered in raised voices until early evening when
they drove into a town with two establishments: Mike's
Garage and Greta's Motel and Diner. Mike's had closed;
Adam would have to fix her tire tomorrow. While Carly got a
room at Greta's, Adam scoped out a place to unroll her sleeping bag, explaining that she wanted to sleep under the stars.
They agreed to meet for dinner in an hour.

The management's idea of wheelchair accessible was a room
with only one narrow double bed to allow more maneuvering
space. The bathroom was normal size with no grab bars, but
Carly could manage. After sitting behind the wheel all day,
Carly was stiff, her muscles tense. She dumped her bag on the
bed and went out to take a strenuous push, forging her way
down a steep, dirt road behind the motel until her arms and
neck were streaked with grimy sweat. Back in her room she
lowered herself into a steamy tub, rinsing the dirt off her
arms, tanned from the sun. She sighed, thinking of Adam's
body, brown all over, imagining her warm skin. Carly com-
pared her dense frame to Adam's sinewy one as she scrubbed
her thick neck, then ran the soapy cloth over her broad shoulders, lathering underneath her arms. She spread her fingers on
the surface of the water, contrasting her thick hands to

Adam's slender ones. Then she flipped them over and smiled at the rough calluses on her palms, just like Adam's.

Carly had seen the outline of a nipple ring through Adam's shirt. She fingered her sensitive breasts, pinching the flesh at the base of her nipple to see what it might feel like to have one. Washing between her legs, she imagined Adam's firm thighs. How would Adam be as a lover? Was she a stone butch like Joan, or would she let Carly touch her?

Carly leaned back, submerging herself up to her neck. She closed her eyes and enjoyed a slow replay of the basketball game. Then she retired the possibility of Adam into her box of missed opportunities.

After she dried off, she threw on a shirt she had picked up in Salt Lake City and pulled the tie out of her hair, letting it fall around her shoulders. Then she crossed the parking lot to the diner to meet Adam.

As they chatted over their open menus, Carly, still entranced, glanced at Adam's mouth. She pretended not to notice Adam taking a leisurely survey of her neck and shoulders, her steady gaze settling on Carly's breasts. When their eyes accidentally met and Carly caught Adam staring, Adam just smiled appreciatively, not embarrassed in the least. Over roast beef and mashed potatoes, Adam announced she had telephoned her family, and her grandmother had stabilized. Adam was relieved and looked forward to a good night's sleep. The two women talked about their lives back in San Francisco, the type of customers Carly sees at her flower stand, Adam's caseload at the clinic. Adam suggested another basketball benefit. "I'd like another chance," she grinned.

"We could work on that," Carly said, feeling her cheeks get warm.

After dinner, Adam ordered a fresh raspberry shortcake, the special dessert of the house. With each bite, Adam's mouth grew darker and Carly's eyes grew wider, gaping at Adam's crimson tongue as she licked the cream from her lips. Adam nudged the plate toward Carly, who obligingly sunk her fork into the spongy red cake. Adam asked Carly how she and "what's her name" were doing. Carly carefully wiped her mouth, then looked Adam in the eye. "Joan and I are splitting up," she said.

Adam leaned forward, her fork poised above the plate. "I'm sorry—did you say you're splitting up or that you had split up?"

"Well, she should get my letter tomorrow," Carly said.

Adam raised her eyebrows. "So, you're *going* to split up."

"No," Carly said adamantly. "We have split up."

Adam nodded slowly and asked for the check.

The air outside had cooled; the sky was black with a smattering of stars. Cricket chirps mingled with the stomp-crunch as first Adam's boot, then her peg hit the dirt path. Pushing back to the motel, Carly's head felt heavy. Judging from her silence, Carly figured Adam must be tired too.

"Are you sure you don't want to just crash in the motel?" Carly asked.

"Yeah, I'd really like to take advantage of being out of the city and sleeping outside," she said. "But a hot shower would be great."

* * *

Carly flopped into the middle of the bed and turned on the television. Adam took her backpack and crutches into the bathroom and closed the door. Carly's mind drifted to images of Adam standing in the shower, crutches under her armpits, water streaming over her shoulders, between her breasts. She pictured Adam throwing her head back, eyes shut, water pouring over her face.

Carly woke up with Adam perched beside her on the bed, her hand on Carly's belly. Carly sat up with a start, propping herself up on her elbows.

"I must have dozed off." Her face flushed, as if Adam had been a spectator to her fantasies. Adam pointed the remote at the television, turning it off.

"Long drive. You must be tired." Adam spoke softly.

Carly relaxed against the pillows, watching the drops of water gather on the tips of Adam's black, spiraled locks, then splash onto the shoulder of her plaid shirt. The room smelled of Adam's spicy deodorant. "I just wanted to say good night," Adam said, grabbing her crutches and getting to her feet. "Mind if I leave my stuff here and get it in the morning?" She hoisted her sleeping bag onto her back, propping her crutches under her arms. "My backpack and my leg?"

"Sure," Carly said.

"Thanks. See you in the morning." Adam walked out, turning to smile briefly before closing the door behind her.

Carly curled up under the covers, still in her shorts and tank top, leaving the dim lamp on. She drifted off to visions of Adam's naked body stretched out under the stars, the moon's rays shining on her dark skin. The wind whirled around Adam, lifting her off the ground, and she flew through the night sky. Then Carly flew with her; they approached San Francisco's skyline. Adam told Carly they were going to Hawaii but that she had to stop at her apartment and get some things. When they got there she took her key out and tapped on the door with it.

The same tap, tap dragged Carly out of sleep. "Carly?" Tap, tap. "Carly? It's Adam."

Carly jerked up and looked around the dingy motel room, remembering where she was. The lit room tricked her into thinking it was morning, but the digital clock told her it was three minutes after 3 A.M. She slid into her wheelchair and went to the door. "Adam?"

Adam hobbled in on her crutches, her load lopsided on her back. "Are you still up?" She was breathless. "I saw your light on and thought maybe you were still awake."

"No." Carly rubbed her eyes. "No, I was asleep. What's wrong?"

"Some cowboy was hassling me," Adam said. "Telling me I wasn't in a campground and..." She waved her hand. "Forget it. I'm sorry I woke you up. The office here is closed, so I can't get a room. I'll just go crash in the van, if that's OK with you."

"OK." Carly dug her keys out of her bag but didn't let go when Adam's fingers closed around them. "But the motorcycle is still in there." Carly motioned to the narrow bed. "Just stay here—it's all right."

"Are you sure?"

"Yeah," Carly said. "That guy might be watching you. This would be safer."

"Look, I'm not afraid of some redneck with a badge—"

"He was a cop?"

"*Sheriff* is probably what they call them around here," Adam muttered.

"Don't fool around with that stuff. It's not worth it." Carly was stern. She wheeled to the door and threw the deadbolt.

Adam drew in a few pensive breaths, blinking her eyes

slowly. Then she dropped her sleeping bag to the floor and slumped into the tattered armchair. "You're right," she sighed. "I just hate all the stupid laws about land, you know? Why should anyone get to decide whose it is and what anyone can and can't do on it?"

It was the closest thing to a frown Carly had ever seen on Adam's face. Her eyebrows were pinched, her eyes narrow. "Hey, you should go back to bed," she said finally. "I'm gonna stay up and write a little bit to cool down."

Carly wished she could cool Adam down. She climbed back into bed and closed her eyes, her heart racing. Soon Adam would be lying next to her, just inches away. How could she resist the desire to reach out and touch her? Carly wished feverishly that Adam would make a move on her. Carly lay still and listened to Adam scribble in her journal, furiously at first, then slower. Adam chuckled, scrawled a bit more, and sighed. Then a long silence. Had she decided to sleep in the chair? Had she just been playing and now was afraid Carly would call her bluff? Carly couldn't bear the suspense.

"Feel better?" She sat up and looked at Adam.

"Yeah. Taking a little time out to write always puts things in perspective." Adam pulled off her boot, dropping it to the floor with a thud. She hesitated beside the bed. Carly pulled the covers back. "So you think you can sleep now?" Carly asked.

"Yeah." She sat on the edge of the bed, still fully dressed, carefully lying her crutches on the floor. "I'm sorry I woke you up."

"That's all right." Carly laid back down. "I'm glad you came back."

"Feeling lonely?" Adam stretched out beside Carly, stuffing the pillow behind her head.

"A little," Carly said. She rolled onto her side, propping her head on her elbow, looking down at Adam. Adam's loose curls, spread across the pillow, softly framed her face. "I like being with you," Carly mumbled, biting the corner of her lip. A sly grin flickered across Adam's face. Carly leaned forward, gently pressing her lips to Adam's. She peered into Adam's face. Adam's gaze moved from Carly's mouth to the wall, avoiding Carly's face. Drawing in a deep breath, Adam shook her head slowly. "Carly," she began, but before she could say another word, Carly kissed her again, slowly sliding her lips over Adam's mouth, her lips as plump and soft as Carly had imagined. Carly's tongue danced around Adam's, the tips of their tongues teasing one another.

Adam rolled on top of Carly, sliding her stump between Carly's thighs, her tongue darting between Carly's teeth. Adam's hot, wet kisses covered Carly's ears, then throat, her breath on Carly's sternum. "Carly, I've wanted to touch you for months," she whispered. "I can't believe I finally am." She tugged at Carly's neckline.

Carly sat up, rolling Adam aside. She pulled her shirt over her head, her nipples hard under Adam's gaze.

"Carly, this is the first time I've ever been with anyone who's...disabled." Adam looked into Carly's face. "Is there anything I should know?"

Carly's fingers worked the buttons on Adam's shirt. "I can't feel much below the waist," Carly said. She felt her throat constrict. "So it needs to be hard. Rough," she said, speaking clearly. She peeled Adam's shirt over her shoulders. "And I need to keep track of my legs."

Carly pulled Adam on top of her, and they tumbled back onto the bed. Adam buried her face between Carly's breasts, nibbling the soft flesh. Adam's long, firm tongue followed the pink curve around first one taut nipple, then the other, sending tingles through Carly's gut. Throwing her head back on the pillow, Carly cried out when Adam's lips tugged at her nipple. Carly rocked her chest toward Adam's mouth, urging her to suckle harder.

Adam's scratchy palm roamed over Carly's belly, then Carly felt a faint tickle between her legs. She watched Adam finger-fuck her, stroking her inside and out, murmuring how wet and soft she was. Cupping her palm around Adam's small, firm breasts, Carly slipped her finger through the gold hoop and twisted, clamping her lips over Adam's other stiff nipple, suckling between tongue and teeth.

Carly clasped Adam's wrist, thrusting her hand further inside. "Harder," Carly whispered. "So I can feel you."

Adam got up and hopped over to her bag. Tugging her jeans down to her thighs, she strapped on the biggest dildo Carly had ever seen.

Kicking her jeans off, Adam climbed onto Carly and pushed into her, slowly sliding in and out. Carly squeezed Adam's cheeks for her to thrust harder, deeper. Adam rolled onto her back, letting Carly ride her while she bucked underneath, driving the dildo deep inside her. Grinding her hips to Adam's, Carly felt filled to her core, little whimpers escaping her throat. Then Adam tossed Carly on her back, fucking her swiftly, firmly, their bellies hot, thighs sticky with sweat. Latching onto Carly's breast, Adam suckled hard and quick, groaning as she came again and again.

Adam rolled them onto their sides, nestling between Carly's breasts. Carly held Adam between her thighs, petting her from the crown of her head to the small of her back.

Carly tilted Adam's face toward hers, pressing her mouth to Adam's. Adam responded with a sloppy, languid kiss until Carly pushed her lips apart, wrapping her tongue around Adam's. Adam's lips came alive, sucking on Carly's tongue and chin, then making a wet, hot trail down her front to her bush.

"I can't really feel that," Carly breathed.

"Do you want me to stop?"

Carly shook her head and watched Adam dip her face between Carly's thighs, licking and sucking her clit, her cunt. Carly chewed her lips, wanting to taste between Adam's legs. When Carly pulled Adam toward her, Adam braced herself, resisting. Tightening her grip, Carly dragged Adam on top of her, sliding beneath Adam's thighs. Adam grunted and lowered her cunt onto Carly's eager mouth. Carly buried her face in Adam's musky scent, drinking in her juices, then pounding her tongue deep inside her. Sucking Adam's stiff clit, Carly followed Adam's rocking hips until Adam gasped and pulled away. But Carly held Adam firmly, flicking her tongue against the tip of Adam's throbbing clit, her juice dribbling down Carly's chin. Moaning Carly's name, Adam's body quivered as one powerful orgasm rolled through her womb. Panting, Adam collapsed, pulling Carly into her arms, pressing her lips to Carly's temple.

At daybreak Carly got up to pee. When she crawled back into bed, she watched Adam sleeping, studying every inch of her. Adam lay on her belly, a pillow tucked under her chest, her mouth a pucker. Carly examined the tattoo on her bicep, an intricate design of a snake entwined in a double women's symbol. Looking closer, Carly noticed a tattoo of a purple iris on Adam's shoulder blade. Adam stirred and opened her eyes. Focusing on Carly's face, she smiled sleepily. "Carly." Then she rolled onto her back, hugging the pillow to her chest. "Damn!"

"Something wrong?" Carly asked.

"Too late now," she muttered.

"Too late for what?"

"Broke my moratorium," Adam said. "No more rebounding babes."

Carly frowned. "I'm not rebounding."

Adam chuckled. "Right," she glanced over at Carly. "You haven't broken up, so how can you be rebounding?"

"I have broken up," Carly asserted. "I'm leaving her," she declared.

"You haven't even..." Adam sat on the edge of the bed, her back to Carly. "OK," she said. "Never mind." There was a thick silence. "I've just had some bad experiences." Adam brushed her hair from her forehead.

Carly scooted across the bed, wrapping her arms around Adam's waist. "Was last night one of them?" she whispered. "A bad experience?"

Adam leaned her head against Carly's, the curve of her cheek giving away her grin. "No," she sighed. She threaded her fingers through Carly's. Running her lips over Adam's shoulders, Carly slid her hand between Adam's legs.

Carly pulled Adam back into bed, looking around for the dildo. Maybe Carly would wear it this time. If not this time, she was sure there would be another.

Chosen

Renette Toliver

Being a night person, I was always used to seeing the stars burn in the Louisiana sky. Still, nothing could've prepared me for this.

* * *

The French Quarter has always allowed people to become lost if they so choose. It's just too easy. Around almost every street corner is a dark hole in the wall where you can listen to music or get a drink. Lately after work I have found myself doing this more often, though it seemed I would go and just be restless. At night I'd stare out of my window overlooking the Mississippi, watching the eerie night sky, and feel this desire to walk along its dark banks. My friends thought I was crazy. It's not the brightest idea for a black woman to roam the streets of N'awlins after the sun goes down. But there I was; *searching,* I called it. For what, I don't know.

Even as a child I often snuck out of my bedroom window, caught up in the sounds of Dixieland jazz that seemed to float in the wind. I had never been afraid to venture out in the dark alone. The demons in my dreams haunted me the most. Seemed like when it was dark you could see a different side of people—how they acted when cut loose from the ties of the real world.

Most times I wandered around until I got to Ms. Cora's house over by the cemetery. She often let me sit on her front porch with her while she told stories of the "old ways." A lot of people in the neighborhood didn't like her. They called her the old gypsy woman and a witch, though Ms. Cora just laughed when I asked why. Even my mama didn't like me hanging around her, but I didn't care. I'd go anyway.

Ms. Cora told us children (and anyone else who would listen) about the people of the night. She said there were those of us who were different—a special group of people who roamed the night in search of others like them. And when the hunger hit they searched for those willing to be seduced into the dark side. It sounded like the demons I dreamed about, the demons I searched for.

Real as it seemed when I was 12, as an adult I found stories like that hard to believe—that is, until the day *she* walked into my life.

I was in one of my moods again, walking around the tattered streets of the French Quarter. I unconsciously headed toward the Night Owl, a club I had been finding myself at lately. A small jazz group played in the corner, while smoke from a machine filled the humid air. Overall it was the perfect place to get lost in. On this particular night, though, something strange happened. *She* walked in.

She was uncanny. Tall and slender, she had almost a regal look about her. She wore all black down to her boots, and her cocoa-colored skin contrasted with her deep black hair, which was pulled back from her face. Her most striking feature was her eyes, gray like a cat's and staring straight at me. Instantly a chill came over me as our eyes met and locked.

She smiled briefly, then took a table in the far corner. I couldn't help feeling her presence; the air around me grew thick with the feel of this stranger. To tear my thoughts away from her, I tried to lose myself in the music. But even with the horns blowing—a loud pulsating rhythm that vibrated through the floorboards—I still found myself distracted.

A strange feeling came over me—one I'd never experienced. I felt her eyes pierce through my soul with a heat all their own. The feeling was so intense that my nipples stiffened underneath my T-shirt, and my panties became wet with my desire. Something had definitely begun.

The music faded into the background as this sensation intensified. I felt compelled to turn around; once again she was staring straight at me. I took this as an invitation, or maybe a *summons*. Whatever it was, I decided to talk to her. I wanted to play it cool and casually make my move, but like a character in a bad movie, I stumbled over my own feet trying to get to her table.

Before I could say anything, she spoke. "I've been waiting for you."

Gathering my composure, I continued the conversation. "Oh, really? Do I know you?"

She smiled. "Don't you?"

Intrigued for the moment, I decided to play the game. "No, but I'd like to."

"Then let me introduce myself." She held out a long slender hand. "My name is Maya."

I don't remember seeing her lips form the words, and yet I distinctly heard them. As I took her hand, a bolt of electricity shot through me as a vision of the two of us intertwined in

a moment of uncontrollable passion raced before my eyes.
Then the vision was gone just as quickly as it had come. Trying to shake off the feeling, I let go of her hand.

"My name is Tanya," I breathed.

I couldn't tell whether the room had gotten warmer or if
my body was reacting to Maya's touch. All I knew is that I
wanted, almost needed, to feel her touch again. Maya looked
up at that moment, reached out, and gently stroked my hair.
"You're very beautiful, Tanya."

I couldn't speak. I found myself captured by her eyes and
lost in the music of her voice. The band played, and people
came and went as usual, but here at this table time stood still.

Her voice again whispered in my head. "Would you like to
go for a walk?"

I nodded.

The cool night air was a welcome relief from the heat of the
club. My head began to clear from the fog it had been in. An
old garden patch stood a block away, and the soft summer
breeze blew the sweet smell of roses through the air. The
moon wasn't quite full, but its presence reflected off the sides
of buildings. For the most part the streets were deserted—just
a few drunks here and there trying to find their way home.
Nothing unusual for Bourbon Street at 3 o'clock in the morning. Feeling more comfortable and confident, I asked Maya
where she wanted to go.

"My place," she whispered.

The wind began to blow harder, and again my head started
to spin. When the world around me stopped moving, the
street was gone. The walls around me were made of earth.
They were cold to the touch, and my body was shivering, but
the room itself was warm. Candles burned in a corner, giving

off an amber glow that softly illuminated the room.

The room was sparsely furnished with an antique four-poster bed covered in thick satin bedcovers and a matching dressing table without a mirror. I wanted to ask where we were, but when I turned around she was gone. My head was still spinning from our journey, and I sat down to gather my senses. Not only did I not know where I was, but I also had no idea how I had arrived there.

As a sudden gust of cold air brushed across the back of my neck, I jumped. I turned around but saw no one.

"Maya, is that you?"

The answer—the eerie sound of silence—hung in the air. I got up and looked around, searching for a door or some other way out. There was only one large pristine window, completely covered by thick black drapes. Then I felt her hot breath against my ear.

"Tanya, I hope you weren't leaving."

I turned around expecting to see her, but like before no one was there. The candles flickered wildly, and when I turned back I was startled to find her standing in front of me. She had changed clothes and no longer wore the form-fitting jeans and bodysuit she had on at the club. She now wore a long, black silk gown that clung to her body like a second layer of skin. Her straightened black hair hung loosely down her back—an endless river of black water.

"You startled me."

She glided over, as if her feet, hidden under the gown, never touched the ground. She carried a tray with two metal goblets.

"I thought you might want a drink." A warm smile formed, and my uneasiness started to fade. Her gray eyes continued to stare through me as the sweet yet unfamiliar warm liquid flowed down my throat.

"Where are we? And how did we get here?" I questioned, more intrigued than angry. Waiting for an answer, I continued to sip from my now half-filled glass.

Her long arms stretched out in an exaggerated gesture, and speaking in distinct Creole French, she answered, "Why, Tanya, you're here at my place...just like you wanted, just like you've always wanted."

A chill ran up my spine as she repeated the last part of her sentence, and a new feeling of vulnerability washed over me, as if she were bringing some dark secret of mine to the surface. I quickly took another drink, attempting to swallow back the demons that had plagued my nightmares since childhood. *Who are you?* I thought. Feeling woozy, I sat on the edge of the bed, my body melting into the thick red satin.

"What's in this?" I asked, holding up my drink.

"Oh, that? That's an old family secret. Some have said it is an aphrodisiac. I tend to think it warms the blood."

She grabbed her silver-and-pearl-handled hairbrush from the dressing table and joined me on the bed. "May I?"

I nodded. Long fingers released my thick shoulder-length hair, which I had carefully French-braided before going out, and I felt the weight of Maya's body against my own. The hearty scent of musk floated from her as she leaned in even closer. I inhaled deeply, caught up in her scent, her magic. The brush came down smoothly against my scalp. Her arms moved in time with my deep breathing—long strokes from top to bottom.

Up, down. Up, down. I felt her breath on the back of my neck as she moved my hair easily to the side. The brush paused for a moment. A warm hand found the side of my neck. I grew hot beneath her touch, my skin tingling. *What are you?*

"Tanya, I am the breeze that travels through the air. I am the shadow that leads to nowhere. I am the flame that heats many souls in strife, the silent watcher in the night. I call on those throughout space and time, hoping they'll join me and be forever mine."

The heat from her words burned through to my core. The shadows of the demons I had grown up believing in rose against the wall. The force of my blood rushed through my body; its pace quickened. I felt her breath closer on my neck. I wanted to give in, to surrender. To what, I had no idea.

"Maya?"

The spell was broken, the demons gone. The brush resumed its lulling pace. Up, down, up, down. I turned to face her, unsure of what I would see. Her skin, almost translucent now, glowed in the candlelight. Her gray eyes gazed deep into mine. Her face slowly started toward mine, and my heart began to pound. The moment seemed to last forever. Her eyes never left mine, and my dizziness returned. The closer she came, the less in control I felt. My body was betraying my mind.

I felt the familiar flush of desire rise to an uncontrollable level. I didn't want her to stop, but part of me hesitated. Had she captured me under some sort of spell?

The familiar whisper echoed inside my head. "I could take you that way, Tanya, but I'd rather have you come...willingly."

A flood of emotions enveloped me as her soft, sensual lips caressed mine. A vision of Maya sucking on my peaked nipples flashed before my eyes once again, weakening me. My body ached deep inside. A need I had been searching to fill all these nights was suddenly making its presence known.

Maya smiled softly while my hands eagerly explored every part of her willing body. Maya left me momentarily exasperated. My breathing grew rapid and shallow, the moisture gone from my throat, only to be found much lower. She stood tall and graceful in front of me. Within seconds, the black silk garment slid to the floor, exposing her delectable curves. Full breasts and shapely hips sat atop her long legs—dancer's legs, thick and muscular. The mere sight of her clouded my mind.

"Tanya, may I have you?"

Before I could answer I felt her weight surround me. Her tongue plunged deep into my throat, and my body succumbed to passion. Maya's movements, swift and languid, overtook me. Fluid hands reached under my shirt and released my breasts from my lace bra. I fumbled to unsnap my jeans, but before I could finish she had them in a pile with the rest of my clothes.

Skin to skin, we embraced and kissed. Each time her lips met mine, I sank deeper into a new level of submission. Maya's hands ran across my body hungrily, studying me, memorizing me, reminding me I was now her possession. Soft lips captured my breasts, sucking them until the prophecy of my earlier visions was totally fulfilled.

"May I have you?"

She bent down and kissed my thighs, starting an upward journey to heaven. My body trembled as her lips found my sex, wet and inviting. Maya continued her exploration slowly, her eyes closed, her body hot. Her tongue, long and thin, penetrated me deeply. Instantly my walls constricted around her tongue as it moved slow and steady. My clit, swollen and throbbing, waited eagerly for the moment Maya's tongue would embrace it.

Maya, I'm ready.

"I know, Tanya."

Firm licks attacked my clit, and my mind began to blur in the thought, the feel, the presence of her. I sensed the oncoming explosion of desire. Understanding my need, she removed her tongue and replaced it with two fingers. Her pace quickened, and our shadows began to grow against the walls.

Reality faded, and inside my head I heard the voices of thousands of souls captured by her rejoicing.

"You know, there are those of us who are different, Tanya. Some of us live and feed in the dark."

Was that old Ms. Cora's voice? Steadily Maya's fingers moved in and out of me. Somehow through the haze I found my way to her own sex. Three fingers slipped inside easily, her wetness oozing down to my palm. It was time. My search had brought me to this place...to her. A long arm encircled my neck and pulled me close. Our lips met once again.

"Tanya, come with me." Her lips escaped mine as my orgasm approached. The roar began in my throat, heading toward the surface. Her tongue encircled my breast, preparing me, searching for the right place. As a scream of release escaped my lips, sharp teeth penetrated my breast.

I closed my eyes, caught up waves of pleasure that completely racked my body. The pain intensified the pleasure. The pleasure intensified the pain. Minutes, hours, years—nothing seemed to matter except this moment. Our hearts beat in time while Maya drank from me. Our bodies swayed. My orgasm passed from me to her in long deep draws from my breasts.

Her body grew flushed, my essence freeing her from her hunger. Darkness started to come behind my closed eyelids. She then released herself, my life essence dripping down her lips in a trickle of crimson.

For moments after, my body was sensitive. I heard people's voices from the street echo above. The bedcovers beneath my flesh made me tremble in a mixture of pleasure and pain. My eyes saw faces in the shadows, and the candlelight reflected in Maya's eyes burned through my skin. The world I once believed in was now a memory.

I lay in her arms, my body recovered, waiting for sleep to capture me. Our worlds connected; our heartbeats slowed back to their normal pace. She handed me my goblet, now refilled to the top. The familiar warm liquid burned pleasantly down my throat. My thirst seemed endless. She smiled.

"We should go. I must get you home before sunrise," she whispered.

"Will I see you again, Maya?"

"There will be a next time. I promise you that."

"You never told me what this was," I said, holding up my glass.

She smiled again. "Blood."

She kissed me deeply, stifling any words I might have been able to utter. My head began to swim in a mixture of blood and lust. I closed my eyes, drugged by the magic in her kiss. Weak from our lovemaking, I drifted off to sleep in her slender arms.

When I opened my eyes again, I was in my own bed. My head was pounding as if I had drunk one too many of something. The sun was up; it seemed to be at least 80 degrees already. The clock on my night stand read 8 A.M. I jumped out of bed and headed to the kitchen.

On the table stood a vase with a bouquet of crimson roses. Suddenly I remembered last night. The club, the sex...Maya. I picked up the card from the vase and ran to the mirror in the hall. I pulled down the T-shirt I always wore to bed and inspected my chest. Underneath my right breast was a tiny red mark.

As I ran my finger over it, a small pulse made me shiver with pleasure. I read the card I still had clutched in my hand:

Until next time...Maya

I ran my finger over my wound once again and smiled.

Thank You, Jackie James
Caitlyn Marie Poland

I must have been 18 before I realized I was not the owner of some unfortunate disease, that I did not possess an illness so contagious it would envelop others and corrupt them, with its cells multiplying so fast they defied physiology. Beyond belief, I know, but before the tender age of 18, I was a timid teenager, shadowed by convention and, as such, by conventional thoughts. I never had the strength to state my convictions, let alone stand by them.

I followed suit even though I felt different, and I treated this difference as a phase I would eventually outgrow. Fucking pathetic in retrospect, I know, but there I was, slaving endlessly to satisfy my peer group's membership criteria. Not one of my friends mentioned lesbianism, so neither did I. I tried desperately to blend into my surroundings, to mix and match with my comrades, and I think I succeeded. I actually enjoyed it at times. I remember laughing a great deal, so something must have amused me. Well, lots of things really…except for what I sarcastically called the "couples market." Any equal number of males and females together in a house unoccupied by parents equates a market. Inevitably male and female would pair together and heterosexuality would dominate the scene, while the lights became dimmer and the music became louder. Sometimes lips would meet, and sometimes they would not. I preferred the latter, and it was only following the rumors relating to my, shall I say, "dislike of boys" that I chose to protect my reputation. I chose to lip massage with David, an 18-year-old captain of the football team.

It was horrible, and in truth I felt sick. I mean, it was not just that I wanted David to magically metamorphose into a buxom brunette who smelled of Gaultier perfume, but he also had to be the most vile kissing partner I had ever been with. Granted, my experience was limited, but his actions were purely self-satisfying and even aggressive at times. His tongue dominated my mouth, and when I finally suctioned him from my face, strings of saliva broke uneasily and snapped back to his lips. My chin felt as if it had been stripped and dipped in salt, since his cheap aftershave reacted explosively with my soft, moisturized skin. I must have resembled the victim of a very suspicious facial-hair-removing salon. Admittedly, though, I would be lying if I said my cunt didn't react slightly. With my eyes closed, with complete concentration, and with my sexual confusion, I treated David's hard and still-trousered penis as an inanimate object as he rubbed against my inner thigh. In masturbation I had often teased myself with a roll-on deodorant bottle, and David's prick felt similar...except not as good. No one knew my cunt like I did; no one had been that close. No one knew how to slip a condom over my 50%-larger-size bottle, how to smear it with K-Y, how to rub it on my clitoris, then slowly penetrate it farther and farther with each stroke. No one had heard my cries of pleasure, increasing in volume as I forced entry with increasing urgency. And no one had heard me come or watched me shake or felt my juice through their fingers and down their arm. No one. Yet in relation to David, even the most creative minds can weaken, and as I instinctively opened my eyes—due to near suffocation via David's tongue invasion—all was most definitely lost.

Poor boy. An erect penis, a crimson face, and testosterone overdrive, and I had just chosen to suppress his sexual flow. David obviously did not want to stop, and as I opted for conversation over a grope in the dark, he grunted uneasily. While my friends and their partners declared undying love for each other (until the next day), I discussed *Henry IV* and *Far From the Madding Crowd*. Unfortunately, David had dropped English literature the previous year, and my monologue did not claim his interest. The night collapsed from then on, and I was not surprised to not see him again. He had served his purpose, though, in that he most definitely protected my image for a while, and he kept my name from being linked to certain girls in school, whom we lovingly called "those fucking lezzies." I appreciated that. I mean, my school was far from progressive, and as my sexuality was little more than a ball of confusion, I more than willingly declined the title of "dyke" or "fucking lezzie"—the former title of which I only use as a term of endearment today, ironically so.

I was simply a bag, no, a fucking suitcase, of mixed emotions that fought against each other with amazing stamina, and for years I actually thought I was "not normal." But I pretended well, and up to and including the fifth form (or year 11 as it's known now) I was only subjected to one more "couples market" and one more "David"…until I met Jackie.

Following fifth form, I was strangely enough granted permission to continue my education into the sixth form, and along with this status came the sixth-form comforts. I

clearly remember observing the lower-school gatherings outside my privileged sixth-form block during their infrequent
break times. They appeared cold—while I was most definitely warm—and I watched as the heated breath from their
mouths created artificial fog in their immediate social space.

I was always content to be inside, comfortable, relaxed, and
usually occupied with a chicken and sweet corn Cup-a-Soup.
Catholic Reorganization, though, was not as much fun. It
meant sharing my wall heater with 40% more students, but at
least I could console myself with a heating appliance by my
side, as opposed to a cold looking friend. A crowded interior
was far superior to a spacious exterior with fully automatic air-
conditioned comrades.

Nevertheless, Catholic Reorganization did bring one
major positive—well, one major—person, Jackie James. I
recall her as tall, brunette, and fucking attractive but also
aggressive. Incredibly aggressive. She bullied me constantly, and for months I feared going anywhere alone: to the bus
stop, to the cloak room, and even to the toilet. Eighteen-
years-old, I was just beginning to experience the power
games that "freshers" faced at age 11. But, believe me, she
was aggressive. She intimidated with simply one look, and
as I sat directly in front of her during sociology, I swear I
could feel the burn of her stare drilling parallel holes in the
back of my head.

A stereotypical bully, Jackie always moved in a group.
Surrounded by her pack, she'd terrorize the corridors and
stairways...and for some unknown reason I was always the
main target.

Then one day Jackie stood alone, isolated from the herd
she held together to perfection. She had been excused from

physical education to retrieve her asthma medication from her locker, which unfortunately stood next to mine. Now, if there is a God, she plays some strange tricks at times, as Jackie's attack of breathlessness uncannily coincided with my late arrival following a long-overdue dental appointment. My mouth felt swollen, and I could clearly taste blood combined with the coffee breath of an overeager dentist. Not surprisingly, then, the image of Jackie next to my locker did not appease me at all.

Then the ogre spoke. "Move, bitch."

I guessed Jackie was talking to me. I had worn that tasteful pseudonym since her arrival at my school.

"I said fucking move, bitch." Now, at that point, I could have corrected her. She had actually said, "Move, bitch," not "Fucking move, bitch." For some reason I thought best not to. Then it struck me: Why not? Jackie was alone; her fan club was in class. She was vulnerable—and she was a prime target. She was my prey.

Still, I went with my first thought...best not.

Unfortunately, though, I had shown Jackie a weakness, in that I wasn't going to retaliate. My underbelly was on display, and Jackie attacked with a vengeance. Spinning me around, she calmly placed one hand on my shoulder while the thumb and forefinger of the other squeezed either side of my mouth. She spoke again. "Have you got some sort of fucking hearing impediment or something?" Her words amazed me. She squeezed again, but this time she had made a fatal mistake of enormous proportions. The injection I had endured to remedy my cavity and toothache had begun to wear off, and daggers of pain jabbed at my face in all directions. I lost control, pulling away from Jackie's grip and mimicking her stance.

"Bitch? You called me a bitch?"

I had been at a loss for words, so reflecting back on Jackie's statement had seemed as good a starting point as any.

"Do you find it amusing? Does intimidation give you some sort of kick?" I was rambling and well aware of it, but I was so angry I honestly did not give a fuck. I was on a roll. Jackie did not initially react, though, and as her face changed it began to reflect both her and my own shock at my actions.

"What? What the fuck are you looking at, Jackie?"

She did not respond, and for a lifetime there was silence. Then ever so slowly her top lip curled slightly upward until a smirk spread across her face. I again responded according-ly, mimicking Jackie's Presley impersonation until we were both grinning inanely. Then, strangely enough, we were laughing, giggling uncontrollably. My breathing—and Jackie's—became erratic, and then it happened. Jackie calmly leaned forward and kissed me. In shock, I remained still, somehow not feeling the aftereffects of my dental treatment. For what seemed an eternity Jackie lingered on my mouth. Her tongue played gently on my lips, sensually teasing my tongue to do the same. My stomach did somer-saults, and the feeling in my cunt was intense, made obvi-ous to me by the juice that spilled from my body, dampen-ing my pubic hair and inner thighs.

My throat tingled, and my nipples hardened to such an ex-tent that the lining of my bra rubbed them almost sensually. I probably could have come within seconds, without further touch there and then, but I thought not. Why should I? Why? Why peak so quickly when it was inevitable that Jack-ie was going to fuck me, and fuck me with passion? I could almost feel her tongue inside me, tasting me, drinking me, and sucking me. Why free my orgasm when the anticipation was far superior?

Then I felt her hold, and Jackie woke me from my trance. Her right arm gripped my waist while her left crept under my shirt to stroke my midriff and right breast. She was obviously far superior in knowledge than I, but I was willing to learn and eager to follow her lead. Jackie urged me to the floor. She was gentle yet rough, dominating each move. Soon we were breast upon breast, until I found myself sucking savagely on her nipple—which she forced into my mouth as she simultaneously began to stroke her own thigh. She wore thin stockings with suspenders, and to my shock—but also to my delight—she wore no other underwear. Perhaps I may have enjoyed removing hers as she did mine, immediately before she sat astride me and placed her cunt on mine, parting both her own and my lips to allow two desperate clits to rub and grind together. She gyrated with skill and perfection faster and faster until suddenly she came. As she did, so did I. I welcomed Jackie's wetness mixing with my own. We came together, then silence reigned until Jackie kissed me. I was at a loss for words, and a lifetime passed again as she lay on top of me. Then she spoke.

"Shit." Strange postorgasmic conversation, I thought, but then she elaborated. "Fucking hall monitor. Listen."

Some other poor fucker must have faced the hallie's wrath before she reached Jackie and me, and luckily we had enough time to dress before her arrival.

"Have you girls got hall passes?"

Jackie gave her reason first and left suddenly, then I supplied my explanation. The hallie responded, "Next time you decide to fuck, try to be quieter. Anyone could have walked past and watched—maybe even masturbated." Shit.

My third lesson that day was sociology, and as usual Jackie sat directly behind me. This time her eyes burned through me for a different reason. We never did develop a relationship, though, nor did we embark on a friendship. Nevertheless, I was no longer the target of her aggressive phases, and neither was anyone whom I personally asked her to leave alone—which was everyone really. I did thank Jackie, though. Not verbally, but cognitively. I could tell from her performance this was not her first lesbian liaison, but it was mine. My Realization. She lifted my veil of confusion, and I came to accept that I was most definitely not diseased. Instead I was simply one of many in a world that is itself physically unwell at times.

Thank you, Jackie James. Thanks again.

Black Vinyl

MR Daniel

When I first started doing erotica readings, women who didn't really know me came up afterward and said, "Girl, I had no idea! I always thought you were such a 'good girl.'" They would do a mildly tortured-looking Pollyanna grin on the "good girl" part. "Now you acting all wild, reading about fucking in all these different positions. Damn!"

Then they would call out to their friends, "Hey girl, can you believe that was Cecelia up there?"

Poised to put in her two cents, the friend would cock her head, "OK! I was on the edge of my seat—I just couldn't believe my eyes!"

Then girlfriend number 1 would counterpoint with, "You remember when she first moved here? She was so quiet and proper acting!"

Girlfriend number 2 shot back with, "Didn't I *say* I almost didn't recognize her?!"

It was like being at a family reunion, trapped between two aunts who since time immemorial had dueled over who was the first on the scene at your most vulnerable or humiliating moment.

("Well, I was there when she was delivered—first baby in the family born bald as an ape's behind!"

"Well, I was the one who helped her when she had her first period and bled through her drawers when we were opening up the Christmas presents."

"Oh, please, everybody was there for that, but I was the one who drove her to her first dance and saw her get her first kiss from that Eric—what was his name? Isn't he in the army now? Cecelia, you and him woulda made some pretty babies."

"Don't listen to her, Cecelia girl. Now, he does have a sister....")

The only relief is in the recognition—often just before you de-evolve into a state of 12-year-old preteen utter humiliation—that you're just this moment's fuel for a verbal duet that began long before you were born.

But at least these two sistahs were ready to believe I might truly be the person they saw on stage. My friends acted like the cousins who expect you to still be the goofy one years after the end of adolescence. (Not to say goofy is bad. I can get behind a goofy-sexy woman—she's not afraid to fall off a table and stay on the floor to get you on your knees.) In my family, cousins cultivate the spoken word like nobody's business, emulating the verbal sparring they saw around the holiday tables of their youth, when the previous generation would come together to pick apart turkey and childhood foolishness. Like making up new names for the cousin who as a toddler used to invade the compost pile and dress up in banana peels. Or acting out the tale, with full sound effects, of the sibling who at 5 years of age ripped down part of a wall when wearing nothing but Wonder Woman underwear and a sheet tied around her neck and jumped off the back of the sofa holding the curtain cord, proclaiming herself Panty Girl, come to free all children from the tyranny of nap time and lima beans.

Somehow without consciously attempting to do so, I find my closest friendships are with girlfriends who have made a priority of acquiring these same oral skills. No development goes unnoticed, and they give me grief about every change I make, taking my self-consciousness to new heights. There are times when I feel I am walking into a high school reunion with nothing on but tit clamps and a G-string. I don't mean to say there is an absence of love. They have my back and love me dear, but you know, on occasion girlfriends can be a little too attentive to each other's lives. We have all been there; sometimes it's just more compelling to get all up into someone else's business than to be concerned with your own. Like when you know you need to be thinking about applying to school or changing your career or taking a computer or art class, but instead you're worrying if Sheila has the right beeswax candles for her romantic date. Or is that gold ball really what Jordan wants dangling from her labia? And if Micaela blindfolds Gertie and takes her off for a fuckfest at the beach, has she scoped out their rendezvous point so that they won't be bothered with that annoying sandy-pussy problem? Admittedly I was changing, but not as much as they seemed to believe; I was just becoming more myself.

Avoiding their banter was my aim in coming to the club alone. The other times when I had come with J.J. and Samara it was ridiculous: On the last occasion they kept a running commentary the whole time. Since they both had been dating recently and I hadn't, they decided the evening was all about finding a fuck for Cecelia. That's what I get for going out with two ex-lovers who are now best friends. In the end they were all over each other ("a bit of lusty nostalgia," Samara said). But by that time in the evening they had rated my outfit, my

come-on lines, and, much like my protective aunties, had
managed to loudly appraise every woman in the place before I
could as much as say "boo" to anyone. When I dropped them
off they were licking each other's juice off fingers, snuggling
and humping toward the sidewalk (oblivious to puddles), and
barely avoiding slipping on the slick, rain-soaked steps to
J.J.'s apartment. Adding insult to injury, the pungent scent of
their good-time sex smell seemed to have soaked into the
damp back seat, and the car heater recirculated the remnants
of their pleasures the rest of my pissed-off ride home. *Never
again*, I said to myself. It's too much to go out for some anonymous sex in the company of sistahs who have shared your lipstick *and* the other side of your bedroom wall and don't care
who knows it.

By myself I could leisurely take in the textures and curious
smiles of the women coming toward me, for once feeling bold,
like "What the fuck? What's the worst that can happen?"
Now that I've gained weight and my *tetas* are spilling out of
my laced-up charcoal leather bustier, I feel more grounded in
my body. Some of the extra inches even had the foresight to
go to my behind, which was looking smoky, black, and buoy-
ant—a round shadow in my skintight velveteen miniskirt.
But I reminded myself, *Cecelia, no one sister, no matter how fine,
is attractive to everyone every day of the week*. So letting go of that
fear, before I came I promised myself I would meet the eyes of
every woman who caused my nipples to harden and sent a par-
alyzing twinge to my clit. Next thing you know you feel like
you can't put one foot in front of the other 'cause your brain
forgets how to send the message. I always end up looking
down, disoriented and embarrassed, lamenting the loss of
what I take for granted as a basic bodily function. I pray no

one notices me furtively trying to make eye contact with my feet in the hope it will help my brain remember where to fire those neurons.

I decided that instead of freaking out because I couldn't feel my legs, I'd just take a deep breath and look forward, undaunted and unafraid, and breathe low—from the diaphragm, baby, just a pause to let me get my bearings and fully appreciate the passing view.

Still, my hands always feel gangly and unwieldy—I can never figure out what to do with them. I end up unconsciously fingering the drawstring of my skirt with one and caressing my leather-bound breast with the other—absentmindedly caressing the skin on my arms, the exposed skin on my thigh, in between my laced-up stretch mini and my thigh-high hose. As a virgin I used to feel the slick smoothness of myself in the shower. I was studying my own pleasure, wanting to know in advance where I desired a stroke, a squeeze, a grasp, and how good my body felt under my fingers. I took the opportunity to give myself luxurious kisses wherever my tongue and lips could reach, the water flowing, dripping from mouth to skin, and making my lips feel full and silken against flesh. It seems like the minute after I got some sex I gave up my water rituals, and I forgot about the value of my own caress. Now I don't mean fingers to clit—I could wear myself out on that. I mean the significance of touch: skin to skin, body on body.

* * *

Attractive women passed by, but their presence didn't generate that slow burn under my skin. And then I could hear the blood in my ears. The treble in the club's soundtrack seemed to fade back, and I felt the bass in my knees. Damn! Big 'fro, black vinyl tank with breast zippers, stomach showin' with a little belly-button ring, and black vinyl hip-high pants. Work me, girl!

Something about her reminded me of the woman I first had a crush on. Truthfully, she wasn't really a woman. I was 8 or something, and she seemed like a woman of the world to me: 16! But she was probably only 14—after all we were both at a summer day camp. Girlfriend was tall, bittersweet-chocolate dark, slender, and kind of muscular. Her power and effortless grace play back in my mind, as I see her striding down the sidewalk wearing a pale pink, almost ankle-length cotton sun dress and black and white Converse high-tops, giving off an intriguing combination of early black boho mixed with a butch-femme androgynous vibe. But I wouldn't have known anything about that back then. I just knew she didn't look anything like the relaxer-coiffed-up, heavy-lidded-eyeshad-owed, Bonnie-Bell-lip-smacked girls at school and choir prac-tice. She had jet black hair—long and kinky-coarse, like Chaka's was in the '70s—and a shock of dark hair coming out of each armpit, which probably accounts for my thing for un-derarms. Not licking on some Secret or Sure, but a fresh hol-low that's just started to get moist with a fine sheen of new funk, while breasts are being licked and rubbed between sali-va-covered fingers.

One really hot afternoon during that day-camp summer, we were holed up alone in a car, one of those late-'60s American models with the you-can-do-it-to-me-all-night-long, ribbed-for-pleasure bucket seats. My bittersweet girl-woman was a vision of knowingness and cool as she kicked up her feet on the dashboard. She pulled out a pack of menthols, and with a display of good, if misguided, home training glanced to the back seat and in a husky liquid-burnt honey voice offered me a cigarette. I barely squeaked out a trying-to-be-cool, "No thank you," and that sensuous arm with the languid fingers withdrew from the top of the seat. Then without bothering to scope out the adult supervision, she lit a smoke in the *front seat* of the camp counselor's car. And of course there were those rebellious underarms.

But getting back to Our Lady of the Luminous Black Vinyl…the sistah in front of me now was honey-brown complected and had more curves than my girlhood crush. But her vibe, let me tell you…that tank top went up to her neck and gave me little chills. I imagined my come caught between her shiny creases and slicking down the teeth of her zippers. She stood against the wall next to a doorway. Shit, and here was the test: She was giving me a look like, "You want it. Let me see you come and get it." I wished at that moment I could fly, 'cause pushing off and taking flight seemed a lot easier than the prospect of making my legs work for the entire time it was gonna take me to get across that hall. The feeling was starting to come back into my toes, so I put my hips into it— my body picked up the rhythm and began to follow. It occurred to me that the dare to come and get it might have given her a chance to see how I moved and to get the blood back into her own toes. That second thought gave me the courage to speak first.

"My, you look very shiny and delicious tonight." Damn, she was licking her lips, not self-consciously, but as if it were an afterthought. They were full and brown, and that pink tongue looked agile, like it had a mind of its own.

"Thank you. I like your lacing. Is that a double knot?" She

had a full, sweet voice: a big ole saucy pepper, with a little bit of honey.

"Hmm, well, I hope not, since I have a hard time taking out tight knots. I'll probably get a cricked neck trying to work this one by myself." I put on a crooked, coy little smile.

"Oh?" She flashed me a big grin: pretty teeth and a little overbite. "Well, here, let me test it." She hooked her index finger through the two loops of the tied laces and led me through the dimly lit doorway. There were pillows on the floor and a futon or mattress of some kind with a black rubber fitted sheet; nearby stood a table with various sex supplies. This time I got to see how she moved; those full hips were working me, and I saw the hint of a powerful booty. She leaned me into the wall and took one end of the bow between her thumb and index finger. A little snap of the plastic tip against a rivet, and I felt the knot come undone.

"Lucky that was easy—you must be relieved." She smiled and arched her eyebrow. Cocking her head to the side, she asked, "So you like my vinyl?"

"Yeah," I said gazing at the light playing off the zippers and the shiny blackness as she moved. "I'd like to lick it."

My mouth parted in silent laughter, but I was looking directly into her eyes. Like a dare. They seemed to get big for a moment. I thought maybe she wasn't used to women having a thing for vinyl, or not while she was wearing it. But then her eyes went sharp and curious.

"So do it," she said.

I moved from the wall. I didn't touch her. I put my lips forward and kissed the shiny material right below her collarbone. I had to turn my head to the side so I was directly under her chin. I stuck out my tongue and licked her up to the edge of her top, just nicking the skin above her throat. I went lower, licking near the zippers, circling the outside of them. The vinyl was smooth and slick against my tongue. I left little islands, little peninsulas of saliva on her; they separated into clear drops of light. Going lower, I had to bend my knees; a shadow outlined the hollow of her stomach as she caught her breath. I looked up at her as my tongue grazed her stomach and circled the loop of her belly-button ring. She was watching me, her mouth a little open. She pulled me up, unraveling my laces and putting her fingers between my breast and the leather. I felt my muscles tense and release as she worked her fingers around me. She pulled sounds of pleasure from my throat. I bent my head again to stroke the other side of the zippers with my tongue. I wanted to tease myself with the anticipation of the size and taste of her nipple—and her with the attention I was going to give it. I began sucking her through the vinyl. I sucked her on both sides. It felt so good, I let out a moan of satisfaction. The material bore the twisted imprint of the force of my lips around her nipples. I raised my head and began to work my tongue on the little bit of exposed skin on her throat. She began to moan with me, putting her fingers in her mouth and putting them back in my bustier.

As I put my hands on her hips for balance she said, "Now unzip me."

Sometimes—but only sometimes—I like to do as I am told. I pulled down the right breast zipper and pushed aside the flap, diving onto her with my full mouth, noisily filling it with with her firm breast. We sank to the floor; we didn't quite make it to the bed. I was on top of her working that other zipper. She had my bustier practically off, and we were sideways, sucking and licking.

As I was bent over, hardening her nipples into little balls, she outlined my ears and painted my neck with her tongue. When I sucked harder she bit my shoulder. She pulled away and drew back from me, smiling mischievously. I looked at her, curious, and rolled to my side, rising up on one elbow. She cupped my chin in her palm and drew her thumb over my lips. Suddenly she sat up, came closer to me, and caught my lower lip between her teeth. She bit me some, just hard enough to make a mark—something to let me know she'd been there. Her teeth parted quickly, and her lips held me. I sucked her tongue into me, and I tasted that peppery sweetness as I undid the zippers that led on both sides from her neck to her shoulders. Finally free, she pressed against my leather, rubbing her nipples against the laces. Spit covered our lips as our tongues slowly, forcefully wrestled each other.

She began to work the second set of laces, the ones that went up the front of my skirt. I had chosen not to wear any underwear so I could feel less restricted and, of course, bold as fuck, but now I was having second thoughts as her naked hand was moving closer to my pussy.

"Oh, we...we need some gloves, baby."

Her voice was muffled, her juicy, firm mouth still against mine. We did a sensuous and hungry mouth-fucking (I was right about that tongue), tit-rubbing, walking-on-our-knees two-step over to the table of plenty, lined with toys and various forms of latex. With sidelong glances we figured out where the gloves were, and with a little teamwork we both got one on the appropriate hand. She undid enough laces to get comfortably at my pussy and began working the juices around my labia, running two fingers through my folds at once. Then going in for more juice and running them back again, narrowing them against either side of my clit as she slid back up.

"I'm a sensitive one," I breathed.

"That's OK," she whispered back. "I'll just have to work my way to the edge of your pleasure. You tell me when to stop."

"Oh, shit," I moaned, as the tips of her fingers came closer to my clit and then quickly dove, circling between my increasingly sensitive cunt lips.

Not to be outdone, I worked my digits into her hip-hugging vinyls. I went for one of the side zippers, stripping back the material. There was skin and a nappy bush, shining damp with sweat. I felt the curlicues of her hair beneath my gloved hand and inched my way to the part between her bush to her pulsing little mound. My fingers found her well-creamed and hard, and she shoved her crotch onto my thigh.

"I like the pressure," she said, coaxing me with her deep brown gaze.

Her raspy moaning and the feel of her fingers stretching inside me gave me incentive to push my hand deeper into her tight pants and get to her pussy. She pressed her swollen clit into my palm and rode the length of my thigh, rising up and trembling and back down again. I looked at her face, high on her own rhythms and mine, as I pushed into her deeper. She strained against my palm, and my thighs were wrapped around hers.

"Wait! I don't want to come yet," I said.

"What is it?"

"I want…" Ever so slowly she drew her fingers from between my legs, and I almost came on her hand.

"Mmm, don't come yet, baby." Fuck. The way she stretched out the word, she could call me "baby" all day long. She smiled and drew little circles on my breast with my pussy juice.

"I want you to get on your hands and knees," she said.

Would doing as I was told a second time make my wish come true? She began to loosen the third set of laces that went down the back of my skirt. I heard her sigh.

"Your cunt and ass look so good through that lacing. Damn, you're so wet and swollen, it's making me want to fuck with you."

She was like a wolf at my door. I felt her biting and fingering me between the thin cords, heard her sniffing and breathing me in deep. The breath of her exhale was jagged as she ravenously dug her teeth deep into my behind then traced the bites with her tongue. My skirt came completely undone under all this attention, and she moved it to one side as it fell on the floor. As for me, I was so wet she could have spun me around the floor on my cunt.

* * *

With my naked ass in the air she asked, "Now, baby, I want to know: Have you been bad?"

I closed my eyes, feeling an unspeakable fury of heat—a desire that raged beneath the skin of my ass.

Pausing for only a second, I growled, "Baby," my voice a low rumble, "make me *wanna* be bad."

Her hand came smack on my ass. She drew her wet mouth over the searing where her hand had been and then smacked me again until my ass felt hot and electric. Humming, like every nerve was alert, like each nerve could individually receive each sensation she was giving my ass as she bit and nibbled me, drawing her nails down my butt as she trailed her tongue to the edge of my crack and slapping me again. Then I felt the cold sensation of lube dripping between the cheeks of my buttocks. I heard the snap of the old glove coming off and a crinkly sound as she adjusted a new one. It made my nipples hard all over again. I shivered as she spread the lube over my anus.

"Are you feeling like you wanna be bad yet?" She teased the rim of my asshole with her finger.

"Mmm, oh, almost," I moaned as the finger probed my hole.

She pulled out her finger and grabbed some of the toys and latex from the table. I felt her working what seemed to be a butt plug into my asshole. She was biting my cheeks and rubbing and spanking me again. "What about now?"

"Uh-huh…"

The plug started to vibrate, and she began to push it in deeper. "What about now?"

"Mmm, yes."

"What?"

"Yes!" The word roared from my pelvis.

"Say it louder!" Her rasping voice was insistent.

"Yes!" Now I was screaming, my ass wildly bucking trying to find more of the butt plug.

"Say you want it." She was pulling the butt plug out so just the tip of it was against my rim, pressing it in a little deeper and then pulling it out again.

"I want it! Fuck! Give it to me, give it to me now dammit!"

She thrust it in deep, and my ass swallowed it whole. I didn't hear the zippers while I was pleading for her to ram it up my ass again. But she must have taken her pants off, 'cause the next thing I know she's flipping me over on top of some pillows and sliding against my thigh. And I'm slippery against her, and she's biting my nipples while I'm twisting hers, and we're hanging on as we cram into each other's thighs and hips. She's got that damn butt plug on high, and her teeth are on my lips while I'm screaming my come, and her mouth covers mine as we howl into each other.

Dream Mammal

Sarah Van Arsdale

Did you come on dream waves
slicked with lake water,
hoist yourself from the depths
and fill the bow
with your strong shoulders and your scent?

Did I dream your shout
swallowed by lake's rough wind,
by water washed lavender and blue,
mainland's gray ridge sinking
into night?

Did I dream you hauling
canoe from waves
onto a rocked beach, dark water rising
around your ankles, pant legs
wetted to your calves?

Did you pull me from the boat
and deep into your chest
your hands and arms
angled constellations bracing
in a pulse high above the shore?

Maybe you appeared
only as I drifted in toward sleep,
deep in your bank's burrow,
nestled into your nest of leaves,
warm reeds and grass

you solid motion
lake waves above me,
steady as I slept safe, blue
waters smoothing out the grassy sheets.

Did you come on dream waves,
night mammal, licking my face
for lake water?

The Healing

M.N. Schoeman

I was introduced to Zodwa at a private party. When I asked, she smiled.

"Being the youngest of five daughters, my name means 'only girls' in Zulu," she answered, then laughed about the accidental intertwining of her name and her sexuality. "My mother must have had a premonition! So, you don't speak Zulu?"

"No."

I spoke English with a slight South African accent and felt a twinge of embarrassment flash up my neck.

"You don't speak any black vernacular?" she stated more than asked. "I see."

As the evening progressed I found myself being constantly aware of her. I noticed when she poured another drink—Scotch whisky—and followed her hands as she lit a cigarette. While she was conversing with friends, I smiled at her expressive gesticulations, and it seemed her body and voice completed each other in perfect rhythm. Often her voice opened up in rolling laughter, her head shaking and sending her beaded hair scattering like a sea star around her head. Only once, moments before she smiled, did her mouth sag slightly, looking tired and vulnerable.

Later that night as I closed my eyes and started stroking

myself, I visualized how her eyes would look like right before she would say, "I want to make love to you." Of how her lithe body would glint like dark oil as she curled herself around me, moving and swelling against my hand, then opening herself up for me to thrust my tongue deep into her, drowning in her provocative body odors. After I had an orgasm, I closed my eyes tightly not to cry.

**   *   ***

"Don't kiss the maid," my mother with her thin cold mouth scolded one morning over breakfast. I was 7 years old.

"But I was just greeting her," I said.

"Beauty, you can bring the coffee now," my mother called in the kitchen's direction, and her face became harder. She leaned forward and hissed, "You will pick up all kinds of germs. Now finish your breakfast."

"But why? She's clean...really, she is."

Whenever I recall my childhood, I can still invoke the strange haunting songs the domestic worker sang while dusting. It reminds me of a burning green landscape being ruffled by a warm wind where one could run and run forever and never become tired. And she smelled of freshly crushed thyme.

From the kitchen came the sound of splintering glass. My mother sighed, rolled her eyes, and stood up.

"Just don't kiss her, that's all," she said to me, and then to no one in particular, "Let me go and see what she broke this time." She slammed the kitchen door behind her.

Through mutual friends, Zodwa and I came to see each other often. Slowly we became friends, hesitantly starting to trust each other with glimpses of our lives that played off at two different poles of a continuum that spanned a schizophrenic society.

Zodwa had an image of her father as a strong man with hands like a tree, smelling of dark, freshly plowed soil after rain, almost as she imagined a black God would be. But the African National Congress was banned under Vorster, God was not allowed to be black, and her father was detained under the Internal Security Act during the 1976 riots. Every day her mother's face was strong. Her high, sickle-moon forehead and oblique cheekbones seemed cautiously chiseled from rich ebony. But after she started dressing in a domestic servant's white uniform and *kopdoek*.[1] her eyes could only follow her feet. One day the authorities informed her mother that her father committed suicide in his cell.

They could not say how he did it.

My childhood lazed by in slow motion, or so it appeared to me. Summers were hot and colorful; winters were put to rest under layers of blankets. I did not know that smoke and despair darkened almost every morning, in most townships, like thunderclouds, rumbling warnings and cracking the air with lightning.

Zodwa never forgot the gray that greeted Soweto mornings. Every memory of her youth seemed to present itself through pale layers of dust, fog, and smoke. As the bleached sun struggled to free itself from the gloom, dull orange candlelight splintered through door casings and sackcloth curtains. On Zodwa's way to school, the haggard dirt road stained her white socks a rusty ocher. Occasionally she looked over her shoulder at where she lived: House 2587A, Zone 5, Meadowlands, Soweto. The house was painted blue—a colorful drop in the monotonous environment—with dusky plants in empty

Dulux paint tins on the windowsills. Rubbish festered in ditches along the road, and the air smelled of sour milk and burnt plastic. Past the squatter camp, where roughly constructed shacks of corrugated iron, carton, and wood shivered in the cold morning air, the stench became worse.

It was at the school's prize giving of that same year that I received a book prize for the neatest handwriting in Standard 2. I also started taking piano lessons, although I clearly did not have the graceful hands of a pianist, but my parents believed that every cultured Afrikaner girl should be able to play at least one instrument.

After school Zodwa used to play top-top, soccer, hide-and-seek, or housie in the rusty wreckage of an old car. Playing housie initially posed a dilemma for her since she was not sure whether she wanted to be the mother or the father. First they only kissed—soft, curious kisses, lips trembling and bodies not always knowing how to react. Once one of the older women took Zodwa inside, pulled down her pants, and examined her to see if she was an *isitabane.*[2] Later they started touching, and one night under the blankets they masturbated each other gently, not to wake the other children who shared the small dark room with them. But every day the political turmoil grew, black schools closed down one after another, and children had no time for playing housie anymore. The clouds grew gray with the burning smell of tear gas and the dry repetitive shots of R1 machine guns.

As Zodwa and I moved closer on an emotional level, my body desperately wanted to follow. At night my hands became hers.

"I fantasize about you often," I told her.

"I know," she said and shrugged. "I hope that your fantasies are set in the right political context."

The nagging feeling of incompleteness then started, as if I were missing something without really knowing what. And every day I spent with her I learned more about a history I was part of yet never experienced. It felt as if I were waking up from a faintly familiar nightmare but not able to remember what I had dreamt about.

More and more frequently the skyline of Soweto erupted with marching crowds, rhythmic voices, and piercing red sirens. The air grew saturated with the smell of boiling hot lead and exhaust fumes from clumsy Stability Unit vehicles.

For my 16th birthday my parents gave me a motorcycle. Sometimes I drove past the black townships but did not dare go too close. I once gave a young black woman dressed in overalls a lift to the bus stop. I clenched my legs tightly around the fuel tank as I moved forward on the seat to make space for her and felt the deep rumbling and tremors of the engine. The woman held me tightly from behind. When we went round a sharp bend in the road, I could feel her breasts against my body, and for the first time I knew I could only love women. But between us spanned a lifetime that attempted to rip the soul from all its inhabitants— black and white—a soul both of us needed to recover in our own way. From that day I addressed our domestic worker by her African name, Sibongile, although my mother persisted in calling her Beauty.

The crowd swayed like a stormy sea while it chanted *Amandhla Awethu.*[3] A young woman (was it a girl?) lifted her fist, and a nervous policeman started shooting. Four killed, an unknown number wounded, the television screen flashed. We've got her, the fuckin' faggot and her friends, the trouble makers, a policeman said as he kicked her into the back of the van. We are going to have some fun, boys.

The blackjack[4] shoved a club inside her until she was swollen and spongy. Afterward, her friend begged for water to rinse the blood and teeth from her mouth. He put his boot on her throat until she started choking, guffawed that he would help her clean herself up and then pissed in her mouth, then forced her head backward and aimed for her nostrils. Blood trickled down her legs and into her shoes.

"There is so much you need to know before we can go any further," she said on the night that we first made love. She started to unbutton her shirt. As she pulled her shirt over her shoulders I could not move. The scar, while healing, shrunk her skin together in a bundle of white, knotty pieces of flesh, hanging like a ghostly full moon against the night of her skin. She began talking, and her voice for the first time seemed tired.

"When the ANC took its first breaths of freedom as a legal political organization, some members declared that black people are not inclined to homosexuality, that it is an un-African import and a decadent white contamination of the black culture. Some gangs in the black community took this to heart and appointed themselves as lesbian bashers. And the *tsotsi*[5] boys only knew one cure—the same as the blackjacks."

Then she undressed, baring her smooth body, hair thickening between her legs. With trepidation I reached out to her, at the same time feeling too embarrassed to touch her, perhaps too angry or too scared. Her fingers unbuttoned my shirt, moving down to my jeans. Then I was also naked.

I crouched in front of her, and she parted her legs slightly for me to lick the pink slit that opened. Then she groaned, strangled her fingers through my hair, and lifted my head.

"No," she said. "I want to see your eyes. And I want you to look at me."

She rubbed my clit, round and round, harder and harder, until I felt my blood thickening between my legs. I closed my eyes, felt how her one finger disappeared in me, pushing deeper and deeper into my body, later two, then three fingers. I groaned for more. She opened me like a wound. *More please. I want more of you. I want to open myself and suck your world inside mine.* Her whole hand disappeared in my cunt, her fingers branching out in the thick fluids of my body. She then clenched her fist, firmly moving and kneading my insides, anchoring herself in me. This time no shots were fired; we both felt safe. *Amandhla Awethu.* Her body was like soil, and I was growing out of her, her mouth like a flower in my ear until my grip around her arm stiffened, again and again. For a short, explosive moment I felt completed. Long after she removed her hand I could still feel her. With a smile I noticed her hand and arm were moist, covered with my thick white fluids and the smell of butter. She tasted her fingers, smiled as I softly started licking my way down to her scar.

"Sometimes," she said, "just sometimes it feels as if I have known you forever."

1. Afrikaans for *head scarf.*
2. Zulu word for hermaphrodite, one who has both masculine and feminine organs. It is widely believed in the townships of South Africa that homosexuals are hermaphrodites.
3. Power to the people.
4. Slang for *policeman.*
5. Black gangster.

Love Play

Myra LaVenue

"Go into the kitchen. Remove your clothes. Tie both ankles
to the front legs of the table, then put the blindfold on. Lie
face down on top of the table and wait for me," her voice whispered in my ear. The hot breath that accompanied the sharp
but soft commands excited me almost as much as the thought
of the instructions I was about to follow.

My long legs swung off the couch as I stood to obey. I
turned briefly for one more glance at my lover. Her beautiful
face appeared flushed and stern. High cheekbones and dark
spiky hair framed her brown eyes, so expressive and forceful
that her soft lips need never move. I bent over and picked up
the bandannas, the soft leather blindfold, and two candles.
With one more glance, I turned and made my way through
the dark house to the kitchen.

As I undressed, removing first my gray silk blouse then my
black jeans, my clit throbbed. When I unhooked my bra, the
cool air in the kitchen hit my nipples. My tall frame easily
managed the task she had given me, bending over one side of
the table, then the other, to tie my ankles to the table legs. As
I placed the blindfold's inner soft fur over my eyes, I heard a
rustling sound behind me. The cold Formica tabletop received
my weight as I lay quickly across it.

I felt rather than heard her approach, the hair on my skin prickling with anticipation. She pulled a chair up behind my small, bare ass. I drew in a sharp breath at the feel of her hand slapping it sharply. She stroked the just-spanked area until the stinging stopped, then slapped the other cheek. The spanking continued for a few more seconds, each sharp slap accompanied by my soft whimpers of pleasure. She paused and let my breathing return to normal, then softly rubbed my back and teased me with what felt like a feather. I felt the wetness drip from my pussy onto my thighs. "Hmm, did I say you could get excited?" Her voice floated to my ears over the pounding of my heart. I managed to whisper some answer before I felt her large breasts move over my ass, the hard nipples brushing my skin in pinpointed circles.

She moved away to reach for a small vibrator, which she began rubbing against the inside of my legs. She teased it upward. I moaned with frustration, unable to move closer to its vibrations. Suddenly she thrust it upward, onto my clit, as her thumb inserted itself into my wet pussy. I gasped at the pleasure and pushed against the vibrator with the small mobility I had. As fast as it had appeared, it was suddenly withdrawn.

"Oh, you think you deserve to come so soon?" she asked me softly. "I'll tell you what I think you deserve. You'd better lie still, or I'm going to stop altogether." Again the vibrator was turned on, and its pulsating presence slid up and down my inner thighs. It dipped down to the back of my knee, where the sensations of tickling and torture merged into one. As the intensity increased I strained to move away from it, pushing that leg slightly to the left, but it followed my movements. Then the other leg received the vibrations as she moved it from behind my ankle and up to the back of the knee. By this time I was whimpering in both frustration and excitement. Once again she moved it to my clit, and the explosive intensity of the vibrations nearly made me come. Instinctively, she moved it away just before I could release.

I heard her move closer to me and felt her soft breath touch my ear. "How about a hard, slow fuck? Hmm? Would you like that?" she whispered. I heard the sound of her buckling and snapping the strap-on belt and knew she was about to fuck me with her warm latex dildo. She pumped the lube bottle vigorously, then rubbed the lube all over my cunt. God! This wetness meeting wetness was overwhelming. My ass moved around, begging for her touch.

She teased my pussy with the tip of the dildo, swirling it around and slightly in, then out. My moans grew louder as my desire rose. I wanted her cock in me, fast and hard. She slapped my ass again and told me to stop whimpering. "I'll decide when you need this." She moved the dildo up and down the crack of my ass as she teased my clit with the vibrator. I became distracted by its throbbing and began to moan from the increasing waves of ecstasy. Then, when I least expected it she thrust herself inside my pussy. She let the cock rest deep inside me as my pussy expanded around it. She moved slowly, letting the dildo slide in and out of me gently. Emotions welled inside me as I felt my whole body come alive and my pussy grow hungry.

I finally mustered the strength to say, "Please, fuck me hard." This time she responded and began moving the cock in and out, faster and deeper with each thrust. My G-spot was receiving an incredible rubdown, which finally caused my pussy juices to spurt as I came hard. But she did not stop. Next she returned the vibrator to my clit as she continued fucking me.

My entire body was pulsating with orgasm as my clit exploded, and my pussy clenched around the thrusting cock. She kept the vibrator pressed against me for about a minute, keeping me coming until I was shaking and weak from the intensity.

She slowly withdrew the dildo and placed her hand over my pussy. The warmth of that hand was comforting. When I heard the lube bottle pump again, I opened my eyes and peeked behind me from beneath the blindfold. She covered her fist with the lube. "I need to feel you come on me," she whispered when she saw me watching her. She slowly worked her fingers inside my still-swollen cunt and at the right moment moved the hand all the way inside me past her wrist. I gasped at the fullness. My cunt relaxed around her hand as she formed a fist and began moving slowly in and out. Oh, my God, the pleasure! I felt became overwhelmed by emotion again, tears welling as my lover united with me. She moved her fist faster and faster until I was screaming, "Oh, God, I'm coming!" She pulled her hand out as I ejaculated my warm come all over her stomach. Weak from emotion and physical pleasure, I lay there breathing heavily and holding back tears.

She untied my ankles, turned me, and pulled me onto her lap as I wrapped my legs around her torso. With my arms around her strong shoulders, I buried my head in her neck. She held me, whispering softly into my ear, as her hands stroked my shaking body. "Oh, my sweet lover," she purred, "I love you." Later we walked to the bedroom. Lying on the bed, she reached for me as I began moving my hands to pleasure *her*.

First Time

Isadora Stern

I already had a bad reputation. Maybe it was a good reputation. I had a sexual reputation that preceded me: I had sex;
I had sex on my terms; I had sex on my terms with whomev-
er I felt like—and I liked it and was good at it. I talked about
it, and I talked about how I was good at it. Now, I knew other
girls who got in crazier scenarios than I, but they had the ability to keep it to themselves. I, with my loose lips, was a known
commodity. I was discovering how to use this to my advantage. What's the fun of having an outrageous reputation, most
of it based in the imaginations of others, if it doesn't lead to
getting off?

Sometimes I had to work faster than was safe for me. I'm
one of those schemer femme girls who stares at butch girls for
six months until the butch gets up the nerve to come over and
tell me she's ready. Sometimes people, moments, things have
to be acted on quickly or they disappear and the experience
goes unexperienced. Sometimes I have to move out of what
I'm good at if I'm ever gonna get pushed.

She was hot. I was the only girl in town who had never seen
her before. She was back for summer vacation from one of
those East Coast schools whose name impressed my grandmother. She deserved to be there. She rattled off words that
made my brain feel vastly underutilized. She intimidated me

intellectually, which never happens. But I discovered I intimidated her. See, I worked in a sex-toy store. I sold items of desire, which implied I knew how to use them (which is the God's honest truth). I was in the right business. I could sell a couple a dildo that would leave the bottom seeing stars. I could sell a top a harness that would have her feeling in her rightful place, clit pressed to the back of the dildo, leaving her convinced it was her dick. Which, by the way, is God's work.

I had done all of this, but it'd become old hat. It never got me off. In fact, it kind of pissed me off. What do I get? When do I get to get turned on? When does the girl with knowledge, who's makin' $7.50 an hour, get something for all the energy spent?

Whine and ye shall receive.

For all her years out in the dyke world, for all the dykes in academia, she'd never strapped it on. She'd never felt the power, felt the knowledge of fucking another women with a dick. She'd never known. And I, for all my instructions given in front of shelves of dildos, had never been invited home for a private lesson, skills honed on the collective dyke need. Though we intimidated each other and I was working out of character, the idea seemed to get us both really hot and bothered.

It's good to fuck for the first time. It's good to fuck for the first week. And when you only get a week, every fuck reeks of total breathless heat. The act of fucking only to say good-bye makes every moment feverish. Adrenaline pumps, and the skin swells on the pulse of what is fulfilled in the dawn hours.

I let her take me hard. She pressed me into the hardwood floor of my tiny apartment and asked me where the gloves were. When she got four fingers in, she asked what was next.

I informed her, "Your fist in my cunt, on this, our first night."

The lack of time was keeping me up even on the nights I didn't see her that week. It was complicated; it was the summer—hot and fleeting; it was building and blurring my brain.

All of this culminated in snapping a harness on her for the first time. It's the moment femmes live for: "Let me show you, baby. Let me give you the power to fuck deep into me. Let me take it and give back like only a femme can."

* * *

It was late at night, and my mind was sharp. My hands knew exactly what they were doing. She stood at the edge of the bed, her body breaking me hard. She was built thick, and her arms were deeply muscled. She stood there, waiting—waiting for me to know every intricacy of what was to happen next. The black Stormy Leather Brief-Style Harness (they don't make it anymore), with the cock ring in the back to make it tighter on the body (my modification) and in it a seven-inch black rubber super ballsy cock from Doc Johnston. A dick length at a good price. My cunt knows that equipment well. She looked sweet in so many ways, sweet like the first time, sweet like "here today, gone tomorrow," sweet like "now, ain't she sweet." I positioned the leather harness on her body as best I could with all my desire stirring in my brain. There she stood in my tiny studio apartment, the place of so much sexual reclaiming for myself, a space I created because I knew I needed to become a deep sexual deviant. There she stood feeling a place inside that those butch girls never turn their back on once they learn that by putting on a cock their sex grows tenfold and their tricks always cry for more. There she stood....

All this ceremony lead to the sex.

"Come on back to the bed. Let me lube that up for you—that long cock. Let me gaze up at you. Let me lie back for you." *Let me speak from the place I've created, the things I know that will change you deeply, that thing you can't walk away from in yourself.*

She made me feel small. I lay on my back, and she climbed over me. I felt her breasts, saw the desire in her eyes, and knew all about the cock between her legs. I knew more about it than she did. I knew it was too big for most girls. I knew it would hit me deep. I spread my legs for her. With her fingers she guided her cock into me. *Yesss, yes, yes. This is why it's good to go beyond what makes sense; this is why it's good to fuck beyond the known. This is why.*

Her youth and strength meant she could keep up a fantastic rhythm for an inexhaustible amount of time. I let my cunt fill with the rhythm, knowing that on nights like this I could take a cock twice that size.

"Lean back and stay still. I want to show you something," I said at some point too late for the sun not to be rising. I was giving away too much, but that's my style. Sometimes with the right people, in the right moment, you can give it all away. That moment of trust comes back as gifts unexpected. The gift is giving it up in the face of everything you know. She knew herself butch, pulsing cock inside me. And I knew it felt strong and complete and that I'd gotten in deeper than I knew what to do with.

Feel it, feeling it, felt it. Deep.

The Wedding Present

M. Damian

Of all the places for a single, on-the-prowl lesbian to get randy. I mean, really. What is it about weddings that gets my juices flowing?

My cousin Felicia was finally marrying Anthony. It was a splashy affair, one of those big, showy, expensive Italian jobs, so of course it had to be an event. Eight bridesmaids, a maid and matron of honor, and two flower girls. The bridal party was so big it commandeered its own freaking bus.

Being Felicia's first cousin on her mother's side, I was a member of this crew, but because the wedding was being planned by one edgy bride-to-be, seven buttinsky bridesmaids, one excitable maid and one ditsy matron of honor, one nervous mother of the bride, and one touchy future mother-in-law of the bride, I stayed in the background, undercover. Just tell me where and when to be and I was fine.

So 18 months from the engagement party, the wedding day eventually arrived. I was between life partners, shall we say, and more or less on the hunt. I would hit the bars every week, sometimes getting involved for varying amounts of time, but always it was the same hot sex and plenty of it; eventually I'd cool off.

Well, the big day arrived, a sparkling clear day in mid August, one of those special perfect days where the temps are in the mid 70s with no humidity.

My uncle's house was a flurry of activity with bride and bridal attendants and mother of the bride all getting ready and all bumping into each other. Sal, the neighborhood hair-salon owner, had closed his shop this Saturday morning. He was a personal friend of the family, and he and his wife, Cecilia, were guests. This particular morning, he and his workers took wedding attendees in shifts, starting with the bride and attendants beginning at 8.

When 2:30 rolled around we were all coiffed, made up, and dressed. The limo and bus were waiting outside the house to take us the ten blocks to the church for the 4 o'clock Mass.

For the next hour we posed for pictures, and at 3:30 we were herded back onto the bus. The driver stopped at Anthony's house and picked up the male half of the bridal party. Then it was off to the church and the nuptials.

The ceremony went off without a snag; 45 minutes after entering the church, my cousin and her high school sweetheart were hitched. Then it was off for another round of pictures.

Now that the pressure was off, everyone began to relax. The bus was loaded with liquid refreshment, and by the time we were dropped off at the reception hall, a few of us were on our way to being pleasantly loaded, present company included. I went stag to the reception; I didn't have to drive home and figured what the hell, I'd have a damned good time.

After the cocktail hour, we all made our grand entrances, the bride and groom were announced, and the wedding feast got seriously under way.

I shouldn't drink. I know this for an irrefutable fact. When I do, I get reckless and do things I wouldn't normally. Everyone made a toast to the happy couple—there were 300 guests. By the time half the people had spoken, I was pretty well blotto. When the 13-piece orchestra started playing, I allowed myself to be dragged onto the dance floor by my bridal partner, my cousin Jimmy. We danced fast, my gown swirling, my feet tapping away. The dance floor was huge, but so was the crush of bodies on it, people moving back and forth, caught up in the wild beat of the music. I was feeling no pain and, thanks to the champagne, no inhibitions.

Doing a fast, shoulder-shaking boogie backward and laughing in joy, I collided with someone behind me. I threw a quick glance over my shoulder, blurted out, "Sorry!" and kept right on dancing.

Eventually, though, it all caught up with me—the rich food, the drinking, the madcap twirling on the dance floor. My head and stomach were in direct competition with each other, each vying to distress me more. I needed solitude, a place to lay my head for a few soothing moments. I went into the abandoned waiting room where the bridal troupe had hung out during the cocktail hour. A small oil lamp burned on a bridge set between two pier cabinets, the mirror behind it reflecting the flame back into the room. Closing the door behind me, I eased off my three-inch heels and sank gratefully onto the couch.

I don't know how long I lay there before I heard a light knock on the door. Figuring someone had missed me and sent a search party, I called out, "Come in." The door opened; glancing into the mirror, I made out a silhouette in the doorway, music from the wedding seeping in around her.

"Please close the door," I whined weakly, closing my eyes again. "My head's ready to split open." I was virulently suffering from the evening's excesses.

"I hope I'm not intruding," her voice said over my head. "But I saw you leave a while ago and wanted to know if you're OK. I was afraid the collision we had on the dance floor might have done something to you."

I hazarded opening my right eye to get a look at the speaker. It was indeed the woman I had knocked into. I vaguely waved my hand in the air, generously dismissing her from any responsibility. "No, that's not it. Just a little too much overindulging."

"Poor baby," she murmured. "Weddings seem to have that effect on people. I expect quite a few babies will be conceived tonight. I have some aspirin in my purse. Would you like a couple?"

I nodded feebly and waited while I heard my benefactress pour a glass of water from the carafe on the French provincial sideboard. The rug muffled her footsteps as she returned to the couch, but her perfume delicately tickled my nose as she got closer. There was just enough room for her to sit next to me on the edge of the cushion.

"Here you go." She placed two small capsules in my palm and then put her hand under my neck, lifting my head a little to help me swallow the water. As she held the cut-crystal tumbler to my lips, I opened my eyes. Her short dress had ridden far up her thighs, revealing silk stockings held in place by garters. Suddenly my stomach started flip-flopping, and it had nothing to do with my headache.

A trickle of water traveled down my chin. I felt my guardian angel lightly touch my skin with her fingertip and wipe it away, then watched in fascination as she flicked the droplet off her finger with the tip of her pointed tongue.

The turmoil in my belly started kicking side to side. Even buzzed, I knew this woman was coming on to me. And though I don't go to weddings to cruise, liquor had erased my better judgment. So when she leaned in for a kiss, I didn't hesitate. The band had swung into a slow song, and our kisses followed suit: burning, deep kisses.

When she relinquished my lips, the mysterious nurse looked deep into my eyes, her own burning like dark coals. Her full lips teased me with their poutiness, making me hunger for more kisses. But kisses were not on my temptress's mind, at least at the moment.

"How's your headache?" she asked softly, lightly touching long tapered fingers to my forehead.

"It needs TLC," I responded. (Hey, I was sick, not stupid.)

"I think I have exactly what you need," she told me, talking in that same soft voice as she undid the lone button at the top of her black dress. She revealed honey-colored skin, golden in the candlelight, warm, inviting a caress. I reached out and gently touched her bountiful breasts, trailing my fingers to very generous nipples, a definite plus in my book. I began salivating at the thought of wrapping my lips around those turgid tips.

She read my mind. "Would you like these?" she asked, coy now, cupping her breasts in her hands and arching her back, proudly thrusting them at me. Those dark hard knobs beckoned me with their beauty. Lust spread from my belly to my cunt like wildfire; my clit swelled.

When I nodded wordlessly, she leaned forward, placing those tasty treats within reach of my hungry mouth. When I got the first feel of nipple on my tongue, my clit jerked. A steady throb worked between my legs, and I felt the moisture in my panties.

Her raven hair brushed against my face soft as angel wings while she gave me first one, then the other breast to play with. I reached up and captured them both between my hands, dragging my sharp teeth across her sensitive skin. She moaned, deep in her throat, a hungry, primal sound.

I enjoyed listening as I suckled her. The flickering oil lamp's flame bounced back from the mirror, bathing us in a golden glow. Soft music added a lulling background to the scene as I contentedly lay there, a grown woman nursed by another grown woman.

When the music picked up tempo, so did my lust. A pulsing beat matched the throb between my legs; suddenly, I wasn't satisfied with just nipples. I wanted more.

"Get on my face," I whispered huskily, afraid to change position in case my stomach acted up.

She looked down, cocking one eyebrow inquisitively. "Mmm...hungry, aren't you?" she murmured, straightening up.

"Famished," I answered honestly. It had been over a month since my last lifelong relationship.

She stood up, the top half of her dress hanging down, dangling around her waist. Looking down at me, she slithered out of it and stood in all her glory for my inspection. She wasn't wearing panties: Her ebony fur was a neatly trimmed triangle nestled between her thighs.

I reached out and grazed her bush with a finger. "Nice," I whispered, letting my fingertip lightly trail the inside of her leg. I was rewarded when I saw an involuntary shudder pass through her body. Black garters held up sheer black stockings; her heels were four-inchers.

The smell of vases filled with roses mingled with the scent

of her perfume and her pussy. Our eyes zeroed in on each other, her dark brown, almost black, ones meeting my deep baby blues; my own hot lust was reflected in her gaze. Mutely she knelt on the very edge of the couch, and then using the armrest behind my head for support, she swung her left leg over my body, straddling my chest. She stayed up, supported by her bent knees, one on either side of me.

"I'm afraid my wetness will leave a big stain on your beautiful dress."

My first reaction was, Who cares? I'm never gonna wear this again. But I realized when our fucking was over, I'd have to go back into a well-lit room filled with people.

"Then climb up here," I said throatily, almost choking on my desire. My fingertips wandered over her smooth-as-silk back, and I was rewarded again by feeling her muscles ripple convulsively under the pads of my fingers.

"Like that, baby?" I watched her throw her head back and nod, the column of her throat long and lovely. I fantasized being on top of her, naked cunt to naked cunt, branding her with burning kisses down her neck and throat. But I was helpless, on my back, and had to await milady's pleasure.

I didn't have to wait long. She started inching up along the couch, making the voyage to my mouth. The closer she got to her goal, the more powerful her cunt smell got. Arousal swept through my anonymous partner; there was no denying that. When she was close enough, I eased my arms under her bent knees, first one leg then the other. That's when I got my first glimpse of the ruby nugget hidden in the folds of her puffed-up cunt. I felt the warmth of this beautiful woman's clit as she hovered dead center above my mouth before gracefully sinking to it.

Wetness, heat, and swollen lips suddenly engulfed my

mouth. I settled myself in since I was going to take my own sweet time with this sexy beauty whom fate had directed to me.

"That good, baby?" she asked solicitously, peering down. When I nodded my head, my nose slid up and down her wet slash. "Oh, yeah," I breathed into her very center.

Her perfect honey-hued breasts pointed out at their dark brown tips. Her flat belly went in and out quickly, mutely displaying her desire—she was actually panting, waiting for me to begin. Such a captive audience was worthy of not being kept waiting. As a preview of coming attractions, I teased the tip of my tongue, lightly—oh, so lightly—around her moist opening, rimming it slowly.

She obviously enjoyed the preview. A low moan escaped her. "Do it, baby. Please."

Your wish is my command, I thought as I continued rimming her hole, going in a little deeper this time. Whoever this horny bitch was, I was going to make her ride my mouth like there was no tomorrow. Because in actuality there wouldn't be for us.

With my hands resting lightly on her hips, I was in control. I got to work. With the flat of my tongue I licked her cunt, starting from her hole, stopping right below her clit, and then back down again, getting a fresh batch of juice on my tongue every time I dipped into her opening. I knew the exquisite torture I was putting her through, and I could tell by the way she scrunched down a little when my tongue traveled upward that she was trying to force contact between it and her clit. I wouldn't let her. When I felt her move, a quick hand movement thrust her back up, keeping her burning clit just out of reach.

"Oh, don't be such a cunt tease, baby. I need you." Her soft pleading words went south, right to my clit. And if mine felt like that that—pounding, huge, and burning for release—then I could just imagine what hers felt like.

I closed my eyes and gave in to passion. Fastening my lips around her fat clit, I sucked on it, feeling her plump knob grow in my mouth, becoming more swollen. I circled my tongue around the delicate morsel, loving how it felt against the softness of my tongue. Gently and then more forcefully, I beat her love bud with my tongue, making my horny partner rock her cunt forward and ride my mouth.

"Yes, baby, yes, baby, yes baby," she chanted.

Not wanting her to come too fast, I stopped what I was doing and slid my tongue down to her hole, again dipping into its honey. Then abruptly I plunged it in as far as it would go, exploring her innermost cavern with its tip. She gasped and squirmed her ass down so I could snake more of it up there. I was too fucking horny to keep it going. Racing my tongue back between her swollen lips, I found her clit and stroked it with my tongue, fast, slow, in between, until her legs started to buck and her hands sank themselves into my blonde hair. I grabbed onto her hips and kept her prisoner, not letting her get away from her fleshy assailant. She moaned while I kept up my tempo, the tip of my tongue driving us both wild.

I flicked faster; she bucked harder, until I knew the moment of truth for her had arrived. With her body shaking as if in a fever, she let out a squeal and then collapsed in a heap on top of me. Pussy juice was slathered all over my face, and my makeup was ruined, but I didn't care.

After a few moments, which I spent stroking her heaving

back, she looked at me and gave a tired little smile. "You were wonderful."

"You ain't so bad yourself," I quipped.

"Mmm, I could lay on top of you like this forever. But," she said resignedly, starting to unglue herself from me, "I have to go. I've probably been gone too long as it is."

With much regret, I helped her off and watched as she slithered into her dress, pulling it over her head, her body wriggling as it settled around her curves. With her arms up in the air like that, her beautiful breasts and delicious cunt were vulnerable, completely exposed. She looked lovely.

"Are you sure you're OK?" she asked. I knew what she meant: Did I want her to do me?

I was on fire. I'd be lying if I said I wasn't, but suddenly it didn't seem so important that she return the favor. I was getting pleasure just looking at her.

"No, thanks. I'm fine. You better get back out there." I paused, then added impishly, "Thanks for dessert," and I gave her a big personality smile.

She smiled back, then slipped out the door.

I did what I could to repair my makeup, straightened my dress, then rejoined the reception, still in full swing. I glanced at my watch: It was 10:30. Still two hours to go.

When I returned to my table, I answered the inevitable question of where had I been, then scanned the dance floor for my anonymous sex partner, knowing instinctively she'd be there. Sure enough, she was kicking up her heels with the guy she had been skipping the light fantastic with when we had bumped butts. A surge of jealousy shot through me when I saw her smile at him—envy, too, knowing what was under that dress was all his.

My queasiness was gone, my head no longer befuddled with drink. I tore with gusto into wedding cake and tea, all the time casting surreptitious glances at her. Watching her. Reliving our mad 30 minutes of unbridled passion. I had never done anything like that before, and the bittersweet feeling coursing through me made me doubt I ever would again. The more I watched the interaction between her and her date, the more jealous and disgruntled I became. I know better than to dip into bi waters, but to paraphrase an expression I once heard, "A hungry lesbo has no conscience." I shouldn't have given in, but circumstances had made me one horny bitch.

Oh, well. I shrugged off my morose thoughts. I'm a big girl; I knew what I was doing while I was doing it. I was the one who would have to live with regrets, because I was already regretting that my honey-hued seductress would be walking out of my life within the next 20 minutes.

The big celebration was winding down. Groups were breaking up, revelers tiredly gathering their belongings and arguing over who would get the floral arrangements. Felicia and Anthony were making the last round of the room; the bridal party members had left with with their spouses or significant others. Time to pack up my own tent and hit the road, find Mom and Dad, and hitch a ride home.

"Hey, hold up a sec, Cuz," someone called out. "I want you to meet someone."

I turned to see Felicia walking toward me. No escape. She had been haunting me for the past two months to meet one of her coworkers. No way! I'd been to Felicia's office. There wasn't anyone there I'd want to go out with.

"Not tonight," I said, trying for a nice brush-off. "I'm too tired to put my best foot forward." I looked down at my shoes.

"In fact, the only thing I want to do is get these torture chambers off my feet." When I looked back up, my cousin was standing in front of me, and with her was my very recent sex partner.

My face must have shown my confusion because she gave a delightful mischievous giggle.

"Taylor, this is my cousin Connie. Connie, this is Taylor."

I looked into twin pools of molten sexuality, tinged with impishness. This is who Felicia wanted to introduce me to?

"Pleased to meet you," Taylor said coyly. "But I feel as if we already know each other. You just have one of those faces."

Her double entendre shot a blush through my entire body. Oh, she was a playful one, wasn't she?

As Felicia drifted off to her new husband after playing matchmaker, I said to Taylor, "Why didn't you just tell me when you came into the room?"

She gave me a dazzling smile and responded teasingly, "But look at the fun that would have ruined."

We sat at the table, heedless of the departures around us. "So, I've been dodging Felicia for two months, and all the time she had the woman of my dreams ready to meet me?" I offered ruefully. Taylor simply nodded her head gravely at my dim-wittedness. But suddenly the bulb burned brightly. "Hey, wait a minute," I said sharply. "Who was that guy you were so cozy with tonight? That's what threw me off. I thought he was your husband or boyfriend."

Taylor sat back and studied me as if I were an exhibit at an art show. "But surely, Connie, you've heard of brothers?"

"Yeah," I responded, galled by her sweet sarcasm, "but you're dark and sexy, and he's blonde and bulky."

"Different fathers," she said simply.

Ah, everything clicked into place then. "So, you really are up for grabs, aren't you?"

"Depends on what you want to grab."

I looked at her, remembering our sweaty session. "How about what I grabbed before with this," I said, pointing to my mouth. "Only this time, let's do it long and slow. And without me being trussed up in a gown."

She gave me a lengthy look full of promise and said in sotto voce, "Maybe not in a gown, baby, but you will be trussed up."

The Cookie Sheet

Ouida Crozier

The late-afternoon sun slanted in through the long wall of windows, bathing the sixth-grade classroom in a deep orange-gold. The room's sole occupant, Lorin Hegge, was bent over a long table in one corner of the pool of sunlight, scraping at the remains of the day's celebration of the autumnal equinox.

In front of her was a large cookie sheet of the type used in institutions for baking cookies, sheet cakes, and the like. With a stiff, short-handled spatula she chipped and wiped at the caramelled residue of the nuts, flour, and molasses pumpkin her class had concocted—with the help of the ever-obliging cafeteria staff—in sweet salute to the coming harvest. As chunks came loose under her prying, she snicked them up with the fingers of her left hand and popped them into her mouth, licking her sticky fingers slowly and with great relish. Once or twice she had already chuckled to herself over a memory of the dinner table with her family of origin, where everyone had loved the baked-on residue of food as well or better than the item that had originally occupied the pan, bowl, or baking utensil and where intense scrambles to get the most goodies had taken place. Here she need not scramble, for she had the entire pan to herself.

The room was still except for the noises of her scraping and the crunch of caramel and nuts. In the hallway the usual sounds of the janitorial crew faded and died. Unknowingly, Ms. Hegge had been left alone in the building.

As she worked, the pan kept sliding sideways, and she struggled to brace it against her thigh at a very awkward height for a tall woman. She sighed softly, pausing to straighten her back for a moment, in no hurry, feeling she had all the time in the world. At the exact moment that she arched her back—the spatula dangling in her right hand, her eyes briefly closed, her left hand held at waist height safely in front of her—a shadow joined hers across the cookie sheet. Scarcely a second later a pair of arms slipped around her waist, and a body pressed against hers from behind.

"Oh!" she exclaimed, trying to turn to see who had joined her. But the arms held tight; the body molded to hers. A warm, moist mouth touched the side of her neck over her right shoulder, and Lorin relaxed as she glimpsed tight dark curls and recognized the woman's head next to hers. "Marianne," she murmured with pleasure.

The arms loosened, and Lorin turned to embrace her lover. Blue eyes engaged chocolate ones, and the women began a wordless kiss. Marianne's mouth was full, the lips a deep red that when impassioned positively throbbed in the rich brown of her face. Lorin loved the feel of her thin, Scandinavian-pale lips against those generous African ones. Their tongues met, intimate strangers greeting one another in these unaccustomed environs, growing more bold with the passing seconds.

Lorin groped behind her and dropped the spatula with a dull clatter. Her other hand waved irresolutely in the air behind Marianne's head, its sticky fingers uncertain. She felt passion overtake her like a tidal wave, knocking the breath from her lungs, sending the blood pounding in her veins, flooding her belly with the heat of desire. Marianne's strong arms pulled her against her, and she involuntarily ground her hips against Marianne's. She gasped and moaned, wanting to be taken right there: on her desk, on the floor, stripped of clothing, naked to her empty classroom.

Marianne forced her backward against the table over which she had been leaning. She felt the edge of the cookie sheet press against the back of her thigh. "Mmm, wait!" she enjoined, not wanting the sticky mess all over the fabric of her skirt. Marianne peered over her shoulder, scouting the situation, holding Lorin bent half backward in her arms. Her eyes returned to Lorin's with a seductive light in them and the glint of inspiration. She unbuttoned Lorin's skirt and pushed it off her hips. It fell to the floor and was shortly joined by a slip, panty hose, and a pair of undies. All of this was being accomplished by remarkably dexterous fingers; those same fingers managed to tantalize and caress the hips, buttocks, belly, and thighs that lay under these articles of clothing, causing their owner to tremble with anticipation.

When all below her waist lay on the floor, Lorin stepped out of the pile of fabrics and kicked off her low-heeled pumps, her arms across Marianne's shoulders, ready for the next move. Marianne kneaded her twat gently, teasingly, until Lorin's head dropped back and her knees began to buckle. Marianne bent to taste the long, pale neck, tightening her arm around Lorin's back, and then gently lifted her onto the table onto the gooey cookie sheet.

As Lorin sat spreading her thighs, she felt the wetness Marianne had brought smear against the sticky cookie sheet. She wriggled her pelvis in tiny, circular motions, seeking to blend the sweetness of the caramel with her own sweet honey. Marianne's lips engulfed hers, her tongue moving deep in Lorin's mouth, her free hand caressing Lorin's breasts through the soft silk of her blouse and camisole. Forcing Lorin's legs farther apart, she pulled Lorin, cookie sheet and all, toward her.

Lorin took her left hand from Marianne's shoulder and began to stroke her own clitoris, dipping the already sticky fingers into the pool of moisture that formed hot between her legs. She raised the dripping fingers to Marianne's face, who inhaled the woman scent deeply, then proceeded to take each finger one at a time into her own hot mouth, licking, sucking each one clean. Meanwhile, she unbuttoned—and not without some difficulty—the tiny buttons of Lorin's blouse and slid her hand under the camisole, creating another rash of goose bumps and renewed shudders as she grazed the smooth skin of Lorin's ribs with her insistent palm.

When Lorin's fingers were clean, Marianne loosened her arm from around Lorin and bent so that her mouth could attend to the small, full breasts whose nipples had already been teased into erectness. Lorin supported herself with her arms and leaned back, arching toward Marianne's suckling. She moaned with pleasure, feeling her hips respond to the exquisite sensation of that mouth on her breasts with movements of their own. Her buttocks ground into the cookie sheet, where the spreading puddle of vaginal juice made it slippery. Once again Marianne's fingers sought Lorin's clitoris so that the motions of her fingers matched the rhythms of her mouth.

As tension mounted and warmth intensified, growing closer and closer to ignition, Lorin lost all sense of time and outside sensation. Her arms were locked, supporting her without volition, as Marianne's mouth worked its way down her body to finally replace the long dark fingers on the throbbing clitoris. The fingers dipped into the streaming, pulsing vagina, reaching for the nerve center where orgasm is kept, circling, stroking from within, bathing in the torrent, easing in and out, cupping over the pelvic floor, rocking, touching, touching....

Lorin panted and gasped, her hips gyrating faster and faster, pressing into Marianne's mouth, slipping on the cookie sheet, reaching with her seductress, until her orgasm exploded, her long body arching convulsively, her legs locked around Marianne's back, while waves of sensation took her over and over again.

Gradually, like fading twilight, the orgasm released her to the humming silence of the nearly darkened room. Marianne's head lay nestled against her belly, her dusky face shining with the dew of lovemaking. Lorin willed herself forward from numbed arms and cradled her lover's fuzzy head against her spent body. With one finger she wiped the moisture from the café au lait cheek, tasting in it, as she licked, herself and caramel.

Rural Free Delivery

Anne Seale

Jill Beverly Jones-Backstrah is the name of the woman who used to deliver my mail. In a town this small, you get to know not only your public servants' hyphenated names, but also their brand of religion and marital status. Jill had married Danny Backstrah, the Shop-a-Minit Market produce manager, at the Grace Methodist Church about three-and-a-half years ago, but none of that interfered with my purposes.

Each weekday morning shortly after 11, Jill's Saturn wagon would appear as a dot on the horizon, growing rapidly. Since my closest neighbor is more than a mile away, Jill had plenty of time to gather speed. Drawing near, she would brake with a squeal of tires, pull to my side of the road, and stop. From her perch in the middle of the seat, she would reach out the passenger-side window, flip down the mailbox door, and re-move my outgoing mail.

Don't worry, there was always mail for her to remove—I'd made sure of that since that awful day in December when I had no incoming mail, not even a Christmas card, and Jill sped by my unflagged box without even slowing down. After that, it became my habit to scan the morning paper for a newsmaker to write to. Sometimes it was a brave soul who had saved a person or animal from certain death, or someone who had won the lottery or whose house had burned down. More often than not it was the governor or president—they never did anything right.

After locating my target, I'd dash off a note of condolence, congratulations, or scathing criticism. Then I'd run it out to the mailbox and raise the little red flag. Returning to the house, I climbed the stairs to the guest bedroom and stationed myself at the uncurtained window. Soon the shiny black Saturn would pull up, and Jill's right arm would shoot out, dexterously gathering up the letter I had deposited. After a moment it appeared again with my incoming mail, of which there was usually a great deal. In addition to answers from those I had lauded or taken to task, there were lots of bills— I had more than 20 charge accounts, and I charged everything.

One day in February I had a close call. I received no mail except for a spring catalog from Miles Kimball. I broke out in a tense sweat when I realized that but for a catalog I would have missed the second showing of Jill's sweet arm! In gratitude, I sat right down and ordered a sweater drier.

Jill's arm was not the only part of her I cherished. From my station at the second-story window, I was also able to catch glimpses of one shapely knee. Only on the coldest winter days did she keep it covered. Otherwise she wore skirts that skimmed the top of the kneecap or in the summer months short shorts that revealed tantalizing inches of inner thigh as she twisted her torso to toss my outgoing mail into a container on the rear seat.

By now you might be thinking I was doing something disgusting to my body as I watched the lovely Jill plunge and twist. Shame on you! My mother taught me better than to sit and play with myself at a window in view of the passing world. No way! That came later.

Every day after Jill had departed for parts unknown, I flung myself onto the guest bed, legs hanging over, and imagined the Saturn wagon was again approaching, that the delicious arm was floating out through the open window.

(In my fantasy it all happened in slow motion. What had taken less than a minute in real life was now drawn out to last a half hour or more.)

Jill's hand would grope around a bit as if she were giving her attention to something inside the car, then suddenly reach up and flip down my panties. She'd teasingly run a delicate finger around the rim of my dew-damp box until a light rain that quickly turned into a downpour drenched it completely. After playing with my wet, slippery red flag for a while, she'd slide her whole hand into the mailbox and feel up, down, and around for letters. The fingers drove me nearly mad with their stroking, roaming, investigating. Then, at the point that I absolutely had to have it, Jill's hand would begin thrusting in and dragging out, languidly at first and then with a wanton force that had me begging for more, more.

And bless her heart, Jill would never drive away until the mail had been delivered.

Once in a while Jill would take a day off or a week's vacation, and some guy I went to high school with by the name of Doug would speed down my road in his Chevy Blazer and stick out a hairy arm at me. I'd be so repulsed I'd have to wait an hour or two before trying to conjure up the lovely Jill. After a few days of Doug I'd actually start to forget what she looked like and have to turn to the stack of *Playboy*s I kept under the guest-room bed to use as interim Jills.

(One time when my mother was staying in the guest room,

I woke up in the middle of the night in a panic, remembering those magazines with corners turned down and comments penned in the margins of my favorite pages. I prayed that Mom, reaching for her slippers in the morning, wouldn't bump her hand against the stack and pull it out. I guess she didn't—she didn't say anything about it, at least. She would have, don't you think?)

Anyway, one day as I watched Doug stuff my mailbox with his hairy paw, I found myself wishing I'd seen ahead to take a photo of Jill to use when she wasn't on the job. Then it hit me: *Why don't I get a camcorder?* If I had a video to watch, Jill could deliver my mail every day, even on Sundays! I jumped in the car and drove to the nearest Circuit City where I purchased a JVC with a 22x optical zoom, paying for it with one of my Visa cards, of course.

When the Saturn wagon drew in front of my house the following day, I stood at the upstairs window, my camera charged, aimed, and focused. I started filming when the car appeared at the top of the road, zooming in as the wagon squealed to a stop and Jill's hand emerged. Taking my eye from the view finder for a moment, I saw she was wearing my favorite green running shorts. I gleefully aimed the camera at the bare upper thigh. After a few seconds I unzoomed a bit to get the whole Jill in the frame and found that her face was frozen, staring up at me through the windshield. My aiming and zooming movements must have caught her attention. I froze too. Finally she threw my mail in the box and peeled out.

I took the tape to the VCR in my bedroom and played it. It was a little fuzzy at times, and the picture jerked a lot, making me wish I had purchased the optional tripod. The film is adequate for my daily needs, however, which is a good thing because ever since that day two months ago, Doug has been my steady mail carrier.

A side benefit to this whole thing is that I'm going to be spending a lot less money on postage.

The Party

Catherine Lundoff

Ana paced nervously around her small bedroom trying not to look at Frida. She always seemed so intense. Ana risked a peek. Frida looked back and so did the small monkey on her shoulder. She wondered if the real Frida Kahlo would have gone to a sex party. Ana had heard she was pretty wild. But she still felt pretty dumb thinking about talking to a poster, even though it was almost as good as talking to the cats sometimes. At least since Sue left.

Of course, if she hadn't left, Ana wouldn't be sitting there all queasy and just a little bit wet thinking about tonight. Nope, she'd be settling in for a big night of videos and popcorn. Maybe her new friend Max had a point when she told Ana that Sue's splitting with the meter reader was the most interesting thing her ex was likely to do. Sue hadn't liked Max, either, the few times they'd met. Softball dyke meets butch-top social worker. It got ugly.

Maybe that was why Ana liked Max almost at once. She said exactly what she thought. If she'd been dating Max, she would have known about the meter reader before anything happened, if nothing else. Not that she would have been dating Max, of course. All that leather stuff was fun to fantasize about, but she was pretty sure she wasn't ready to try it. Still, when Max insisted she go to this thing tonight, she agreed. Sue left almost six months ago, and Ana knew everyone was tired of her moping around. So she was going, but just to make them happy. Well, maybe she was curious too, she admitted.

She stared mournfully into her closet. What the hell do you wear to these things anyway? The white turtleneck with the little flowers? Definitely not. Not the vast collection of crucifixes on chains her family had foisted on her since she came out, either. They made her feel like a vampire. She continued toward the back of the closet, shaking her head. The little black wool dress? Too formal and probably the wrong kind of hot when she stopped to think about it. One of her cats watched her warily from the doorway.

Finally she settled on the red silk shirt with the buttons, the one she hoped she'd have the nerve to wear without a bra, and a short, full black skirt. Easy access, she thought, and blushed, laughing at herself in the mirror on the closet door. At least she looked pretty cute. The red shirt set off her cocoa-butter complexion, and she posed, modeling the outfit. Plainly it had been too long since she had gotten laid. Who was she kidding? She hadn't even had a date. Her bare feet tapped out an impatient little dance.

She collapsed on the edge of her single bed and squirmed a little. Butterflies were having a blast in her stomach. She lay down and ran her fingers up her thighs, then under her skirt and inside her panties. At least she knew she could do this right. Forcibly dismissing her mental picture of Sue, she let her mind wander while her fingers played in the slick wetness beneath her skirt. No, this would be a special occasion, and damn it, she was going to do herself to another fantasy if it killed her.

There had been a cute butch at the film festival last weekend. She'd do nicely. Ana remembered the woman's long fingers, imagining what they'd feel like inside her. She moaned a little, riding her own fingers. The butch's tongue would be sliding against her now, slipping inside her, then lapping up to tease her clit. Her fingertips circled it slowly, then faster. She took her hand from her pussy and pushed it under her shirt and pinched her nipples into small erect points, squeezing her nails into them just a bit so they would feel like teeth.

Her fantasy butch slid her fingers back inside her, one at a time. Feeling daring, Ana pushed one moistened finger against her asshole, barely venturing inside. It made her feel nasty and sexy, just like those fantasies she never told Sue about. She imagined the butch had a nice hard dildo and was working it up her ass. Grinding her hips into the bed, she rolled them in a slow sensual circle until the heat washed from her clit up her body. Her legs stiffened, and she arched her back, shuddering, frightening the cat away. She collapsed and lay still for a moment, gently grinding her hips against the patchwork coverlet.

After that, of course, there were the cats to be fed and bills to pay and all the other little errands that fill up Saturday afternoons. It still seemed like forever until they picked her up for dinner. "Don't want you chickenin' out on me," Max grumbled as she gently shoved the frantically nervous Ana out the door. Max's girl Erin sat in the driver's seat of their old beater. Ana could see they were both dressed to kill. Literally. Any more studs on that leather and they'd set off metal detectors at the airport a mile away.

Erin grinned when Ana got into the car and slid her short leather jacket off her shoulder to show off the new leather bustier, laced tightly up the sides but open enough to reveal lots of white skin. Ana oohed and aahed, all the while feeling jealous that she didn't have the nerve or the tattoos to show off like Erin did. Oh, well—she figured as she settled into the back seat—they'd have to get dinner at the Cave 'cause anywhere else Max and Erin would have the wait staff fleeing the area. Ana sat back to enjoy the ride.

Sure enough, 20 minutes later the old car pulled up outside the Cave. It was a dark and seedy boy bar that was turned over to the girls once a month for parties. The place had good sandwiches, though, which almost made up for the ambiance. Ana kept looking around curiously in the smoke-filled gloom, checking out the women headed for the back room as they passed under the sickly neon beer signs. They were a pretty mixed bunch: some leatherwomen, a few butch/femme couples, and lots of young, pierced goth types, but no one who really caught her eye. She turned a disappointed eye back to her turkey club. Erin made reassuring small talk until they finished eating.

"Ready?" she asked Ana gently.

"I guess," Ana took a deep breath. She didn't have to do anything she didn't want to; it would be fine. She smiled nervously at Erin and Max.

Things were just starting up when they picked up their latex and condoms at the door to the back room. The door butch sullenly pointed out the safe-sex rules scrawled on the chalkboard over her head. Common-sense stuff, Ana thought, breathing slowly and carefully so she wouldn't hyperventilate. She wondered if the door butch was allowed in to play. The muscular, solid woman with her bleached flat top, tattoos, and leather pants was almost her type, if Ana only had the nerve to ask.

Erin and Max towed her inside, away from temptation. The room was dark and smoky, with just enough light to see women groping each other on the benches along the sides of the room. "You want to play with us?" Max inquired, knowing the answer already. Ana shook her head and wandered over to an unoccupied bench. She watched as Max seized Erin around the waist and kissed her hard, running her hands over her black-leather-covered ass. Max's hand slid lower, reaching under the skirt and displaying Erin's fishnet stockings up to her garters. Ana could feel the wetness growing between her own legs. Surreptitiously, her hand began a slow journey up her thigh. Might as well have fun the easy way.

Erin and Max tossed their jackets on the bench near her, and Max pressed Erin against the wall, arms pinned over her head. Ana watched Max's big, muscular thigh shove into Erin's crotch as Erin spread her legs in their black fishnets and spiked heels even wider to accommodate her. Glancing around, Ana noticed a couple doing a boot-licking scene in the corner. She looked away quickly. Humiliation was not her thing. At least not the voluntary kind, she winced, thinking about her fights with Sue.

The three women across from her, now that was different. The woman kneeling in the middle had her face buried in one woman's pussy while she took it up the ass from a hot butch wearing a harness. The three of them were moaning up a storm, and Ana's hand slid into her own pussy while she imagined she was one of them, preferably the ones getting licked or fucked. Ooh, she was wetter than she'd been in months.

Well, she'd get her money's worth anyway.

"Want some help with that?" Ana looked up to see a handsome dark-skinned butch looking down at her. She hadn't noticed this one before. From the bulge in the woman's jeans, Ana could see she was packing. Rrowl. Must be her lucky night. How was she supposed to act? Should she ask her name first? Wrestling with her nerves, she took a deep breath. Now or never. She took another breath to slow her pulse and smiled invitingly at the woman. Squirming against the bench, she slid her skirt up a little as she slowly sucked her own juices from her fingers and watched the woman pull on latex gloves.

The butch leaned down and pulled her to her feet as Ana strangled the "good girl" voice in her head. The woman's kiss tasted like cigarettes, beer, and peppermint gum. Ana leaned into her and wrapped her arms around her muscular neck. The butch's hand closed over her breast, covered only by a layer of red silk. Her nipples were like rocks. Her leg moved between Ana's thighs just like Max did with Erin.

Ana wanted to lie back on the bench and scream, "Do me now!" But maybe, she reconsidered, that wouldn't be as fun as waiting a little while as the butch slid her hands under her skirt. Those big busy hands peeled off her black lacy panties, slipping them slowly down her legs. Ana kicked them off, not caring if she saw them again. Thick, sturdy fingers unbuttoned the top buttons on her blouse, then the butch lowered her mouth to Ana's hardened nipples, licking and biting them through the silk. Ana ran her fingers through her short dark hair, felt her own head tilt back as the butch ran her tongue over her neck and collarbone. She groaned as the hot mouth nibbled its way down to her breasts.

Ana was leaning back so far that only the butch's strong

arms were holding her up. One hand slid slowly up the outside of her thigh, then worked inward between her legs. She whimpered deep in her throat as the fingers slid into her soaking wet pussy. "Like that, baby?" the butch whispered into her ear. Ana kissed her fiercely, tongues twined, lips smashed together. She was so close to coming, only her fear of falling held her back. The butch sensed this and pushed her down on the bench. Suddenly she was kneeling between Ana's legs, plastic wrap placed swiftly between her tongue and Ana's clit.

The insistent pressure of that tongue stroked up and down Ana's slit until, whole body quivering, she came with a sharp moan. "I bet you got more than that in you, don't you, honey?" the butch growled softly. Unzipping her jeans, she pulled out a large dildo, just rigid enough for what she had in mind. Then she took out a condom and slid it on. Ana reached out her belt loops and pulled her crotch forward. Slowly, sensually, she licked her way down the dildo, then pulled it swiftly into her mouth, wondering where she got the nerve to do this. The butch's head was thrown back, one hand now burrowing into Ana's thick, dark hair, pulling her face closer, driving the dildo farther into her mouth. Ana took it gladly, jerking her mouth quickly up and down the shaft.

The butch pulled suddenly out of her mouth and sat on the bench beside her. She pulled Ana astride her lap and slid the dildo inside her. Its long, hard length pulled a deep groan from Ana's throat as it filled her. The butch's hand slid inside her open blouse, playing with her nipples. They kissed again. Her other hand moved over Ana's ass, then without warning she stuck a finger up her asshole. Ana yelped into the butch's mouth, and she pulled away. "You want me to stop?" the other woman asked between gasps. Ana shook her head and settled in to enjoy the ride.

This was better than before. She could feel the other woman's finger going deeper as she tightened her muscles around the dildo. The butch thrust deeper and deeper inside her. She felt high, breath coming in huge ragged gasps, so full, everything turned on at once. When she came, it was with a yell, nails raking the butch's shoulders through her shirt. Kissing the butch tenderly, she whispered, "What do you like, baby?"

"Do-me queens mostly," was the reply, said with a grin, and she pulled Ana up onto the bench next to her.

Looking around, Ana saw that Erin and Max had taken over the St. Andrew's cross in the corner. Erin's bustier and net stockings were the only clothes she was still wearing, and she was tied, spread-eagle, to the cross. Max pulled a set of tit clamps from her pocket and fastened them to Erin's nipples, slipping them on underneath the supple leather. Erin's head flipped back sharply, and she moaned. Max pulled the decep-tively soft leather flogger from her belt loop and ran it slowly down Erin's back and thighs.

"Hey," the butch called. Ana turned swiftly back to the butch as the flogger began to snap through the air onto Erin's bare ass. "Like to watch, huh?"

Ana blushed. "Sometimes. It's not like I get the chance much. What's your name?"

"Mercedes. And yours?"

"Ana."

"Well, *dulce*, what else do you like? You want me to tie you up to that cross and whip your sweet little ass? Or maybe I'll fuck you while I make you lick off another chick." Ana's involuntary movement and faster breathing told Mercedes what she wanted to know. With one hand possessively stroking Ana's breast, rolling the nipple between her fingers, Mercedes surveyed the room. Finding what she was looking for, she beckoned another woman.

Her fingers continued pinching and rolling Ana's nipple as they watched the other woman approach. Mercedes's fingers dragged a low moan from Ana's throat, which made the other woman smile. She was slight and beautiful, with long black hair and a graceful, sexy walk that resembled a prowl. In her left hand she carried a set of tit clamps that drew Ana's eyes in spite of herself. She imagined them tightening around her nipples. She pictured herself moaning the way Erin was, with the joy of complete surrender, and she shivered in anticipation and fear as Mercedes greeted her friend. "Ana, say hello to Yasmina."

Mercedes's other hand slid Ana's skirt up to nearly display her pussy, while the hand playing with her nipple paused to pull her shirt open to expose her breasts. Ana gasped and writhed and found herself spreading her legs. She looked up at Yasmina under half-closed lids and ran her tongue slowly over her lips. Suddenly she wanted these women to think she was the hottest thing in the room. She wanted to be displayed, even owned, for that one night.

Yasmina studied Ana for a long moment, eyes trailing from her red high heels up her outspread legs to the bit of dark-haired pussy visible below her skirt over her large breasts spilling out of the red shirt to her open mouth and wide, pleading eyes. "She'll do," she concluded and reached down to tweak a nipple, then ran the cold chain connecting the clamps over her breast. "This what you're thinking about, honey?"

Ana nodded, closing her eyes as the cold metal touched her tender skin. The clamp closed on her nipple. She groaned, rocking her hips as the sweet searing pain of the steel sent shooting heat through her, right to her cunt.

Just as suddenly, her nipple was released. Ana's eyes shot open as Yasmina slid off her baggy pants and sat next to them on the bench. "Kneel in front of her," Mercedes growled in her ear. Oh, shit, what had she gotten herself into? If this woman was planning on fucking her ass with that dildo, which suddenly looked enormous, she was in trouble. The two watched her hesitation with amused smiles. That did it. Pushing her fear down, she asked,"You got lube, right?" Her voice sounded like it was quivering, even to her.

"Don't worry, sugar. I'm going to stretch you out while you and Yasmina get acquainted," Mercedes replied with a chuckle. Ana knelt between Yasmina's lean, brown thighs and began tentatively running her tongue along them. As she moved closer, Yasmina reached down and fastened the clamps on her tits, with just enough skin so she could stand the sensation. Ana got down on her hands and knees, trembling with excitement, ass bared for whatever Mercedes had in mind. She licked and nibbled her way up to Yasmina's clit just as the other woman stretched plastic wrap over the pussy hovering before her questing tongue.

The first stinging slap on her round ass cheek made her jump forward instinctively. Yasmina caught her hair and ears and pulled her close, forcing her to hold the plastic with one hand. "Don't stop," she demanded. Ana's tongue pushed into the plastic as hard as she could as several more stinging slaps warmed her ass. A well-greased finger wormed its way into her asshole, just as Yasmina reached down to cup her breasts. Her hands kneaded and rubbed, tugging on the chain and the clamps as the finger slid in and out of her ass. Ana felt her juices spill out of her full cunt and run down her thighs as that finger coaxed more out of her. She stretched to open and greet it. Her tits started to burn.

A second finger followed the first into her ass, and Mercedes began to thrust into her pussy with her other hand. Yasmina tugged hard, then softly on the chain, pulling her breasts from side to side. Ana tried desperately to focus on licking her clit, reaching up with the other hand to hold the wrap in place. Soon she gave up, the other sensations overwhelming her. She came hard, shouting into Yasmina's thigh, thrusting her ass backward as her body begged for more. There were more fingers in her cunt now, driving hard into her, pushing her body out of control.

Groaning, supported by Yasmina's thighs, she floated in ecstasy, the unaccustomed sensations lifting her higher and higher. Suddenly Mercedes pulled her hand from Ana's pussy, then her fingers from her asshole. Whimpering her disappointment, Ana started to turn in protest. Quickly, Yasmina caught her head and pulled her face back into her pussy, with a sharp tug on the chain for emphasis. Ana began licking away energetically. Mercedes smeared lube over the dildo and Ana's eager hole, then slowly and inexorably entered her. Ana growled softly in pain as her hole was stretched wider.

The timbre of her groans and cries changed swiftly as Mercedes entered her. Yasmina's strong hands played with her breasts, sending rivers of fire through her nipples every time she touched the clamps. She came again as Mercedes began driving into her. As her thrusts got faster, Ana felt her shaking as she came. Her ass felt as full as it could possibly get, every nerve ending blazing from her ass to her nipples. She had never felt so well and truly fucked, so thoroughly high from her orgasms that she thought she'd pass out if it went on much longer.

Sensing her exhaustion, Yasmina reached down and un-fastened the clamps. Blood came back to her nipples with an agonizing rush as Mercedes pulled out of her ass and shoved her hand back inside her cunt. Ana was so wet and open that Mercedes's whole hand fit inside as it moved swiftly in and out.

Ana came once again and collapsed at Yasmina's feet, begging for mercy. Mercedes yanked the gloves off and pulled her up onto her lap, laughing as she sat down next to Yasmina. Yasmina got up with a grin and went off to join someone else. Mercedes ran her fingers through Ana's hair and kissed her gently. "Think you'll come back next month?"

Ana grinned and kissed her back, hard. "Dunno. Maybe I'll have a girlfriend by then." She instantly regretted how wistful she sounded.

Mercedes kissed her again. "Here's my number," she said as she handed Ana a business card. "Give me a call if you feel like it." She chucked Ana under the chin, slid her off her lap, and got up. Pulling her clothes back on, she saun-tered out with a quick wink back at Ana, who sat with a be-mused grin on her face.

What a story she'd have for Frida when she got home. The thought made her smile. She smiled even more at the card in her hand. Maybe she'd call Mercedes in a few days. But maybe it would just be enough that she could feel Sue was gone for good. She closed her eyes and, leaning back against the wall, sat basking in the warm smell of sex until Max and Erin came to get her.

This Is the Famous Bath Scene From From Dirty Alice—Revised

Merril Mushroom

"Wait for just one moment." The child released Alice's hand and disappeared into the undergrowth. Alice looked about. She had no idea where they were, how she had suddenly appeared in this forest naked, or where the small child had come from. Before her confusion could take hold, however, the child emerged from the bushes holding two large spheres. "Here." She handed one to Alice and bit into the other.

Alice watched as juice gushed forth, trickling off the child's chin and down the length of her small body. Alice followed her example, taking a small, experimental nibble at first, then biting deep into the fruit, burying her mouth and chin in the succulent, juicy meat. She ate greedily, and the sweet nectar ran in clear streams down her chin and over her breasts and belly. As she finished the last delicious swallow, she blotted her fingers in the sticky trails drying on her body. "I need a bath," she laughed.

"You can bathe when we get to my sister's home," the child said. "She lives on the lake, and sometimes in it or under it as well." She reached out and took Alice by the hand again. Her little fingers were slick with the juice from the fruit. "Come now."

Alice followed her, spellbound by the beauty of the forest around her. There were trees and shrubs of every description, flowers of every hue, delicate bracken and mosses. Bright-plumaged birds flew about, singing and calling to one another, and now and then Alice caught a glimpse of soft fur and black eyes as some small animal peered curiously through the brush at them.

At length they arrived at a large lake that was blocked on one side by a huge beaver colony of dams and bridges. The child stopped by a large hollow stump. "This is where my sister lives, and here is the door to her house."

"Where?" Alice looked about, seeing nothing that even vaguely resembled a house. She suddenly felt strange, insecure, and she wondered why she felt such trust in this little girl.

The child swung open a section of the stump to reveal a steep staircase. "Here." She began to descend the stairs, holding her hand out to Alice, and slowly with much trepidation Alice followed.

The staircase opened into a large, bright room with floor, walls, and ceiling of hard-packed earth. In the center of the room was a low wooden table. A fire burned in a fireplace that had been cut into one wall, and over the fire hung a pot that gave off delicious-smelling clouds of steam. Across from the fireplace was a doorway hung with strands of bright beads through which, as Alice stared in amazement, a woman entered the room.

"Good day, my dear." The woman's voice was low and sensual. It flowed from her throat with the same fluidity that her body had as she moved across the room. She was tall and strong-looking, with silken hair that hung down her back to her knees, hair that seemed to be all colors at once, changing hue as it rippled with her movements. Her smooth skin had a pale green tone and shone with her energy. The one skimpy garment she wore was bright blue, draped in gauzy folds from shoulder to knee, and did little to conceal the lush body beneath. Her legs were muscular, her feet bare, and Alice realized with a start that the woman's toes were webbed, as were her slender fingers. Her gaze rose to the woman's breasts, full and high, dark, ripe nipples outlined by the flimsy fabric. She flushed and raised her eyes to the woman's face only to find that the woman was watching her intently.

Alice flared scarlet with embarrassment. She was suddenly acutely aware of her own nakedness, and a slow bubble of panic began to swell within her.

The woman laughed at Alice's discomfiture. She crossed over to where Alice stood, took her face in her hands, and kissed her on the lips. "You are indeed a treasure, my dear," she murmured, her lips soft against Alice's mouth. Then she moved away. "Come, my little one," she said, taking Alice by the arm, "and bathe."

In a half trance, Alice followed the woman. Her head was spinning, and the beating of her heart threatened to throw her off balance. She could still feel the gentle pressure of the woman's lips against her own, and she was aware of a scent and taste of violets on her mouth. The woman drew her down a long passage and through a low doorway into a smaller room, and Alice was startled to see a number of large rabbits scampering about on their hind legs and carrying various objects in their forepaws. The woman stroked her hair, soothing her, sending tiny currents of energy to prickle their way into her belly where they formed a little nest of excitement.

"Don't be afraid, sweet Alice," the woman said. "My little

servants have been preparing your bath. Here," she drew aside a curtain to reveal a wooden tub filled with fragrant, steaming water. As Alice watched, spellbound, a rabbit poured scented oil into the tub and stirred it around with one paw. Then it scattered a basketful of flower petals on the water, nodded to Alice, and left the room. "Now, into the tub with you," the woman ordered. "I will help you bathe, and this will clear your head." She lit a censer that stood on the table near the tub, and clouds of heady smoke billowed forth and spread through the room.

Alice climbed into the tub and allowed her body to relax in the hot, soothing water. The heavy scent of the flowers, oils, and incense filled her head, and as she breathed deeply she felt herself recover from her surprise and shock. She was no longer concerned with where she was or how she had arrived at this place. She felt happy and at peace, ready to accept all and everything that might come her way. Lazily she stretched her limbs through the caressing fluid and sighed with pleasure.

The woman bent over the tub, holding a large, sudsy sponge. She slipped her hands under Alice's arms and raised the girl to a sitting position. Alice's nostrils quivered delightedly at the heady, violet aroma as the woman leaned close to her, lathering Alice's back, shoulders, arms, and chest. Suddenly she dropped the sponge in the tub and slid her slippery hands over Alice's breasts. Alice gasped at the sharp jolt of pleasure that coursed through her body at the contact. The woman massaged the lush fullness of Alice's breasts, rubbing the delicate webbing between her fingers over Alice's puckering nipples, then moved her hands down over Alice's belly and through the hairy triangle between her legs. She pressed the throbbing lips apart and probed into Alice's secret place, slipping her fingers deep inside her sex while she massaged the girl's stiffening clitoris with the heel of her hand.

Alice felt as though she were about to be consumed by the raging heat of her passion. She moaned loudly and thrashed her body about in the water. Suddenly the woman's hand was gone as she retrieved the sponge and began to lather Alice's legs, lifting first one and then the other out of the water. "Oh, no," begged Alice as waves of heat and cold washed through her, "please don't stop touching me. Please."

The woman smiled. She leaned close to Alice and again kissed the girl on the mouth. Her lips were cool and soft, with a steady pressure that slowly parted Alice's own lips. Alice closed her eyes and opened her mouth to receive the woman's soft tongue. The woman drew away. "Don't close your eyes, Alice," she murmured, her voice heavy with passion. "Look at me." With one swift motion, she stripped her flimsy garment over her head and tossed it away from her.

An overwhelming shyness swelled through Alice, and she lowered her lids so that her lashes masked the vision of the woman's nakedness, but the woman took Alice beneath the chin and pressed the girl's head up and back. "Look at me, Alice," she ordered, and Alice cried with longing as she raised her eyes and viewed the woman, devouring the lush body with her vision.

Now the woman laughed, turning about and posing for Alice, her own breath growing more rapid as her desire mounted. Her skin was indeed green, smooth and firm-fleshed. Her breasts were large with lush, dark-brown nipples. Her waist flared into generously rounded hips and a muscular belly. The hair that covered her private parts was a shiny copper color, and Alice could see a glimmer of pink moistness

where the woman was beginning to open in excitement. Alice
realized that she was the cause of the woman's mounting passion, and the thought aroused her more than the memory of
the woman's touch upon her body. She felt a throbbing in her
chest and between her legs, and she reached out a soapy hand
and stroked the woman's sleek thigh. The skin felt like hot
velvet beneath her fingers.

At Alice's touch, the woman tensed and began to make a
low crooning sound deep in her throat. She climbed into the
tub with Alice and pressed the girl's knees apart. She sat down
between Alice's legs and wrapped her own legs up around
Alice's waist. Alice began to tremble as she felt a soft tickle of
hair against her inner thigh. She raised her knees high, moving her throbbing vulva forward, and pressed her heels hard
against the bottom of the tub. Then with a violent shock she
felt the woman's intimate flesh pressed hard against her own
inner membranes, the woman's belly squeezed close to her
own, the woman's arms holding her tightly, the woman's
breasts crowding hers, their nipples rubbing over one another, as the two of them ground their bodies together, the oils in
the bath easing their movements.

Faster and faster they moved against each other, panting
and moaning. The woman massaged herself between Alice's
legs and squeezed the girl's body rhythmically with her strong
arms. Alice watched the woman's face, seeing her own passion
reflected there. The woman's eyes were slitted, her nostrils
flared. Her mouth was slightly open, and her tongue moved
about between her teeth and over her lips. She sang their
rhythm of lust with soft, moaning grunts, while Alice accompanied her with a high, keening wail.

The woman mashed her mouth against Alice's, grinding

their lips together, thrusting her tongue deep into the girl's throat. Alice sucked hard on the woman's tongue and bit her lips as her passion mounted uncontrollably. Hot flashes streaked through her thighs, and a great weakness descended through her arms and chest. She tightened her grip on the woman's body and dug her fingernails into the flesh of her back. She was dimly aware of the woman trembling violently in her arms. Then her entire body went rigid, and a blinding light exploded in her brain. Through the roaring in her ears, she could hear the woman's loud cries a half-octave deeper than her own screams. She buried her face against the woman's wet, fragrant neck, sobbing as her tremors slowly subsided.

Water splashed over the side of the tub as the woman disengaged herself and moved away from Alice. "I could remain in this tub with you for the rest of the evening, delighting myself with your enchanting body, but dinner will soon be ready, and the others are waiting for us."

"Lady," spoke Alice, gathering all her courage, "by what name may I call you?"

The woman laughed and kissed Alice lightly on the eyelids. "I have no name, my dear. However, if you must, you may call me by any name that pleases you." She stepped out of the tub, and Alice caught her breath as the sight of the woman's nakedness sent a pang of remembered pleasure through her. She gave a little whimper and pressed her hand against her throbbing cunt. The woman laughed again. "Sweet, little Alice," she said softly. "I promise you more delights later on. Now get out of the tub."

Alice stood up and stepped from the water. "I shall call you 'Lady' then," she said with satisfaction. "Where are the towels?"

"Towels? No towels? Never mind, our bodies will dry in

the warm air. Come on now. She took Alice by the hand and led her back into the passageway. "It's time to eat."

The floor climbed gradually beneath their feet and finally opened into a huge room with domed roof. "Aah!" Alice hesitated in the doorway, spellbound. Gigantic candles standing on the floor illuminated the interior. The walls and ceiling were hung with magnificent fabrics and tapestries, and the floor was littered with cushions. A large silver burner hung from the high lintel, and from it billowed clouds of the same incense Alice had smelled in the bath.

Slowly Alice entered the room and walked over to one of the curving walls. She pulled a curtain aside to better peer out of the curiously shaped aperture over which it hung and gave a loud squeak of surprise as she discerned in the fading light that they were over the waters of the lake. As she looked further, she realized that they were inside what she had earlier thought was a beaver dam.

The woman walked up behind Alice and embraced her, and Alice was intensely aware of the woman's breasts boring into her back and of a soft, fuzzy tickle against her buttocks. "Do you like my house, dear Alice?" she asked, her warm breath stirring in Alice's hair and against her ear.

"Oh, Lady, yes," the girl stammered.

"The beavers built it for me when I came to live at the lake. The rabbits, moles, and woodchucks dug my tunnels through the earth, and all the little animals serve me. It is their pleasure, and it will be your pleasure too, sweet Alice, if you wish." She stroked Alice's belly loins with her fingertips, and Alice wanted nothing more right then except to serve the lady for the rest of her life. She clutched one of the woman's hands and brought it to her lips, feeling the soft, pliable membrane of webbing between the woman's fingers against her mouth. Her heart pounded in her chest, and her eyes brimmed with tears of joy.

The woman laughed and danced away from Alice, breaking her grasp. "Do you love me, Alice?" she demanded.

"Yes, Lady," Alice's voice was husky with her longing. "I do love you."

"Good!" Lady whirled over to a table of carved wood inlaid with gemstones. Her silken tresses caught the light from the candles, rippling down her back in a kaleidoscopic stream. She picked up a tiny bell and shook it. Delicate silver tones rang out, permeating the room with a microcosmic tintinnabulation.

At the sound, the same child who had brought Alice to this place appeared in a doorway hung with a long drapery of sea-blue, billowy, diaphanous fabric woven together with tiny slivers of abalone. She pulled the curtain aside and bore in a tray holding a small bottle and two tiny goblets. She set them on the floor near a pile of cushions and then without a word retreated behind the curtain. The woman beckoned Alice. "Come, my dear, and sit with me." She drew Alice down beside her onto the soft pillows and handed her a goblet filled with sparkling amber liquid. "Refresh yourself. Then I want you to dance for me."

Alice raised the goblet to her lips, sipped, then drained the cup of the cool draught. It was delicious! She was relaxed, content, and she wanted nothing more than to please Lady, to do as Lady wished. Rising to her feet, she swayed sinuously before this most beautiful of creatures. Her thick black hair crackled about her as she arched her back and drew her fingers sensually up her thighs, her flanks, her belly. She touched her breasts and ran her hands down her sides, feeling desire rise hot inside her. She danced before Lady, watching the woman's face, seeing the flush that rose beneath the emerald complexion. Alice danced, feeling every cell of her body tingle with desire. She knew that she was beautiful, that Lady liked her dancing, and she was happy.

Then Lady reached behind her and pulled a cord that hung from the ceiling, and a heavy drape fell away to reveal a large, curved mirror. Alice stared, spellbound, at her own naked reflection and that of Lady, magnified and illuminated by some magical quality of the glass.

"Enough!" ordered Lady, and Alice stopped dancing and stood quivering with restraint. Her body felt as though it were being consumed by cold flames, and a heavy moisture seeped from between her thighs. Lady took her by the wrist and pulled her down to the cushions, pressed her back so that she must look upon her image in the mirror, and descended upon Alice's cunt with a hot, greedy mouth, taking her suddenly, fast, and hard.

"Oh!" screamed Alice. "Oh, Lady!" And then she had no more breath for exclamations, because Lady was doing the most amazing things to her with her mouth and fingers. Suddenly she stopped, and Alice moaned and sobbed and tried to grind her cunt against Lady's mouth; but Lady was only turning her body, taking a moment to swivel about so that she could present Alice with the magnificence of her sex. Reverently, Alice touched the hot, throbbing flesh with her fingertips. Then with a loud sigh she bent forward and buried her mouth in the sodden copper hair, sliding her tongue between the swollen lips to taste the woman's succulent wetness, feeling Lady's thighs trembling against her cheek.

The woman crooned her pleasure, her voice muffled against Alice's own cunt, and the vibrations of the sound palpitated Alice's inner membranes, sending little flashes of delight shooting up her thighs and into her chest and belly. She felt her own sounds of moaning deep in her throat, and she drew Lady farther into her mouth, seeking to merge their flesh together. Faster and faster they moved against each other. The nectar of their sex ran down their chins, and they smeared their faces and hands in it. They were coming, coming, riding each other's pleasure in spasm after spasm, filled with the feel, the sounds, the tastes, the scents of themselves, and each together, coming harder, harder, and then after one brief transcendent lull, coming again.

Lady rolled away, turned around again, and propped herself on an elbow. She looked down at Alice's face. The girl lay still, drained, exhausted. Lady laughed. "Poor Alice. We'll have to work on building up your stamina, won't we?" She bent and kissed the girl on the mouth, and Alice could smell the scent of her own sex on the woman's cheeks and taste her own juice slick upon the woman's lips. She moaned, feeling a fire begin to rekindle in her loins, but Lady pulled away and laughed again. "Later, dear Alice. I, for now, need a *real* dinner. Come with me and eat some of my food." She rose to her feet, reached down, and drew Alice up after her.

The Tarantula Mind

by Nyondo Nadi

"Hey, want a tarantula?" my boss asks.

"Sure, OK," I reply. I only half wonder why she has se-
lected me for this. There are plenty of oddballs and people
who are more "out there" than I am, but maybe it is my reputation for reading weird books at lunch or seeing under-
ground cult movies that gets me elected. As it is, I happen to
be in the mood for anything—any kind of mind fuckery at
all. It doesn't happen often, but when it does the strange and
the ordinary switch places, performing an "After you,
Alphonse." And no matter what is requested of me, I just say,
"Sure. OK."

Terry steps into my paper-laden cubicle to explain why she
has a tarantula to give away. It first belonged to her husband,
and they have kept it for years. Now, however, they also have
a bright-eyed, hyperactive 2-year-old with a supernatural tal-
ent for putting her hands on things and opening them up. The
place for peanut butter, obviously, is the TV screen. Cold
cream belongs inside coffee cups and on dresser handles. It
will only be a matter of time, Terry says, before Sandra will
figure out how to open Dierdre's cage.

Three days later Dierdre is riding home with me, her cage
secured on the floor in the back of the car. Along the way I

stop at a pet shop for supplies and a tarantula guidebook.

Dierdre, I discover, is a Mexican red-legs. *Brachypelma smithi.* She is a dull brown all over, except at the joints of her legs, which are ringed in bright yellow. The highest set of leg joints, next to her body, is bright red. As she delicately picks her way through the sand in her cage, I watch the red spots move back and forth. The colors are bright, Terry has told me, because Dierdre has just shed her skin. I wonder if Dierdre knows how limited her little world is. Just sand, a stick to climb on, some water. She doesn't seem to mind it.

The following Saturday Nancy comes over and decides to stay the night. She makes appropriate squeeling "ugh" sounds at Dierdre. Our relationship has progressed to the point where Saturday night has a regular schedule. Dinner at 8, the club by 10, home by 12:30, slow dancing in the living room by 1, lights out in the bedroom by 1:20.

For some reason on this night Nancy simply lies on her back, her panties still on. I pull on the elastic, but she won't lift up to let it slide.

"If we're going to make love, you need to get those off," I say.

Her voice, smug and drowsy, drifts out of the darkness. "Make me."

Stunned and a little appalled, I stare in the direction of her voice. After all, she is a strong, independent woman, and so am I. Ripping the panties off her just doesn't seem right. But bullying her into doing it doesn't seem comfortable either. I ponder the problem for a minute, then settle on a compromise. I insinuate my hand between her legs and into the panties. My middle finger slips neatly into her vulva. The insides of my knuckles and my palm settle into familiar places.

I work her to a climax. For the moment I have managed to mentally and physically sidestep the panty problem. I know I will have to attend to it later, like a popcorn hull stuck next to a back tooth.

According to the guidebook, Dierdre is actually a shy, fragile creature; her only weapons are two large fangs on her underside, in front of her mouth. At times she will lever herself up on her back legs, plastering her underside against the glass. I study the fangs protruding from the dull brown hair. A bite won't be toxic, but it'll be no joke, either. I watch her walk. If she walks with her legs hunched and her hair fluffed up like a cat's, that means she is angry or hungry and definitely untouchable. Otherwise, she can be handled.

When I look in the mirror, this is what I see: a small brown woman dressed in sensible clothing. A pleasant, open face. The shoes are always flat, comfortable, and never red. A peaceful person. Fragile. But always able to fix the leaky tap, the stuck window, the blown fuse.

I can sympathize with Dierdre's looks only so much.

I spend an afternoon reading up on Dierdre's sex habits. Kinky! Oh, my God. Tarantulas, you see, do everything backward, and then they fist-fuck. Says so right in the book: The male tarantula finds a safe spot somewhere to build a web. Then he ejaculates into it. He carefully gathers every bit of his own seed into his "hands"—hollow spaces in his front two legs. Then he walks back over to his lady and stuffs these appendages into her genitals, alternating right and left like a boxer.

Afterward, the female tarantula beats him up.

"I don't blame her," I say, putting the book down. It's time to check on dinner. Nancy will be here soon.

That evening we go out to a play. It's a good play, a funny play, a play about gay people, naturally. What else would we see? It's about these two lesbians and their relationship and their friends. What else would it be about? As we wait for the lights to go down, Nancy leans over to say, "You know, I don't see many people of color here."

She's right, of course. Mine is one of maybe three dark faces in the audience. During intermission, the playhouse puts Marvin Gaye on the sound system. I decide that if I must go through life looking small, brown, and innocuous, it might be better to be a tarantula instead of a mouse.

Later over coffee Nancy brings up an idea. I reject it out of hand.

"Tie you up?"

"Well, it might be exciting, you know, just an experiment. Use scarves or something...not anything ugly like rope or chains, for Pete's sake."

"Yeah, but I've never done anything like that. I'm a complete moron with knots, remember?"

"If I get into trouble, we can just cut them...."

"My scarves? Cut them up?"

"Veda, sweetheart, you've got 20 of them, but you only wear two or three. Can't you spare a few for this—for me?"

I want to say, "Make me do it." What I actually say is: "Sure. OK."

A friend of mine who was once a Girl Scout lends me her old handbook. I spend an afternoon with the book and a piece of string. Tying and untying. Cutting knots loose and starting again. Tying and untying. During a break from string practice, I wander over and study Dierdre. She is always up to something new. Right now she's spinning another web. She never hangs them anywhere, which doesn't seem normal for a spider. She spins them on the sand and rolls them up, over and over again.

At least Dierdre's through eating. I have watched her, during her first meal in her new home. Tarantulas have this tendency to move slowly and deliberately—until dinner is right in front of them. Dinner, I have learned, must be a live thing, like a cricket. And crickets are abnormally stupid: Three or four of them have to disappear before the rest figure out they're trapped in a cage with something dangerous. Nonetheless, one will forget eventually and wander out to be snatched by Dierdre. Then she will sit, her hair fluffed and threatening, while she works over her catch.

On a Saturday night at 1:20 in the morning, I go over my knots for the last time and check my handiwork. For some odd reason I have chosen my most exotic scarves to use on Nancy. The combination of cotton and skin looks better that way; she is a well-padded earth-mother type with an olive complexion and curly black hair. I have tied her up with brilliantly dyed creations, the work of nameless female hands, from Gujarat, Belize, and Mexico. I wonder if the colors will run. Then I start in.

The kisses turn into nips; the nips turn into bites. What is usually a thin trickle turns into an entire chaliceful, brimming and then overflowing onto the sheets. I gently take her clitoris and suck on it, flicking my tongue back and forth. The vibrations pound through her ass and into my hands. Without warning, I lift my head and start nibbling my way to her breasts. Curious. I have never seen her nipples this hard. I

tweak them, pinch them, twist them this way and that. The
breath rushes out of her in small gasps. Worried, I turn on the
light and study her face.

She hasn't forgotten the little code word, has she? The one
that means she wants to stop?

Her breasts are a puzzle I try to solve. The nipples have
turned to stone sculptures, secured to moldable pedestals.
Hard and soft, together. A steady pulsing reminds me of another hardness, another softness. I combine the two, squatting
carefully. It's OK for a while, but nipples don't move on their
own. They have to have help. Nancy's tongue darts in and out.
It gently laves her bottom lip, as if searching. Aha. I continue
to slowly work my way up.

"Please lick my cunt again, please, please, please, I'm so
close, Veda! How could you make me do you *now*?"

Without another word, I untie her and flip her over. I
quickly retie her so her hands are raised higher and she is on
her knees. Then I reach for the other thing, the thing I had casually looped over the bedpost while getting undressed.

Dierdre is the one who decided me on it. One night I
couldn't sleep and got up for a glass of water. I looked in on
her and was shocked to find her hanging by her feet from the
mesh lid of her cage. Dierdre is not supposed to be a very
good climber. She has these tiny hooks on her feet that
shouldn't be any good at all for climbing glass walls. Somehow, I don't know how, she had managed it and was now
walking upside down along the ceiling of her bare, sandy
world. It ran counter to everything I knew about her. What
she was doing was dangerous. So dangerous, in fact, that she
was beyond rescue. If I touched the cage, she might fall. Mes-

merized, I stood with my glass of water and watched her do the impossible for 45 minutes.

It's only a leather belt. It is black and about two inches wide. It's good leather—it's the belt I wear with my good suit to job interviews. It's folded up, a loop of it hanging from my fingers. I show it to Nancy. I rub her cheek with it. Her eyes widen; she trembles...and says nothing.

"Pick a number," I say.

She picks a number. Lucky for both of us, it is a small one. I don't know what would have happened otherwise. I am new at this, so the first slap of the belt is too soft, and the next one is too hard.

"Maybe—maybe you'll need one more scarf," she says. Her breathing is uneven.

Why? Her wrists are tied; her ankles are tied. There's nowhere else for one of my scarves to go.

O-o-oh.

"Sure, OK," I say and get one more scarf and gag her with it, making sure her nostrils are clear. The next few slaps are more even, on target, and the right pressure. Nancy bucks, struggles, does not quite scream; and yet when I play with her I find her sopping. What was a river is now an ocean, with a single island lapped by foaming waves. My fingers glisten when I remove my hand. At the end, heat rises from her ass, and there are pink marks. She flinches when I remove the gag and turn her back over, but she doesn't fight. Unbelievably, she protests again, and I quickly use the belt to flick and snap. Once. On the inside of her thigh. A nest of brown hair muffles her voice. Then it is silenced and finally replaced by a moist, sucking sound and a churning that fills the stomach and resembles, but is not, food.

Tarantulas eat very, very slowly. I timed Dierdre once, and she took all of two hours to dine on a cricket no bigger than the end of my finger. With just two fangs and nothing else to open up her meal, she has to massage her food with her front legs, press and squeeze, to make sure she gets every last drop. If one area dries up, she turns the cricket around and starts all over again. I give her six or a dozen crickets at a time. Sometimes it's as long as a week before the sweet, pastoral chirping comes to a stop.

After what seems an eternity, I finally let Nancy have what she's been asking for. She's been pleading in tones of voice ranging from a wail to a desperate hushed whisper. The bed trembles. I watch her pull and jerk. Moisture runs back from her eyes into her hairline. The facial expression—what is it exactly?

She does her best to push her head backward, throwing her neck up and forward. Her breathing quiets, slows; at last there is nothing but quiet. Something is wrong with the quiet; something is missing. I realize what it is; I decide not to compromise.

I stroke her throat, working to make my voice as hard and cold as possible.

"You know," I say, "your lack of politeness is appalling."

Shocked, she twitches and looks fearfully up at me. It is so hard not to let my expression change. She lets her head sink back.

"I'm sorry." The throat works convulsively under my finger. "Thank you—for everything."

The next morning we are both silent as we move through my apartment. The scarves, just scarves once more, are buried in the pile of hand washables. I get an extra kiss and a scary but thorough bear hug with my coffee. I return the kiss, but it is hard to keep my mind on it. Where Nancy cannot see, I have a bright yellow memo note in my hand.

The thing about the hand laundry is, there's no room around my building for a real clothesline. So the laundry dries on a folding rack made out of plastic-covered wooden dowels.

I have never needed clothespins.

And yet, if I look down into my hand, I will see the yellow paper with my handwriting on it: "Clothespins. Kmart? Monday P.M."

I wait for Nancy to wander back into the kitchen before I slip over to the tarantula cage. Dierdre is cuddled up on her climbing stick, motionless, looking for all the world as if she were in a mid-morning doze.

"You can't fool me," I whisper harshly to her. "You will *never* fool me."

Sand

—For C.S.
Lana Pacheco

Today we went to the ocean and built a sandcastle. A marvel of grainy architecture, really. Three levels of intricate towers and barricades, with a moat all around it, filled with sea water and ferocious creatures we made up in our wicked little heads. I fell in love with you all over again when you used half a paper cup and two popsicle sticks to make a drawbridge that allowed my scallop-shell soldiers entry to the fortress.

At dusk we folded up our blanket and tried to shake the sand from ourselves. We headed back to the car, tired and happy and satisfied with our day spent playing hooky in the sun. I saw in your eyes how sleepy you were, and I hated not knowing how to drive. I would have driven you home, *nena,* while you lay back in your seat and drifted off to sleep. Instead you had to force yourself awake and watch the road as I read aloud from the *Weekly World News* about the Chicken Boy in Florida, Michael Jackson's clone, and the "Ten Strange and Haunting Things Elvis and Christ Had in Common." You laughed when I got to the page advertising a Beverly Hillbillies collector plate.

The one bad thing about a day at the beach is sand. It gets everywhere. We were both itching to get out of our clothes the moment we pulled into the driveway and jumped out of the car. I can't remember whose idea it was to just hose down in the driveway in our shorts and T-shirts, but it was a good one. We took turns spraying the cold water at one another, each of us shivering but glad to get the sand out from behind our ears and between our toes. It was you who thought to strip off our clothes in the garage where the washer and drier are and make a beeline through the side door that leads directly to the kitchen, through the house, and straight to the bathroom. I chased you through the house, running after you in the dark, almost slipping on the shiny linoleum. When I reached the bathroom you already had the water running. You looked at me over your shoulder and gave me a wicked grin.

"Turn on the radio," you said. "Music to bathe by, please." Lordy, you're so cute when you're like that.

I walked over and turned on the old transistor radio you keep on the toilet tank, a little plastic jobbie that runs on a nine-volt battery and is good for little else except singing along to in the shower. Tom Petty was singing about free-falling over some good girl, and we both made faces at that. Flip, flip, flip, and I found a station playing Spanish guitar. That was more like it! The sounds of Segovia, falling water, steam rising from the tub, and the smell of the ocean that hung in the air: Is this the recipe for some magic soup?

I watched as you added fragrant salts to the bath water and then stepped into the tub. I reached for the ratty robe that hung from a hook on the door, but your voice stopped me.

"Don't be silly, woman," you said. "Get in here and wash my hair."

Me not being a small woman and it not a large tub, you and I were a tight fit. You scooted forward, and I slipped in behind you, legs around you, the small of your back looking at my belly. You reached forward and handed me the Waterpik that dangled from the showerhead. I ran the warm, gentle water over your head, drenching your long and abundant hair, the color of chestnuts. The tub nearly full and your hair wet, you turned off the water and took the hose from me, letting it dangle back in its place.

"Shampoo!" you ordered.

"I was getting to that, brat." I answered, both of us smiling.

I poured the shampoo onto your hair and went to work with my fingers, massaging your scalp, working up a rich lather. I heard that tiny noise you make, that happy little groan I love so much that means "I love what you're doing, please don't stop." Just the incentive I needed. More than happy to comply, I washed your thick, long hair with zeal: fingers playing over your scalp and running the length of your soapy locks. You tilted your head back as if to say, "Here I am. I'm yours. Take what you want." I knew exactly what I wanted. I wanted to eat you for lunch. I wanted to crawl inside you and call your belly home. I wanted to take you to a place that only women in love can visit. I wanted a goddess to come down and make it so I could make a baby with you, so that we could share all the things other couples have with one another.

I washed your hair, *mi querida,* and the act of my fingers running through your long strands was like a promise of the caresses I planned to lavish on the rest of you. Once this luxurious shampoo was done, I reached over and turned the water back on, letting a gentle, warm stream wash the suds away from your hair and down your back. You kept your head tilted back, resting on my breastbone, even after the suds were gone and the water had stopped running. I bent to kiss your forehead, and I saw a smile take over your sweet, strong, wonderful face. I slid my arms under yours, reaching up to cradle your breasts in my hands, when I felt your back arch, pushing yourself out to meet my fingers, silently begging me to pay you the same attention here that I'd paid to your long mane. In case I've never told you, I'll tell you now, woman: I love your breasts. I love the way they perfectly fill my small palms. I love how they are soft and hard at the same time. I love that you are the only woman I have ever known who wants her breasts caressed and massaged and made love to as much as I love to do these things. I love...your breasts. And so today when you arched your back and sought out my fingers, I gladly obliged, taking your little mounds in my hands and massaging them, feeling your nipples grow under my palms, finally using my fingers to tease your delicious little knobs, making them harder than I'd ever felt them before. My mouth hungry to taste some part of you, I leaned down and bit into your shoulder. Did I hear the word "please" escape your lips then? I think yes, because then you pulled one of my hands away from its sweet job and pushed it between your legs, grinding yourself against my fingers.

"No," I whispered in your ear. "Not yet, not here. Let me take you to bed where we can do this right."

"Yes, yes, anywhere," you answered, and before I knew it you were out of the tub, not bothering to take a towel, and offering me a hand to pull me out of the bath.

Not wanting to rush things, I forced you to stay, drying you off slowly with a towel. First your neck, to keep you from catching a chill, then your back and bottom. Next I dried off your breasts, one at a time, loving the way you moaned when the terry cloth brushed over your nipples. Down, down...I passed the towel over your supple skin, making sure not a drop of water remained. You giggled and twitched when I got to the back of your knees, and I stopped to kiss you there.

Quickly I dried myself off and led you to the bedroom. Hand in hand we found the bed in the dark. Crawling under the covers we faced one another; so closely I felt your warm, heavy breath on my chin, your breasts and belly touching mine. I draped a leg over your own, drawing my hand down your back slowly, stopping when I reached your soft, full bottom. I held you there, kneading this place where you are so full and yielding, giving the pressure you always love. You offered me your mouth, ravenously brushing my lips, searching out my tongue, humming a low, guttural, hungry sound into my mouth. After a moment of this I pulled away from you, touching a finger to your lips to keep you from thinking we were anywhere near finished.

Raising myself up on my elbow, I moved you onto your back and looked down at you. I ran my fingers down the side of your face, tracing over lips that tried to pull me in. Bending to give you the hard kisses your throat and neck love so much, my hand worked its way down to your breasts, picking up where I'd left off in the bath. When I pinched a hard, rosy nipple between two fingers, I heard you gasp, hold your breath for a moment, and then let it out slowly. This was what I wanted from you, this sound, this wonderful sound of joy. Such a sound from you is almost enough to make me come. When you are this close to bliss, nothing in the world matters but pleasing you, *nena*.

In a flash I moved on top of you, straddling your hips. I laced my fingers through yours, raising your arms over your head and pushing them down. We were like two wrestlers: me pinning you down for all I was worth, hovering over you, dipping my head down to draw my tongue from your ear, to your neck, and finally down to your breasts, where I took turns lapping at one nipple, then the other. I felt your hips wiggle beneath mine, that warm, wet place begging for attention. I let loose my grip on your hands, knowing that nothing short of a surprise visit from your mother could tear you away from this place, this place where you belonged: with me, under me, so close to me our hearts beat in time with each other.

Keeping my weight on my arms so as not to hurt you, I dipped down and whispered in your ear.

"Say it." I said. "Tell me what you want, and beg me to do it."

"No," you pleaded. "Don't make me say it."

"But you want to, baby. You want to beg me, don't you? Say it."

When you refused a second time I sat up and pretended to stop in my tracks. You reached out for me, pulling me back down, making me smile as you held my face to your breast and whispered, "Please touch me...I want you inside me...please."

Moving off you I lay again on my side, kissing you hard while my hand moved down until it came to the downy patch of hair between your legs. So wet were you from this endless foreplay, the insides of your thighs were covered with a thin film of slippery juices. Unable to take another minute of this tease, you reached down and guided my fingers into your wetness, into your glorious cunt, which seemed to suck me up and pull me in and greet me hello. And at that moment, my darling woman, at the moment my two fingers slid into your warm depths and my thumb found and began massaging your hard, throbbing clitoris, you threw your head back and let out a deep gut-wrenching sound, bringing me more joy than I can describe. I slid my fingers in and out of you, reveling in the feel of your silky wetness, the raging pulse under my thumb, and finally the tight squeeze, the contractions around my fingers that coupled with the sobs that hung in the air signaled your climax.

Long before we became intimate you told me that when especially moved during lovemaking you cry. Today I slid my fingers from you, gently massaging your sweet clit as it went into hiding. When I moved in to kiss you, I tasted salty tears on your lips. I held you close as if you were my own sweet child and rocked you to sleep.

Of Human Bondage

Danya Ruttenberg

"So, do you want to be tied up?" Becky's voice was low and teasing as she untangled herself from me. I took a deep breath. Out loud I squeaked a quiet, mild "yes" and moved my hand to her shoulder to wind the tips of her glossy hair in my fingers. She still smelled rich of sandalwood and sweat, and I breathed it in with a curious kind of nostalgia. I wasn't yet over the general weirdness of being back in her bed.

She asked if I wanted to be blindfolded. I was, to be honest, more than a bit nervous about this whole business and avoided making that decision by stuttering that, uh, she was in charge, wasn't she?

Becky sure liked that one, the little power tripper. Seems she had briefly forgotten she was supposed to be the big, butchy top and was pleased I had so graciously restored her fascist role. Actually, I was fine with that; this whole business was her terrain, and if I didn't know what I was getting myself into, it seemed best to not take responsibility for it.

She reached over me, her tight, apple-shaped breast bobbing in my face (which I licked, since it was just begging for attention), and she somehow managed to open the bottom drawer of her desk without shifting her body away from my mouth. After shuffling papers for a minute or two, she pulled out the box.

I'd been hearing about the box for what seemed forever—at least since we had broken up. It had always struck me as unfair that she waited until I was no longer part of her sex life to start dropping serious cash at those sleazy shops on St. Mark's. But I suppose my remarkably pleasant visit to her town was enough to warrant her bringing out the sacred box. She wanted to show off. And I'll admit I wasn't too averse to letting her show off in this context. I wasn't sure whether I should feel particularly honored or just validated at last, but now I could be at least on par with "all the girls she'd loved before." Or since. Or something like that.

So she brought out a box covered with floral fabric that looked like it should contain craft supplies. She plopped it onto the floor by her side of the bed and whipped out a blindfold she must've stolen from one of those coast-to-coast United Airlines packs. I had been given one just that morning—it came with hand lotion, a pinkie-sized toothbrush, a shower cap, and a pair of those scary ashtray-gray terry cloth socks no one ever wears.

I left mine on the plane. I get spacey when I'm "life antsy," and for a while I'd been feeling that brand of dissatisfaction in which I come home every day expecting something. I'm not sure what it is, but I start to believe that the unnamed object that will prevent my life from becoming sitcom material will materialize on my doorstep, gift-wrapped and pretty. Once it finally shows up, I'll be happy and the cameras can get rolling. Since it seemed unlikely the stewardesses on my flight were part of the Contentment Distribution Team, I hadn't bothered taking the toothbrush pack with me.

Apparently, though, Becky had. With the blindfold in hand and a giggle on her face, she squirmed out of our flesh pretzel, grabbed both my wrists, and forced them behind my head. I was still stronger than she and could've gotten out of it if I had wanted, but I just gave her a defiant look and stayed put. She straddled my waist and scootched the blindfold over my eyes. Then it was dark. I tried to peek, but she saw (she was right in my face, after all) and tugged it farther down. After that I kept my eyes shut. I was getting into the whole thing and for the millionth time decided to let this be Becky's show, that for one night I should be open to trying everything her way. I wasn't ready in the Land Called Before; I dunno if it was intolerance, inhibition, or indifference that kept me content with visions of vanilla monogamy. Whatever the cause, by the time we broke up she was slamming hard up against my walls, and the harder she pushed the thicker they became. Now, I squelched the *if* that came after. The if-I-de-cide-that-I-like-it *if*. The if-her-world-can-work-for-me *if*. I shut it up.

Blindfolded, I was reduced to aural and tactile and could practically feel Becky's ego puff up like a blowfish as she took the helm of the evening. I heard a jangle, and then my wrists were forced into a very cold chain loop. She must've hooked it to her headboard, because suddenly I was held only by the metal, and it all felt a bit tight. I squirmed, trying to get more comfortable—it worked for a moment or two before the damn chain tightened again.

We hadn't said much since the coming of the box; a mellow wash of synthesizers and dulcimer rhythm flowed from her stereo, and it added a nice ambiance to the room. I suspected, though, that after this night ended, I would be sick of Iranian techno for a long time. Which is OK, I suppose—Iranian techno isn't a major part of my music collection. According to Becky, this was because I worshiped dead-white-male boredom. Now, my beliefs on love, sex, and commitment are one thing, but Tchaikovsky is another entirely. As much as I have always adored Becky's penchant for new vistas, a girl must have priorities. And I draw the line at my piano concertos.

So I was tied up with a not-very-comfy chain, and for a while I contemplated mentioning it. Then I decided that since I wasn't in agony at the moment, I could just wait and see if I needed to pipe up later. And while I was contemplating and squirming, Becky pulled out her notorious bunny fur-lined restraints. I had heard all about them during the animated phone chats about her dissertation, my office politics, her sagas with Juanita and Kim, and my irritation with Alex. These long-distance buddy sessions had been dubbed the "Why-don't-more-people-understand-the-pure-drama-of-it-all?" series. They were expensive, usually on my bill, and never without some mention of the box and the bunny fur.

At some point in our relationship I had taken to calling her the Tactile Woman, and as I lay there, hands over head, metal biting into wrists, she rubbed bunny fur all over my body.

"Mmm. Fur," she purred, and I have to admit I was beginning to see the logic of the epidermophile. (I had no idea if this was a real word and made a mental note to ask Becky later. I was sure that if there was an epidermophile community out there, she knew about it and probably hung out with them before the pride parade or something.) The sensation was soft and light and quite a turn-on. Mmm. Fur. Of course, earlier in the evening I had been served miso soy curd casserole and wheat-free, dairy-free carob cake at Becky's friend's potluck dinner, so there was really no question that the restraints were actually made out of fake fur, which was just fine by me. (Though I had gotten over protesting animal rights injustices at the mall by the time I was 16 or so, it was still nice to know I was involved in socially conscious sadomasochism.)

Becky buckled the restraints around my ankles and tied them to the footboard. I was now naked, spread-eagle, and blindfolded in my ex-girlfriend's room. It's a good way to feel completely, terrifyingly vulnerable. (Two words: *exposed orifices.*) But the fur had felt nice, the Iranian techno was sexy, and Becky was softly brushing feathers up and down my torso.

"You are to address me as mistress at all times," she commanded and summoned as much theater and grandeur as possible into her voice—for Becky, this is a substantial amount. "Other than that, you are not to speak. Do you understand?"

"Um, yes." I squeaked. "Uh, yes, mistress." I had been fantasizing about this moment since damn near puberty and was surprised to realize how hokey I felt uttering the phrase in seriousness. Though deciding it was better saved for party banter, I managed with some effort to force my mental door to remain ajar. I was still waiting to see the light—the error of my narrow ways—and figured I shouldn't give up on baptism just because the water was kinda cold.

She spoke again, and this time she sounded more real. Her voice was tender, and it cracked a little.

"Your safe word is *angel.* If anything gets too intense for you, just say the safe word and I'll stop."

Huh. Safe word. I had never really thought about it, but it did make sense. I realized that while I'd been dying to try this stuff for a long time, there probably wasn't anyone in real life whom I trusted more than Becky to do it. At the same time, I wondered what in God's name she was planning to do that required a trap door for escape. My boundaries were being stretched open like a too-small T-shirt, and I suspected I was never going to deal with sex the same way again. It's a funny feeling, seeing the precise moment of crossing into a new level of personal growth. Even with some awareness that change is about to occur, there is no real sense of how, and not a thing can be done except attentively watch as the moment passes.

I'm one of those people who always tries to make her friends pull over to the shoulder of the expressway right next to the INDIANA WELCOMES YOU sign, so I can stand with one foot in the Land of Lincoln and the other in the Hoosier State. I really like the idea of being in two places at once, sitting on a line that's supposed to be crossed at 55 miles per hour. There's a view behind, there's a view ahead, and there's still time to turn around if a state full of corn doesn't seem all it's cracked up to be. But it doesn't usually matter, since my friends are apt to tell me they have no desire to hang out on the side of the highway, thank you very much, and would I please just put on the Prince album already?

So I lay in Becky's bed, naked, spread-eagle, tied up, and felt the sign whiz by at 55 miles per hour as punctuated by a slap on my inner thigh with a leather whip. It stung, as did the subsequent slaps on my stomach and hips. The experience was still erotic, but I was surprised that a whipping wasn't doing much for me. It was too obvious to be arousing, like women with big blonde hair and blue eye shadow. It seemed there should be a large blinking neon sign looming above that read: THIS IS SEXY. THIS IS WHAT DEVIANTS LIKE.

It did get better, though. For the next however long (when one is tied up and blindfolded, one tends to lose track of time), Becky rubbed and dragged various objects—silk, beads, what could have been rubber, and so forth—up and down my body in silence or with an occasional comment. When she laid a fatter metal chain across my nipples, she asked softly, "It's cold, isn't it?" "Yes mistress," I responded. So annoying. Her silence and the Iranian techno turned me on more. My mind had some time to wander, which was both good and bad. My wrists began to throb from the chain around them. I thought about saying "angel" so she could fix it, but again decided to be a trooper and do this whole thing right. I began to obsess about the job interview I had the next day (*oh, fuck!*), and I prayed I'd be functional enough to charm the pants off those people. I also hoped like hell that the cuffs of my jacket would cover the bruises I could feel forming just north of my hands.

When Becky got going with the silk, I thought about how great this was and how I was gonna relocate out here, and we could finally be partners and do this every night and we had only broken up because of the distance and our relationship had been so beautiful when it was good and it was uncanny how compatible we were and she truly understands me and she shows me so many things yet she needs me so badly and my God we needed to be together and we were falling in love again and…*Ow! Holy shit! Ow!* That didn't just hurt, that really fucking hurt! She dripped hot wax onto my already tender nipples. And it stung like hell. She was also splattering the stuff on my stomach and rib cage and then back to the nipples again. I thought about saying "angel" but again decided I should be a good Stoic and suck it up. *Ow.*

And I did not want to give Becky the satisfaction of thinking I was a wuss or not as liberated as she. During much of our relationship it seemed she was trying to prove something to me—or her asshole father or somebody—about how sexually and spiritually evolved she was. I did not want to be the one to cry uncle. I had been long aware that my stubbornness was partly about showing her that if I rejected her polyamorous, oh-so-fringe way of life, it was not because I couldn't hack it, but because I could but didn't want to. Hah. So there.

Ow. Well, I suppose I was tied up spread-eagle and blind-folded because I wanted to try new things, learn new things. And I did, in fact, learn something new at this moment: Searing pain is not sexy.

But then she was rubbing me up and down with vanilla-scented oil ("This might help get that wax off"), and I managed to get past the wall I had put up around my throbbing breasts enough to enjoy it. Despite the fact that my future children may now be forced to bottle-feed, I was still receiving a fair degree of pretty damn good-feeling attention. And it had been a while. After being caressed by all of Becky's found objects, she straddled me and began to grind herself into my stomach.

"How do you feel about my getting off on you? Do you like that? Do you wish you could be part of it?" she asked in her best drama queen, soap star, trying-to-be-tantalizing voice.

"Yes, mistress." I had at one time been crazy-dazzled in love with this woman, and despite this circus I was still aroused by her smell, her shape, the sheer fact of our being together again. I had always adored her body, more than any other lover I'd had. I couldn't keep my hands off her. When we went out I had to have my arm at least around her waist; I was empty if there wasn't a bit of Becky on me. And at this moment all of the lust and stuff that had been accumulating over time was about to overflow like a dam in monsoon season. Shit, in spite of the histrionics, I wanted her full to burst.

And she gave me what I wanted. She stuck her crotch in my face. It was like returning to a favorite hometown coffee shop: familiar in every way. Irrespective of time's passing, some guy named Sean will always be there, on break from his mini-mum-wage bakery job with a bottomless cup of the house roast and a copy of *On the Road.* The tables stay the same, the banana bread remains perfect, and the bathroom graffiti is al-ways about marijuana. Even with the new people on staff, there's a twisted comfort in the place's predictability. I got to revisit the Café Express of Becky's cunt, and I enjoyed it thor-oughly. And so did she.

Then it was my turn, but she told me I had to ask for what I wanted.

"I want you to fuck me." I said. Then I really lost track of time.

At some point I had figured out that by grabbing the wrist chain instead of just lying there, the circulation in some major veins would no longer be cut off. I held on to the chain for dear life—to do otherwise at this stage in the game would have forced Becky to give my family a whopper of an explana-tion as to how I died. The poor folks are open-minded, but even they would have had trouble receiving condolence calls about this one.

When I was done (by that time I was pretty darn done), she untied my left foot, which I immediately used to, um, get her goat one more time, just for old time's sake. Then Becky got around to liberating my other ankle and, thankfully, prayer-fully, my tattered wrists. *Jesus. My sleeves better be long,* I thought. We smooched for a couple of minutes, and I asked if this had been a run-of-the-mill, ho-hum, standard S/M expe-rience for her.

"Well, you're definitely one of the more active people I've slept with," she said, somewhat quizzically, like there was something about my playing the bottom role without being comatose that she didn't get. It complicated her schema, maybe. Seems to me that the breaking down of conventional boundaries doesn't mean much if it just creates new laws about how to behave in bed. I'm all for fun and kinky, but what that has to do with fitting into some precut catego- ry...oh, whatever. I suppose I can't expect much more from a woman who dumped me by announcing I didn't fit into her life paradigm.

She was at the lab when I returned from my interview the next day. I was giddy with the self-confidence that for better or worse comes with external validation. Dancing around her room as I hung up my jacket, I mused about taking the job. *Maybe. Hee hee. How bad do you want me? What are you gonna give me for it?* I hummed to myself. Should I see if my current boss wants to throw in a company car to keep me? Are there any other opportunities into which my talented ass should be looking?

As I took off my earrings and stepped out of my heels I found a notebook bookmarked with a pen on Becky's desk. I'd like to say I'm above such things, but I'm a little sister so there's always been a bit of a snoop in me. Especially given the night we had just had, I couldn't resist. She had written a poem:

a heart, a rose, a diamond
the moon is full tonight.
i want you to fuck me, she said,
her face full of shame and melody.

dawn of the hope, she carries my Phoenix, softly.
her lips call to me,
whispering
a heart, a rose, a diamond
a heart, a rose, a diamond.

Oh, the drama. This was not my first exposure to Becky's Bad Poetry; I will even admit to carrying a bunch of them around in my Filofax in times past. Part of me did feel a thrill that I could still "inspire" her (her word), so I couldn't help but find it sweet, at least in a narcissistic way. And it oozed, it damn near bled, of the intensity and innocence I had never quite gotten out of my system. The fact that I had not once that evening felt remotely "full of shame and melody" was beside the point for me. I wasn't looking for her to define my reality. It's a post-postmodern world, and she can do with it whatever she wants.

I shut the book. Becky was due any minute; she'd probably sweep in, fuming and frustrated with the way her advisor is screwing up the research, the way the data center can't get its act together and send her the right numbers, the way Kim is misinterpreting their conversation yet again, goddamnit, why doesn't she listen for once? After some patient nodding on my part, she'll calm down a bit, maybe ask how my, uh, thing went today. Or maybe I'll just tell her because she'll forget to ask. Although I haven't yet decided, the offer is certainly worth reporting. And then we'll doubtless get back to discussing the data center. Fantastic people do not always great listeners make; I've known this for a while.

I'll loan her some cash so we can eat before my flight home, and she'll promise to pay me back right away because she swears she finally got that mess at the bank straightened out this time. Good thing for Becky they don't check your credit history when they hand out Ph.D.s. I'll try to muster up as much sincerity as possible to show my regret about missing the Twine-Wrapped Rainbow Goddess Drumming Circle. I think it's Find Your Inner Athena night.

But whatever. No drumming today. Instead, my wax-blistered breasts and I will go to our departure gate, and we'll watch people wait. I'll wait, and I'll weigh, and I'll take my time deciding what I want. And while my starry-eyed ex struggles to string together words Hallmark rejected years ago, I'll be air-high and untied across the blue.

Deo Gratias

Connie Fox

"Thank God," she said, her hand wet with her secretions, loving her black lycra legs above all—the thin ankles and anaconda muscles, the highest possible S/M heels, ankle straps, up on the bed as she lay back—and it finally happened after a whole day of angst, hoping it would, could happen again this way, easy, flowing, mindless, totally self-immersed, wanting, even if only for a few minutes to feel totally "profane," whorish, sluttish, transported into pure, excretory fleshiness away from all her usual megathinking about aging, death, god, godlessness, souls, no souls. No ultimates, just an immense secretory *now.*

It was a different kind of sacred than she had experienced before. Like the Siva temple in India she had walked into once, where she saw a 50-foot gilded penis being greased with sacred butter (*ghee*) by devotees of Siva as Fertility God. Or all the statues of the Great Mother Goddess on her back with her legs spread to the sky. They *knew*, the ancients did, what it was all about: rutting, ecstasy, losing your mind in the great, all-powerful image, not merely to procreate (a by-product) but to transcend time and deify everything you are as an expression of the universal urge toward pure, mindless ecstasy (*samahadi*), the Peace that Passeth Understanding.

Down on her knees to the God of Orgasm: *Deo Gratias, Deo Gratias, Deo Gratias, Qadosh, Qadosh, Qadosh, Thanks to God, Thanks to God, Thanks to God, Holy, Holy, Holy.*

Sixty-five, 66, eternity.

Ever since Teri had died six months earlier, she had gone sexless, couldn't get interested in anyone else, and now finally she had gone back into an autoeroticism that she felt liberated her to go on a hunt again. From Self to...?

She got up from the bed and looked at herself in the huge mirror that covered one wall, her eyes so artfully pantherish. OK, 65, almost 66, nice legs, that's what made her so attractive to herself. Plus the experience of the Lover; the fact that she knew all the tricks there were to know; that she was an ecstatic survivor, defying time; that she was going to Death like everyone and everything else but remained defiantly, profanely erotic.

All her money, her house in the suburbs, her books, her collection of exotic heels, drawers of corsets, body stockings, bras, lace panty hose—ever since Teri's death they became ghosts, corroded. She thought only of her dead friends, surrounded by their ghosts. Guilda Bernard and her ponytail: cancer. Fat and sassy Jackie Eubanks: AIDS-related complications. Soft, smooth, blonde Linda...All her grandmothers, grandfathers, ancestors going back to Noah and beyond...she'd started feeling them full-time since Teri had gone.

Only now it was OK. She, herself, was the Great Fetishistic Mother.

She swallowed a couple of kava kavas, sprayed a little kava spray under her tongue, and went just a little back toward ecstasy again.

Deo Gratias
God the jaguar,
God the Opium Poppy,
God Datura,
God Endorphin,
Impossible God who Never begins and Never Ends,
Logical Impossibility God, God who Nevertheless
is and *reigns,* allow me to be with my breasts and
allow me to BE, be flesh, myself, beatific me, be a potato or
a tulip tree, be old, old, old, but give me just a few more years
with my nipples and tiger eyes, with HER whom I will find
and love almost as much as myself
Amen   Qadosh
Amen   Qadosh
Amen   Qadosh

Deo Gratias
Amen.

Marisol

Carla Díaz

I almost always date straight girls. I don't necessarily plan it that way, but I'm totally drawn to real girly girls. You know, the ones with the long hair who always wear makeup, get their nails done every week, and sport the little hoochie outfits that just make a sister go "Damn!" Yeah, they're high maintenance and almost always drama queens, but you put one of those girls in front of me, and it's like putting a rock in front of a base head—I just can't say no.

It doesn't help much that I seem like forbidden candy to them too. You can take the most homophobic honey in the world, turn her on to me, and I'll turn her out within a week. I really don't understand it myself. I mean, I know I'm muy suave and all, but I know plenty of chula jotas who rarely land a straight girl. You have to remember, when it comes to Latinas you're not just up against cultural ideologies, you're up against Catholicism, and we all know Dios doesn't fuck around! But for some reason that all seems to go out the window when I come by.

I think it's because I'm not superbutch, so I don't scare them off, but I'm boyish enough that they're attracted to me. I'm real active physically; my friends call me "Super Sport" because I play so many different sports, so I'm pretty cut, which the nenas seem to like. And I dress real ghetto fabulous—pure Kani, Fubu, Pelle Pelle, baggy jeans, and the newest kicks or Timberlands—but my hair's long enough that people know I'm not a nene. The chicas go crazy for that badass look, and when you mix it with nena sweetness it's all over.

Plus I always keep it real. Even though I talk a mean game, I'm always sincere. If I'm hanging out with a heina, it's because I really want to get to know her, not just because I want to sleep with her. I think nenas are so used to getting screwed over by tiburones that my attitude really turns them on. It's like they feel safe with me, and once the attraction to me as a person starts rolling, the rest just falls into place.

But a lot of my friends clown me for dating straight girls, especially my friend Ana. She's always going on and on, "Oye, Cristina, think about it. You're 28 years old, and you've never even come close to long-term commitment. Don't you think that might have something to do with your only dating straight girls? I mean, come on. They're never going to take you home to mami and papi. Not only that, think of all the diseases you're exposing yourself to. I hope you've been tested for HIV, chica."

She's right about the disease thing. Not that patas are totally clean either, but you really up the risk when you date girls that have been with guys. I'm careful, though, and I get tested every six months or so. As far as the commitment, she's totally off-base on that one. I'm nowhere near ready to settle down, but every straight girl I've been with has wanted a serious commitment and a long-term relationship. I'm always the one who ends it, and I've even been stalked by a couple locas who refused to let me go. One day I'd like to settle down and raise a family, but right now, with the magazine, I don't have the time to be serious with anyone.

I'm managing editor of this new general interest English-language magazine for Latinos based in San Diego called *Latino Lifestyle*. Since it's a new magazine and we're working with a shoestring budget, I do everything editorial. I mean, I am literally the editorial department. I even do some photography when we're desperate, and I'm also doing a lot of the production now, since our graphic designer quit. I tell you, sometimes I'm surprised I even find the time to date.

One of the biggest perks of the job, though, is all the mami chulas I meet. I mean, we're doing articles on actresses, models, musicians, professional athletes, writers—all kinds of famous people. And I'm the one who puts it all together, so I'm the one they deal with the most, even if I'm not doing the article myself.

That's how I ended up meeting Marisol Maldonado. It had been a while since my last fling, and I was flipping through the channels one night and saw a preview for her newest movie, so I decided it was time to try to make my dream come true. See, I've had this fat crush on Marisol ever since her first film in '88. I was a senior in high school, and when I saw her in *Hip Hop Headache*, I swore somehow, some way, I was gonna get with her. Nine years later, I decided it was time to put a plan into action.

Getting the interview and photo shoot was easy. Famous people are easy to get because their agents are always looking for more publicity for them. The days leading up to the interview were the hard part. Usually I'm not nervous before an interview, but because it was Marisol, I was stressing for days before it even happened.

Anyway, the night before the interview, I knew I wasn't going to be able to sleep at all, so I went clubbing in Tijuana and didn't get home until 5 in the morning. I had to leave at 8, so I took a long shower and tried to chill a little until it was time to go. I was meeting her at Marcos's (one of our photographers) studio up in Los Angeles since we were doing the interview and the photo shoot all in the same day. Luckily I missed L.A. rush hour so it only took me two and a half hours to get to the studio.

I was all distracted when I walked in because some crazy guy had been hassling me on the street, but as soon as I saw Marisol, I forgot all about that drama. Even though I had seen all her movies and had a copy of every one of her magazine clips from the past nine years, as beautiful as she was on paper and film, seeing her in person took her beauty to another level.

She was built like a delicately balanced hybrid of perfection, mixing physical traits from both her African and Taino ancestry. Her skin was a smooth chocolate color with a sprinkle of canella, and she had these beautiful lips, all thick and juicy like a ripe mango, which were accentuated with bright red lipstick. Her hair was deliciously kinky, her corkscrew curls so full and tight they didn't hang from her head, they sprung out like little Slinkies.

Marisol was average height for a Latina, about 5 foot 5, and was wearing a pair of old, ripped Levi's and a little silk, sleeveless half shirt. Her body was like a reflection of her lips—thick and full. She had these really wide, gorgeous hips that curved out from her thighs and tapered into her waist, which bordered a stomach so flat and tight you'd think she was a spokesmodel for *Abs of Steel* or something. She also had the tightest, roundest, most delicious booty that curved out at least six inches from the rest of her body, and her breasts were large enough to stand out (literally and figuratively) without being so big they were disproportionate.

As I looked up at her, all I could do was smile. She flashed me a sexy sonrisa back, and I introduced myself.

"Hi, Marisol. I'm Cristina, managing editor of *Latino Lifestyle*."

"Hey girl, what's up? Marcos tells me you're a Boricua too, straight up?"

"Yeah, de Rincón."

"Get out! My family's from Mayagüez. Girl, we're practically neighbors."

Damn! Not only was this girl hella fine, but she also had that Nuyorican accent going, which always drives me crazy. We didn't stop talking for like half an hour. We were just talking and talking about everything, but mostly about California and how much we both hated it because there was nothing caribeño. We talked about how there's no salsa on the radio or panaderias that sell mallorcas or brazo gitano and how nobody can understand our Puerto Rican Spanish and all the Mexicanos seem really confused by the whole concept of Latinegras.

Finally Marcos had to come over and drag her back to the shoot. They did their thing for about another hour, and then Marisol and I went up the street to a little coffee shop to do the interview. Luckily I always prepare my interview questions beforehand—this girl had me so distracted I couldn't concentrate. She kept smiling that smile that turned my insides all soft and warm like avena. She was acting all coy and flirty like nenas do.

Right before she left, she gave me her number and said we should get together. I didn't know what to make of that one because she'd spent the whole morning talking about guys and her ex-boyfriend, whom she'd been with for five years. Even though we totally hit it off, and I picked up the faintest hint of a potential vibe, for the most part she was registering relentlessly straight on my gaydar. With any other nena I wouldn't have had a single doubt in my mind. I would have called her that night and been in bed with her by the end of the week. But I guess because Marisol was so fly and so famous, all these doubts and insecurities I'd never experienced before came creeping up on me.

A few days later I called her, and she invited me to come to L.A. that weekend to hang out, so I drove up and after that we started hanging out as much as our busy schedules and distance allowed. At first my attraction to her was purely sexual. She was so fucking fine I had to work to keep the tremble out of my voice when I was near her. Her fame really excited me too. Not like it would rub off on me and I would be famous too, but because everyone in the world wanted to be a part of her life—and she wanted to hang with me.

After I actually started hanging out with Marisol, however, it was her personality I really came to appreciate. She was so vibrant and enthusiastic, grabbing every moment as if it would disappear if she didn't snatch it and taking it in with this intense passion before blowing it out for everyone around her to share. Even her dark moments and her private moments were lived with a deep intensity. She'd withdraw into herself, embracing pain and sorrow, and you might not hear from her for days, sometimes weeks.

I lost track of time whenever I was with Marisol. Hours would pass, and I wouldn't even think to question when and where I was until she was gone. Just hanging out with her was like this intense, all-consuming sex where she'd just eat you up and spit you out when she was done. After spending time with Marisol I'd lie in my bed all mongo in the head, replaying every moment and wondering when I would see her again. Man, sometimes it took me days to recover from a weekend with her.

Plus, for someone so famous she was really down-to-earth. Most Hollywood stars are really into themselves and their own lives, but Marisol was always doing projects that made our people look good, you know. She did a lot of gang-banging ghetto movies but only ones with positive messages, written and directed by people of color. She never did any of those Hollywood ghetto-exploitation movies, like *Dangerous Minds*, where the whitey comes in and saves all the coloreds. She also did a lot of charity work back in Puerto Rico as well as in East L.A. and New York, where she was from.

Although nothing had happened between us, I was content to just be near her—to catch a glimpse of her bra strap; breathe in her sweet vanilla scent; listen to the sharp, loud voice that personified the ghetto mami she was; feel the occasional brush of her silk skirt against my leg; and imagine how those beautiful mamilicious labios would taste if they ever met mine. She was always talking about this papi chulo and that papi chulo, but I just wanted to give her a taste of how strong and dulce this mami could be.

Cruising around Hollywood in her red sports car, blasting salsa and merengue, I'd forget all my drama and just be absorbed into her plush velvet custom interior and the rhythmic beats of the congas. Being with her took me home to the island and my past; her presence triggered all my ancestral memories and erased the pain inflicted by my people's transgressors. It was Marisol who taught me how to forgive as well as how to love myself for me, not my accomplishments.

One Saturday I was just chilling at home when she called.

"Hey mami, whatchu doin'?"

"Nothing girl, just chilling. How 'bout you?"

"Mira, girl, you wanna go to the Mayan tonight? It's salsa night."

Marisol never had to ask twice. She could have invited me to a lecture on nuclear physics, and I would have gone just to be with her.

"Sure, nena. I'll swoop you up around 10, all right?"

"OK, mami, I'll see you at 10."

I don't know why, but I was even more excited than usual about going up to see Marisol. I didn't leave San Diego until 8, but I was so juiced I made it up to L.A. in like two hours. As soon as I got to Marisol's, I could feel the vibes just flying back and forth. She was wearing this micromini, skintight, red silk dress that made all her curves stand out like a Latino on Rodeo Drive. There was usually a mutual, always unspoken spark underlying our days together, but it never went beyond a current I always questioned whenever my mind prodded me to bust a move. I knew if anything ever happened, Marisol would be the one bustin' it, not me. There was way too much at stake, and I think not knowing if we were ever actually gonna knock boots was half the thrill for both of us.

As soon as we got to the club, we went straight to the bar. I knew I was going to need a few beers to get through a night of being with Marisol, especially while she was wearing that dress. As for Marisol, she just liked to get her drink on. After I'd downed a few Coronas and Marisol had finished her double rum and Coke, she grabbed my hand and dragged my ass over to the corner stairwell and upstairs to the hip-hop room.

The beats were flowing right through me, and I started freaking her, and she was all over it. She was bumpin' her booty all up and down, and I was all up on her like white on rice. As I rubbed up on her, I could feel the outline of her chonies through the nylon of my dress, and after about 30 seconds I was starting to get seriously aroused. I could tell by the look on her face that she was too.

For a minute we both lost ourselves, and I know everyone around us picked up on it because there wasn't an inch of space between us, and all the guys were staring at us while the heinas checked us out from the corners of their eyes. We were moving like one, me all up on her booty and she just pushing into me. I swear I almost blew right there on the floor. Then I think she kinda came to and pulled away from me—slowly enough so nobody else noticed but fast enough that I knew something was up. We stayed in the hip-hop room for a few more minutes and then went downstairs to dance some salsa.

I love to salsa, but I'm used to dancing with other nenas and leading. I am the shit when it comes to leading, but pair me up with an hombre and make me follow, and I am worse than a white girl trying to merengue. I was getting really frustrated trying to follow these guys, but most of them were really nice about my trying to take over the lead. After about an hour of struggling while Marisol flew around the dance floor with all the finest papi chulos, who were literally all waiting just to dance with her (and after a few more drinks), she grabbed my hand again and pulled me onto the dance floor. She let me lead, and we were on fire! When she pulled me to the dance floor, it was like *Boom*, and I was off! My heart was pounding with adrenaline and skipping with lust as I spun and dipped Marisol across the floor.

For a minute the guys just stood there and watched in amazement. I don't think they knew two women could dance salsa better than a man and a woman. But just when we'd really found our rhythm, these two guys danced between us and split us up. The guy I was dancing with was nice, but man I was pissed! I don't think I had ever been so on when dancing salsa, and it was nice to have Marisol in my arms for a minute. Anyway, I really thought something was gonna happen that night, and we split not too long after our brief dance together. Of course, before we left Marisol had to exchange numbers with some actor from the movie *187*, but it was all good 'cause I was the one going home with her.

It was almost 3 in the morning (which is late in California), and we were standing on the curb all dressed up and drunk off our asses, and Marisol says, "Lets go to the Train Station," an after-hours club in West Hollywood. I was hella beat, and I wanted to get back to her apartment and see what was gonna happen, but, of course, I played it off.

"Sure, girl, I'm always down for some after-hours clubbin'."

"Ooh mami, wait! Mira, Roberto's is right across the street, and they're open. Let's get some tacos al pastor and chill for a bit."

"Cool. My feet are killing me—you know I'm not used to wearing these dress shoes."

We sat in Roberto's for a while, drinking horchata and eating tacos al pastor, then headed back to her place. It was a given that I was staying over because San Diego is like 150 miles from L.A., and I was still pretty drunk. Even though I wasn't sure if anything was gonna happen, I figured I'd be sleeping with her in the bedroom since she didn't have a futon or a sofa bed, just a purple velvet couch that reminded me of

Prince. Pues, I went into the bathroom to get ready for bed, and damn if she hadn't laid a cobija and a pillow on the couch for me while I was in there! If I hadn't been so drunk and tired, I would have been pissed. Luckily the alcohol knocked me out, and I crashed until almost noon.

I woke up because Marisol's kitten, Misu, was licking my toes. I didn't trip, though, because I have two cats of my own, and they do the same thing. I got up to brush my teeth and wash my face, and when I came back from the bathroom Marisol was sitting on the couch. We sat there talking for a few hours, acting like nothing at all had happened. I felt a little uncomfortable and kind of wanted to jet home so I didn't have to deal with the awkwardness, but Marisol seemed to want me to stay. I'd half expected her to kick my ass out as soon as she got up, but she sat down on the couch and started showing me her photo album.

Now here was the funny part: She started showing me pictures and telling me all these stories about her pata friends and all their drama and this one guy she had done a movie with who was an ex-banger—tats and all—but a hardcore joto too. Then she told me how sometimes she goes to the clubs with him and how she had gone to the gay pride parade in Long Beach that summer. The whole time I'm sitting there trying to figure out if she's trying to tell me something in coded message or if she's trying to give me an opportunity to come out to her or if she's really just saying whatever is coming to her mind. That was the problem: You never could tell these things with Marisol. Anyway, I ended up just keeping my mouth shut and not saying anything either way. Even though we never discussed my sexuality, I assumed Marisol knew I was a pata, and she never asked me about guys or anything specific about my ex, who I would ambiguously refer to occasionally.

After a while we'd gone through all her pictures, so we got dressed and went to breakfast. Actually, Marisol got dressed, and I put on my same old clothes from the day before. She took me to a little Cuban café in her neighborhood, and we got cafecitos and pastelillos and took them to the beach. We chilled there for like three hours, which passed like nothing, and before we knew it the sun was setting. It was like no matter how much she wanted me to stay or I didn't want to go, without the pretense of sex there was no plausible reason for me to stay when I had an interview to do down in San Diego the next morning, and she had a big screen test for some new movie with Esai Morales. Plus she had a date that night with one of her million and one papi chulos. So we called it a weekend, and I went home, more than a little frustrated— emotionally and sexually.

A few days later she called and invited me to see John Leguizamo perform at the Comedy Club that weekend; turns out Leguizamo's a friend of hers so he put her on the VIP list. It was the last time we would see each other for a while because she had gotten the part in the movie and was leaving for Hawaii that Monday to start shooting. I drove up to L.A. that Saturday afternoon, and after an early dinner we went to the show, which was all that *and* a bag of Chifles! Leguizamo always blows up when he performs. Afterward we went right back to Marisol's apartment, which was unusual because she always likes to go from one event to another, and John had invited us to an afterparty at his hotel. But I wasn't complaining because I was always down to spend time alone with Marisol.

We ended up back on her couch listening to reggaespañol, and all of a sudden, out of nowhere she says, "*Mami,* why don't you stay up here with me tonight." My heart nearly popped out of my mouth when she said that because I knew exactly what she meant. This was our last chance to finally get our freak on—for a while anyway. She'd probably be in Hawaii for at least two months. Even though I was nervous as hell, I kept my cool and flashed her a fat smile.

"Not if you make me sleep on the couch again."

She looked back at me, trying to hide the panic that flashed through her eyes. I figured maybe she was having second thoughts, but I had started something, and I was going all the way with this one.

"Girl, I have never slept on anybody's couch before. What was up with that?"

I knew what was up with that, her fear of what desire might lead her to do if we slept in the same bed. I watched the final decision rest easily on her face, which softened with a calmness I had never seen before.

Her thick, beautiful labios de guayaba opened slightly with her smile, and she reached out to stroke my hair as she said, "Of course, you can sleep with me, mami." I leaned toward her, and a soft, gentle island breeze blew through my heart as we kissed for the first time. She stood up, grabbed my hand, and led me into her bedroom. I did not stop kissing her the entire time I undressed her, from her face and throat as I unbuttoned her shirt, to her chest and stomach as I unhooked her black satin bra, and all the way down her hips, thighs, and calves as I undid her skirt and slipped off her black silk panties. All the while I was undressing her, she had been undressing me, and we fell into her bed in a tangle of tension built up over the course of our friendship.

I fluttered my tongue across her tetas until her moaning was unbearable, and then I traced it down between her breasts and to her belly button. In between kisses I muttered praises that drew her into a wilder frenzy than I had imagined possible. As I ran my tongue over her deep, dark swell I tasted a sweetness so delicious it was unlike anything my mouth had ever encountered. "Ay, mami," she muttered as she thrust herself toward my teasing mouth. I forcefully pinned her hips, remembering she had told me she sometimes likes it rough, and I thrust my tongue far into the depths of her flooding cavern. I circled my tongue inside her, slowly at first, then faster and faster until her body shook and shuddered like an earthquake beneath me, and her screams became so loud I thought I was going to come too. She let out a final "Ay, mami" that was so loud I was afraid the neighbors might call the cops, and then the earthquake within her lapsed into intermittent aftershock tremors as I held her loosely in my arms and she drifted off to sleep.

My Familiar Aphrodite

Sonia Abel

1923.

*I'm tangled in dark beads plucked from the uncertain night, which
again tries to wrap itself against my shrouded desires. I can't say
where these desires come from. A place so foreign to all I've known that
knowledge of their very existence would make my mother turn against
everything she thought sacred and true, which, of course, includes me.
This night is all I've got. Darkness takes away everything—desirous
and not. Coming into this place of letting go while still carrying the
import inside me, I see places I may travel to. I see glimpses of me un-
defined by anything else around me, glimpses of all that was before
transformed by all that will come.*

She came to me in a whisper. I could have dismissed her
subtle voice as the whirl of the ceiling fan or the sigh of one
of the girls, as I had no doubt done in the past. Tonight I was
open to her, my muse, my familiar Aphrodite.

I found myself walking toward Nadia through the opium
haze, ready to take the fan from her hands to cool the soaked
curls trailing down the nape of her neck. As I approached I inhaled a stream of the warm ripe gardenia she had tucked behind her ear. The cream silk chemise clinging to her body was
unresponsive to the current of air. Her eyes were closed as my

hand covered hers to gently remove the fan. We had all been very busy that night, as sex seemed the only diversion worthy of movement in this suffocating New Orleans heat.

Hundreds of men (and at least a third as many who could not yet qualify as men) passed through the place simply known as Madame Satchie's on Rue de Fleur and also—it must be said—through each woman fixed upon the red velvet cushions, sofas, and chairs lining the Grand Room. As Jake's sweaty piano fingers pinged out the last rhythms of something between blues and jazz, there was an unspoken consensus that the usual house soiree would not go on tonight. Though opium and champagne continued to flow as freely as the beads of sweat on our foreheads, no one felt like slinking to the music in this heat.

Nadia's gasp was quickly lost in the smoke as I touched her hand, and she rose from her exhaustion-induced trance. Her lips, swollen from the humidity, could barely form the words, "Frances, that feels divine." She sipped champagne as if to cool them. I gently fanned her skin, glistening and darkly flushed like fresh soil uncovered by the wind, skin so dark it barely allowed a blush to overcome it, but I noticed.

Nadia and I had become increasingly flirtatious since she had arrived three months prior with two other women from the West Indies. She would watch Frederique and Gina dance and share a cigarette with wide eyes and parted lips. Fred, always with strong hands running through sleek black hair, would beg Gina with her smoky eyes.

Many women in the brothel take a female lover at some point during their stay. These are women stripped bare from men, removing layer upon layer from the inside out: layers of skin and softness, trust and assurance. To release a veil of magic, Madame Satchie designates a goddess familiar and a "performance name" for each girl to "simultaneously entice and protect," as she puts it. Though we all feel the cloak of the goddesses around us, abuse and mistreatment from aggressive, unloving men still occur. Often they are the men the women choose to date after business hours.

The lips, hands, and soul of a woman act as a balm against the inflamed skin and hearts of women. Fred and Gina are beyond the simple familiar comforts of same-sex affection; They're inseparable; they're in love. Madame Satchie smacks them on the bottom with her fan if they get out of line in front of clients, but even she is envious of their love.

Nadia unbuttoned the first few buttons of her chemise to allow the current of air from the fan to further penetrate her glistening skin. We both knew the dark moon tonight would carry us far beyond the gates of mere flirting. "Look, Frances, by the candelabra on the piano," she gestured with her cigarette. "I think your Aphrodite is dancing with my Artemis." Nadia looked up at me with her almond brown eyes, penetrating eyes that swept sighs from my sentences. The kohl encircling each eye had melted from the heat and made her look like a Lafitte cemetery vampiress.

"Let's join them," I demanded as I brought her to her feet before she could protest.

We circled the gauzy figures with skirted spins, swirling the sandalwood incense and opium smoke up from the floor. I found myself trying to restrain the urges I felt welling up for Nadia's laughing lips on mine. Nadia suddenly turned her head as if someone tapped her on the shoulder to share the dance. She turned back to me with a half-cocked smile and slowly sinking eyelids.

"I think the Huntress of the Night wants to run through wet grass in the untamed night air," she said.

"Nothing in New Orleans is tamed," I bantered, "but we can't disappoint your goddess, can we?"

We entwined our fingers like threads on a rope and fled the smoky bordello without uttering so much as a hint to the girls of our destination; Aphrodite likes secrets. Mischievous Artemis threw her laugh into the air and grabbed a bottle of champagne from the bucket, leaving a suspicious trail of melting ice as it slid from the bottle. We ran through the ripe magnolia air with the intensity of children growing into their legs, not stopping until we felt duly saturated with the percolating dew from the grass.

Under monstrous live oaks dripping with Spanish moss, we fell into each other and smoothed the wet grass into the earth. We rolled between mausoleums and statues, laughing headlong and steady to keep up with the goddesses. Nadia's desire for me pressed into her dress, flesh drawn out into the cool night air.

"Oh, Frances, I hope the sun never rises," she whispered, tracing my lips with her finger.

"Spoken like a true vampiress!" I hissed jokingly at the wind and softly bit her neck until I heard the welcoming moan of deep-rooted desires.

I cooled my tongue with mouthfuls of icy champagne and allowed the wind to do the same as I moistened the skin on her neck and made my way down to her chest. She entwined her legs around mine, separated my curly hair with her fingers, and grabbed hold to force my head to stay as I reached her nipple. As I drew circles around each areola with my tongue, she pulled my head closer to her breast, inviting me to linger and suckle harder. She stirred the rising steam in the air with her satisfied breath and guttural moans.

She drew my chemise higher and higher with her legs, and I felt the cool night air against my wetness. I unbuttoned the rest of her gown and spread her open like a white-linen picnic ready to be devoured. My gown rose with the wind, inviting our flesh to press together as the goddesses experienced themselves through our sensual earthly abandon. We breathed into each other, feeling lips against lips just as soft, just as ripe and warm and open. Playfully biting and sucking each swollen part, we rested into a slow chase of tongues and lips.

The swelling pant and pulse of Afro-Caribbean drums rose in the distance, echoing the rhythm of our hearts. Dark priestesses with crimson cloaks covering their hair raised magic into the night with their arms and voodoo voices, pulling us into their spell as I poured myself into Nadia.

Nadia's hair fell loose and entwined with mine. We were one: the goddess of darkness, passion, and wild beasts uniting with the goddess of love, purity, and sweetness. I became her Artemis and took my lover with the passion and fortitude of slaying a sacrificial beast: appreciative, respectful, and adept. My fingers rested at the edge, allowing the invitation of her wetness to well up and over her inflamed pudendum. She lay open the love and purity of her heart as an offering as we exchanged familiars in complete union.

I felt her wetness upon my leg as she glided down my body, kissing my breast and nipple and belly with the gentle ease of a woman plucking petals with her lips. She lingered teasingly just above my wetness, breathing moist night air onto my skin, pulling my hips into the darkness like milk from a breast. I felt her breath in my curls as she edged toward me,

inhaling my sweet earthy scent. I opened my mouth to en-
courage her to do the same. Anticipation sat like a weighted
babe in my gut. I trilled a moan like a mourning dove cooing
for her lover, inviting her inside. We lingered for hours, discovering our nature with hands uncovering the true flesh
buried below our taken flesh.

Her moist mouth was made even wetter by my readiness.
She drew me into her with deep suckling breaths, parting my
flesh with her tongue, gently stroking the swelling pulse that
had hardened from her touch. Tender to my needs, she
soothed my swollen pain with her deft and alluring tongue. I
felt blood surge to the tip to cleanse and purify me, the rushes starting deep like a trickling wellspring in the bowels of
the earth, pushing up to the surface—like a bird in a cave
finding the opening just in time, releasing itself into the
world with fluttering waves. I was finally free to scream into
the night air, to hold love close, and draw her inside with
every pull of the womb.

A rain fell into our earth bodies, our hair, our mouths. Our
souls were everywhere, floating above the graves and beds of
our sisters, drawing them out to join us.

We became the dark moon, the night air breathing into
every woman, making love to every woman, every goddess in
every woman. Nadia said what is already known: "I don't ever
want to go back. I want to float here with you, suspended
above the earth, above time."

"You will lover," I encouraged her. "We will. I'll never
leave you."

We stayed that way, feasting on the ambrosia of each other
with the goddesses and women of the night, until the sun
rose, and we could no longer see ourselves.

Desire no longer clings to me like an inescapable sacred wrath. I plunged into her depths headlong, swam through every urge of needing her, feeling her here and there, hungering for what was, what could be. This is where I have found pure peace, allowing myself to purge the depths of desire, to feel all angles, all sides. I have touched myself in places of stored truths tucked behind realities I never meant to share, that I didn't even know were there.

Blood Hunger

Ginger Simon

In the past we savored our girlfriends' bodily fluids.

We delighted in each other's menstrual blood in the years before the plague.

Menstrual blood.

So fragrant. So rich. So enticing.

I dipped my fingers in Renee and then finger painted a mustache on her that I licked off. She did the same to me. We dipped our fingers in our wetness and put red spots on our necks and chests, which we sucked and bit as vampires would. Of course, we circled our own nipples and each other's with blood and licked and sucked hungrily and lustfully.

When Marie spread her or my flow on me, I was in heaven. She'd turn me over and put splotches on my ass, which she'd pinch and bite. She was the only woman who could make me purr and beg. I had the loudest orgasms with her.

Victoria's scent and flow was the heaviest and the most intoxicating bouquet. Better than any champagne and certainly the best-looking vessel to dip a tongue in. No crystal flute could compare to it.

* * *

Each time I get my menses, I celebrate. Alone now, as I play with my blood, I remember.

*　*　*

My high school gym days used to drive me wild. I'd be sitting at my designated spot, hoping for a girl with a strong menstrual odor to walk by. Those were days of sanitary napkins—before the use of tampons—so the odor was sharper when collected outside the body.

Hot, humid days were the best. Mixed with odors the gym always contained—that of dirty socks and sweaty clothes—were the individual aromas I tried to identify. Soaps, colognes, and powders unsuccessfully masked pee, shit, and body odors. As different girls wafted by, I'd sniff appreciatively, sometimes looking directly at a crotch, sometimes looking up to see a face.

I felt disturbed and uncomfortable. The thrilling sensations and the wetness made me turn away, afraid to keep looking. Afraid my secret sniffing and interest would be revealed. Afraid they would think me queer (which they did anyway). Afraid I would become the queer I knew I was already.

Part of my fascination with this was discovering the combination of exercise, my period, my fantasies, and pleasure—intense pleasure. One night I was performing an exercise called the rocking horse on the floor of my bedroom. I was lying down on my stomach and trying to grasp my ankles with my hands and then rock on my stomach. I couldn't get it right. My hand slipped while I was squirming on my belly, only it wasn't my belly. I was writhing and felt such delicious sensations in my pelvic area—my "privates," as I called it. All yummy wetness, a melting. My bones felt rubbery. And while I felt this, for some reason I began to think of my friend Doreen. I pictured her beautiful face and exquisite skin; she looked like Sophia Loren. I imagined biting her smooth, olive-skinned neck. Then I realized I was indeed getting something right. I was bucking like a pony, if not following the rocking-horse directions right. I had gotten my period, and it was dripping.

Only later did I learn what a powerful orgasm I had experienced and how I had stumbled across a wonderful way to prevent or relieve menstrual cramps or discomfort.

So it's no wonder that some strong connection exists for me with menstruation and pleasure—and women, always women. Perhaps I secretly yearn to be a personal-hygiene analyst working for the pubic sector. In fantasy and in role-playing, this too excites me.

*   *   *

"Open the door," I demand.

"What?" Elizabeth whispers, even though we are the only two in the rest room. "Why? What's the matter?"

I was in the next stall while she was complaining about her heavy flow, so heavy that today she has to wear a pad to ensure her tampon doesn't leak through her panties.

"Let me in." What a fantasy come true! "Please," I cajole.

She is standing on the left side of the toilet, facing me silently.

I look at her long, curly auburn hair and once again wonder if her pubic hair matches that lovely shade. Today I will find out.

Elizabeth looks afraid, almost transfixed in that space, like a pinned butterfly. Her mouth is slightly open. This is just how I want her to be. This is just how I want her to look at me, as she has many times in my fantasies.

I look at the wad of paper on top of the metal toilet tissue dispenser.

"What is that?" I point with my right index finger.

She looks at my finger and glances to the object. But she turns back and stares at the red plastic handcuffs I hold in my left hand.

"My tampon. I just changed." She is still whispering.

I want to compare her facial lips with her labia. Color. Texture. Taste. Taste her lower lips with the tip of my tongue. Savor. Tease. Probe. Then plunge. But not these days.

I caress one side of her face with the cuffs. With my other hand, my index finger still extended, I touch her cheek. I make circles marveling at its softness.

Her mouth opens a little wider. Her breathing is getting heavier. I lightly touch the vein pulsating in her neck. I put the handcuffs on the hook on the back of the door. Not with her. Not this time at least.

I close the stall door. Latch it shut. Just in case. Only just now. We can always say I'm helping her with her bra—a hook broke—if anyone comes in. An old excuse for a lesbian tryst at work. The hets won't wonder, and the dykes will smile.

"What are you wearing under your skirt?"

"Panties. Just panties. And stockings."

"Not panty hose?" Please, not that.

"No. Thi...thigh-highs. I feel too bloated for panty hose today." *Thank you, goddesses.*

"Take off your panties...and hand them to me."

She blushes so prettily and lowers her head, turning it away from me as I sniff the sanitary pad stuck to her mint-colored undies. About a centimeter of bright red blood is on them. I'm careful not to let my nose or lips touch them. Very scant blood odor. Mine is stronger and saltier. More raw, chicken-like. Stronger is the gardenia scent, probably from powder. A faint smell of shit, not unpleasant at all, mixes with it.

I ball this up and toss it on the floor. Gently.

"Open that." I point to the wrapped-up, used tampon.

She turns and stares when she hears a squeaky sound. She watches me put on the latex glove I took out of my tote bag. I never leave home without them or condoms or K-Y, which we won't need.

"Give me the tampon."

I touch the side that's completely filled with menstrual blood and some long strands of tissue. My gloved finger rubs a round clot. Better than a pomegranate to my taste buds. But I'm no longer allowed to savor this with my tongue.

* * *

You still with me, sisters? Disgusted? Turned on? Which? Both? Hey, everyone has her own range of erotica. Different experiences. Different ages. Whatever. Different turn-ons. For instance, I don't get hot on fisting fantasies or in reality. Anyway...

* * *

I drop this on the floor too.

Elizabeth is smiling. Barely. It also looks like she's trying hard not to cry.

224

"Hold your skirt up to your waist and spread your legs. Wide."

She complies.

My two fingers circle around the end of her tampon. I am careful not to tug on the string or to dislodge it.

As I stroke her wet, erect clit, I remember back to Katherine, who when I ordered her to get undressed in front of me, stood with a tampon string hanging from her. I softly rebuked her for not obeying me completely and told her she'd be spanked later for her noncompliance.

As I continue to stroke Elizabeth's clit and rub and squeeze it between latexed fingers, hearing her moan, seeing her rapturously tilt her head to the side as she does in my masturbation fantasies, I continue to imagine my tongue replacing her tampon. A few tears appear on Elizabeth's cheeks after she climaxes. I kiss them. Maybe some day she'll talk about them to me. Maybe I'll talk of my tears of missing a time that was. Maybe not. I don't think we'll share that other, deeper kind of intimacy.

It's ironic that now blood-red lipstick and nail polish are "in." The years before the plague, they were politically incorrect. Glorifying in our blood was politically correct: "I am woman—eat my dripping, bloody pussy." So we did; we tasted ourselves and each other. Then, menstruation was safe and sanctified. Taboo was lipstick and nail polish in public. Now latex reigns, and the red dripping down our body is shunned. Ah! The days before dental dams!

After Elizabeth left the rest room, I cleaned up the discarded items. Then I sat down and finished myself off, smelling my heavier, almost time-of-the-month secretions.

* * *

At times like this I like to stay home in bed under the covers, hot and sweaty. I like to not wash. I love to breathe in my crotch aroma. I cup my pubic mound, delighting in its wide, heavy, fleshy size, and sniff my hands, my unique *eau de menses* mystique.

Then when my short, light flow is over, I bask in a scented bubble bath, lie naked between fresh sheets sprayed with cologne, and pamper my after-menstruation body.

This month I'll add the pleasure of reading Anne Rice's vampire story "Pandora." Pandora feasts on blood, and I'll feast on her pleasure and on my memories and fantasies as well.

* * *

I am sitting on the F train now, looking at women. I pay special attention to possible dykes, and I focus on women getting on and off the queer ghetto stops of 7th Avenue in Park Slope and 23rd Street in Chelsea.

I wonder which ones are menstruating and want to smell and eat them. In regard to the lovely, older ones—and the older women do seem lovelier and more interesting—I wonder if they still get their period and what their thoughts and feelings are about all this. What did or do their sexual encounters consist of during these times? I so hope they don't think it dirty or disgusting or wrong or taboo.

I'm starting to fantasize about devouring a short-haired woman who just left on 34th Street. Is she or isn't she? Does she or doesn't she? My blood hunger is still with me.

I'm still eager for that now-forbidden pleasure.

I begin to feel that familiar cramping at my center. I smile in anticipation.

The Closet

Robin St. John and Sandra Hayes

I walk up to the porch and lift the squeaky top on the mail-box. There is nothing. The cat sidles up from a bush near the porch, leaves caught in the long hair of her bushy tail, and slithers around my legs as I fumble with my keys. I get the se-curity screen unlocked and have just put my key into the dead bolt on the front door when it is pulled open. I jump back, startled; she is not usually home first, and I didn't see her car. But there she is, smiling at me, rubbing her short dark hair—which is obviously damp—with a white cotton towel. She smells deliciously of soap and coolness.

"Hey," I say. "What are you doing home?"

She grins. "Oh, just decided to come home early and sur-prise you."

I laugh. "Surprise me, huh? Well, I'm surprised."

"Good," she says, an odd smile on her face.

I'm happy to see her, but mildly suspicious—it isn't like her to come home early to surprise me, and I wonder what's up.

"Here," she says. "Let me take your stuff." She relieves me of my briefcase and the paper bag of empty lunch containers. She sets the briefcase down in its usual spot by my desk in the dining room and heads into the kitchen, where I can hear her removing the containers, filling them with water to soak.

"There's a cold drink for you in the bedroom," she calls out. "Why don't you relax for a few minutes? I'll be right in."

I go into the bedroom, eager to shed my office clothing. I take off everything but my undershirt and panties, hanging things up as I go. A glass of iced tea is sitting on my bedside table, and I stretch out on the cool comforter and reach for it. She has gone all out; there is even a sprig of mint gracing the drink. I smile and shake my head, still wondering.

She comes in, running her fingers through her tousled hair, and sits beside me on the bed.

"So, what's all this about?" I say, reaching for her hand.

"Oh, I just feel like we haven't been spending enough quality time together lately. I wanted to do something nice for you...for us, I guess." She smiles and reaches to stroke my cheek with her free hand. I am surprised—and touched. We have both been way too busy with our jobs lately; some days it seems we scarcely have time to kiss good-bye, much less talk, much less touch.

"Thank you," I say. "I've missed you too." I lean over, and our lips meet, connecting in a long, leisurely kiss, tongues exploring. I feel her hands travel over my skin, along my arms, brushing my breasts. The old fire between us begins again.

"I love you, Shannon," she whispers.

"Yeah?" I say.

"Yeah," she says, her lips eager against mine.

"Show me," I whisper.

"I will," she murmurs, her hands on my face.

"Let me take a quick shower. Not fair you being all fresh and clean."

"OK," she answers. "But hurry."

The water feels good against my skin. I wash quickly, shampoo my hair, and slide open the shower door. She is standing there, holding a towel spread, waiting for me to step into it. She dries me off, slowly, meticulously, as if she is working a puzzle and every drop of water on my body is a piece that must be searched out and put in its place. She is gentle and thorough, working the soft towel carefully into every fold, every crevice—her touch light almost teasing in places, firmer in others. By the time she is done, I am warm, dry, relaxed. The steam in the room has begun to dissipate, and the mirrors have started to clear.

She stands, hangs the towel over the wooden bar beside the shower, and smiles at me.

"You ready?"

"Ready for what?" I say.

She does not answer but opens a cabinet beneath the sink and pulls out a covered basket. She opens it; it is filled with bright pieces of cloth. She looks through them slowly, holding up one, now another, as if considering.

"Hmm," she says. "Yellow, I think." She holds a piece of bright yellow silk against my face, as if evaluating its effect. "Yes," she says. "This will do nicely. Turn around."

I do, and I feel her bring her arms around me. Then she places the yellow silk, which she has folded into a thin strip, over my eyes; she pulls the ends behind my head and ties them.

"What are you going to do?" I ask her, suddenly nervous.

"Oh, you'll be fine, baby. Just trust me."

And I do. She takes my hand, and we walk out of the bathroom into the much cooler, drier air of the bedroom. I expect her to take me to the bed, but she doesn't.

230

"Stay there," she says and is suddenly gone, leaving me standing there, blindfolded, unsure even of where I am in the room.

She is gone so long that I get tired of standing there naked and vulnerable, and just as I am about ready to start feeling my way around the room for the bed or something to sit down on, I hear her come back in.

I feel her move behind me, feel the heat of her body close to my back, close but not touching. She reaches around me, and I feel her fingers on both my nipples, barely touching, and at the same instant her tongue runs down the back edge of my left ear. The current surges through me again, and I feel her breath hot against the side of my face.

"I thought we might do the closet this time," she says, and her words, laced with anticipation, electrify me. She tightens her fingers on my now hardened nipples, squeezing, pulling, and I move my ass back, trying to feel her behind me. She moves out of my reach, laughing a little.

"Hey, you," she says. "Not so fast. Don't be in such a hurry. We're going to make this last a nice, long time. No rush at all." I feel her move away from me, hear the rattle of keys, hear the lock on the closet door open with a solid metallic clink. I am shivering a little now, whether from chill or from the uncertainty of what is about to happen I am not sure.

I feel her at my elbow, guiding me ahead of her. I walk slowly, and through the yellow blindfold I sense we have entered a darker space: There is a heavy, musky, slightly sweet smell, and a feeling of being closed in, shut off. I hear the door click shut.

I know—because I have been here before—that we are in the walk-in closet, approximately ten-feet square. The only light is from a small lamp affixed to one wall; as my senses adjust I begin to see its dim glow filtering around the edges of my blindfold.

I feel her move in front of me.

"OK," she says. "Back up." She puts her hands on my shoulders and pushes me backward. I move my feet slowly, not knowing what to expect. I know she has spent many evenings working in here; I have heard power tools running, smelled sawdust, but she would not allow me to see what it was she was preparing.

I feel a hardness at the back of my thighs, as if I have backed into a table. I start to reach behind me, but she grasps my wrists.

"No," she says. "No hands. Just back up and sit down." I do, and now I can feel that the table, or whatever it is, has a padded top, covered with fabric that is rough and knobby. I lie back, and she is behind me then, pulling me down into a reclining position, so that I am lying on the surface, my legs hanging in front. I feel the air on either side of me, and I realize that the platform where she has placed me is quite narrow.

"Just lie still," she says, her voice barely above a whisper. I lie there, listening to her move around the small room, feeling the roughness of the cloth against my back. The sensation is not unpleasant. I hear the sound of a bottle sucking air and then her hands rubbing together, and the air fills with a new scent of mint and flowers and something else I cannot identify. She takes one of my hands and begins to massage it, covering it with warm oil; she pays meticulous attention to each finger, each joint, rubbing and working the skin between the fingers for a long time. She places my hand on my belly and moves around to the other side, where she gives the other hand equal attention.

"All right, now," she says, finally. "Are you OK?"

I am more than OK. My body feels suffused with energy, warm, relaxed, and so alive I am almost certain I must glow. I make a small murmur of assent.

"I can't hear you," she says.

I murmur again.

"I said, I can't hear you," she says again. "Maybe this will help you speak up."

I feel her fingers suddenly grip my left nipple, and she squeezes hard, the side of her thumbnail cutting into my flesh—not painfully, but enough to startle me out of my cozy complacence.

"Ah!" I cry out, my back arching involuntarily as another jolt moves through me. "Yes! I'm OK."

"Good," she says, her voice softer now.

She releases me, then takes my right arm, pulls it downward, and I feel now that the structure I am lying on has solid sides, like a box. She tightens around my wrist what I can only guess is a leather cuff so that my arm is held in position against the smooth surface that feels like highly polished wood. She moves around and secures my left arm in the same manner so that even if I wanted to get up I could not.

"Comfortable?" she asks. Always she is considerate.

"Yes," I say, making sure this time to speak up clearly.

"Good." I imagine I see her smiling.

She is in front of me now, and I feel her hands on my knees, pushing them apart, then moving down my calves. She straps my ankles in place at the bottom of the table, perhaps to the floor—I cannot tell, but I feel the leather against my skin, feel her adjust its snugness to her satisfaction. Experimenting, I try to move my arms, my feet—I am immobilized, unable to see, unable to move. It hits me then that I am completely vulnerable to her, open, exposed, helpless. Only my deep trust keeps the awareness from shifting over the edge into fear. And yet we have never gone this far before, have never taken things to such an elaborate level, and I wonder....

I feel her fingertip trace a delicate line around my lips, hear her sigh. She continues the trail, just barely touching my skin, down my chin, down my neck, straight down the center of my belly, then continuing along my thigh, along the sensitive inner surface, all the way to my foot, then back up again slowly—like a walking trip through mountains—all the way up to my lips. This time she puts a finger into my mouth, allows me to suck it briefly, then makes the same trail down the opposite side of my body and back up along my hip. She lays her palms flat on my belly, allowing me to feel their warmth. Then her hands move up, her palms brushing delicately over my nipples. Already I am fully aroused, longing for her touch. She cups my breast in her hands, then draws her fingers upward, finally taking the nipples, squeezing, rolling. I stir, unable to move far, but my body makes its own responses to her touch, and my cunt has started to ache with fullness. I want to beg her to touch me there, but I don't; I just concentrate on the sensations running up and down my skin, along every nerve center as she touches, manipulates, strokes, caresses. I feel her breath against the skin of my belly, feel it move upward like a small hot wind, and finally I gasp as she takes my breast in her mouth and sucks it in. Her tongue massages the nipple. She bites gently, then harder, then harder until it hurts, and I cry out. She backs off immediately, nuzzling and licking the wounded spot, and finally she moves to the other one. With her hand she traces a downward path over my belly until her fingers are almost on me, until I can almost feel the heat of her palm against me. She does not touch but brushes lightly over the hair, barely moving it, and I strain my hips upward, wanting her to touch me, but she moves her hand away.

"Not yet, baby," she says. "There is plenty of time."

I groan.

She stands up, and I feel her between my knees. She takes both hands, pushes my knees apart as far as they will go, and I feel her looking at me, feel myself open. I am wet and swollen. She dips one finger into me as if she were dipping a pen into an inkwell and draws on my belly with the wetness, so that I can feel coolness where the air strikes my skin.

My breathing is fast now, and again I want to beg her to stop teasing, to please touch me. She puts her finger into me again, as if exploring, then withdraws it. I hear sounds I cannot identify, then I feel something else, something hard and cool, moving against me. I am desperate now to be touched, to be filled, to be taken, and my body arches frantically as she touches, teases, pulls away.

"Mmm," she says. "I think you want it, darling."

"Oh, yes," I gasp. "Please…"

"Well," she says. "OK. Just a little."

I feel the hardness, the coolness, feel it slowly, so slowly move into me, feel myself open to take it, feel it fill the empty space in me, and she moves it in deeper and out again with agonizing slowness, and then suddenly, unbelievably, it is gone, she is gone, leaving me gasping and frantic. I listen, and I cannot hear anything, cannot hear her moving, cannot hear her breathing, can only hear my own ragged breath, my own heart pounding.

I whisper. "Where are you? Where did you go?"

I feel cold metal against my face, hear scissors snipping, and the blindfold falls away from my eyes. She is wearing a leather harness, and I now see the dildo she was teasing me with: large, erect, glistening with my juices. She turns my head to the side so that I am looking right at it and nuzzles my lips with it.

"Take it," she says, her voice quiet and strangely calm. "I want you to know how you taste."

I lick the wetness from it, then open my mouth to take in more of it.

"That's good," she says. "That's very good." I can see her face now, and I can see she is excited too, her own breath coming quicker, her skin flushed, her cheeks bright with color, her eyes boring into mine. I imagine her cunt behind the end of the dildo, its pressure against her swollen clit.

She moves away and leans over to kiss me, her tongue finding mine, reassuring me.

"I'm sorry, love," she says, smiling. "Just a little bit longer…"

I sigh, wondering what else she can possibly do to put me off, to prolong this sweet agony. My arms ache slightly from being held in position, and my right hip is threatening to cramp. I tense and untense it to unkink the muscles.

She unsnaps the dildo from the harness and moves over to the a small cot-like bed that sits perpendicular to the table where I am strapped. With my head turned I can see it, can watch her as she lies down on the bed. She reclines against a stack of pillows and lays the unstrapped implement between her legs.

"Look at me," she says. "Watch me."

I watch. She begins to touch herself. I watch as her large nipples stiffen under the touch of her own fingers, watch her hips move in response to her own manipulations. Her lips part slightly, and the look in her eyes tells me she is aroused. She moves her hands to her cunt, spreads her legs, opens the lips with her fingers, and I can see even in the dim light how wet she is. She dips her fingers into the wetness, then brings them to her mouth, sucking her own juice from them slowly one at a time.

I did not think I could be any more aroused than I already was, but watching her I feel my body is going to burst the restraints, lift off the table, and float away. I look at her eyes, her swollen breasts, her engorged cunt. I sigh. She picks up the dildo and opening her legs wide inserts it. I watch while she takes her pleasure with it, slowly at first, then faster, deeper, moving her hips, one hand massaging her nipple. Every cell in my body screams, my breath matching hers. She stops suddenly, holding her breath, and I know she is about to come. She closes her eyes as if waiting for long seconds, barely breathing, and I wait to see what she will do.

She withdraws the cock from herself and smiles at me.

"Shannon," she says.

"Yeah?"

She doesn't answer me but gets to her feet. I watch while she straps the dildo back into the harness. She walks over, reaches down, unstraps my feet from the leather, and I stretch my legs out, releasing the strained and cramped muscles. My arms are still immobilized.

She moves in close between my legs.

"Shannon?"

"Yes?"

"Do you want it?"

"Oh, God," I say. "Yes, I want it." I open my legs, making more room for her, and she guides the end of the dildo into me, and oh, God, finally it is there, she is there, filling me, fucking me, thrusting deep and hard, and she is working my clit with her thumb, and we move together until finally I can hold back no longer, and I let the wave overtake me, give myself up to it, and she follows me, our cries filling the small quiet room.

Finally we are spent, are still, and she pulls out of me, unstraps the harness, and unfastens my bound wrists and takes me in her arms. We go out of the still, stifling space into the cool evening light of the bedroom and collapse together on top of the comforter.

"Hey," I say.

She holds me. "Shhh…"

Plastic Pleasures

Nilaja Montgomery-Akalu

I always know when my period's on her way. I get horny.
Granted, I'm always horny, but I'm talking *horny*. I masturbate four or five times a day. I have to masturbate 'cause I can't
keep a woman around long enough—or rather they don't keep
me around long enough. I always meet those U-Haul women.
You know the kind. They're the ones who wanna pick out
Hers and Hers towels 15 minutes after meeting you. No
ma'am, Modelle Charleston (that's me) ain't the one. I don't
plan on being anyone's wife, partner, significant other, companion, or whatever the hell you want to call it anytime soon.
Now where was I? Oh, yeah, my period. When Cherrie (that's
my vibrator) starts getting that extra workout, I know "my
special friend" is coming for her week-long visit.

Take last week for instance. Ol' Cherrie had gone through
a pack of AA batteries in two and a half days. I have a bad case
of procrastination. Can't get rid of it. I knew the batteries
were low, but no, I just had to get in one more orgasm. Just
as I was reaching my peak Cherrie reached hers, leaving me in
mid come. There ain't nothing worse than being brought to
the point of no return only to be yanked back down.

So I got dressed in a plain denim skirt and white blouse. I
didn't bother with a bra or panties. It was the middle of spring

and too damn hot to be all cramped up. I left my apartment in the Mission District and walked the few blocks up to the Castro. A new novelty shop had opened a couple of weeks ago, and I had been meaning to check it out. This would be one of my rare excursions to the Castro. It was mainly a bunch of white gay guys. There was nothing much there for a 40-something black lesbian like myself, but I wanted to see the store and get my batteries.

On my way I stopped by Dolores Park to watch a game of tennis. The players were two young women, probably no older than 23. One was an African-American, the other Latina. I watched for a few minutes as they hit the ball back and forth over the net. The women's young, perky breasts bounced up and down as they jumped around the court. I squeezed my thighs together when the black woman, who had her back to me, bent down to pick up the tennis ball. Her skirt was short enough to reveal lacy white undies. Baby, as the saying goes, had much back. Her friend caught me gawking and pointed in my direction. They giggled like little school girls sharing a juicy secret. I waved and went on my way.

Even though it was the middle of the week and the middle of the afternoon, the Castro was crawling with people. This was another reason I hardly ever went to the queer headquarters of the world. Wall-to-wall people. I fanned myself with my hand. With the sun beating down, people practically skin to skin, and my premenstrual hormones raging, I was sure I was going to have a sunstroke.

"Hot enough for you honey?" a rather granola-looking white woman asked as I walked past. She was leaning in the doorway of one of the many bars that litter the district. I looked her up and down. Her classic lesbian hairdo—military-style crewcut—

did not flatter her square face. White women are not for me. I love my women like my coffee: black and sweet. I smiled politely and kept on until I found my destination.

The inside of Plastic Pleasures, the novelty shop, was a vast contrast to the outside. It was pleasantly cool and deserted except for the young black woman behind the counter. She smiled at me, revealing pearly whites. She was a cutie pie with a dimple in her left cheek.

"Can I help you?" she asked.

"No, thanks. I'm fine," I said, going over to the battery selection.

"I'm here if you need anything," she smiled again. I swore I saw her wink at me.

Was she flirting with me? I was old enough to be her mother...her young-looking mother, mind you. I might be hitting mid 40s, but I ain't one of them old, wrinkly-looking women. I shrugged the thought off. My hormones were starting to make me hallucinate. I did catch her looking at me when I glanced over my shoulder. I got three packs of batteries, the eight-pack kind just to be on the safe side.

"Find everything OK?" the cashier asked when I brought my items to the counter.

"Yes."

"Three packs of AA batteries; your vibrator musta cut out on you, huh?"

"Excuse me?" I felt myself blushing.

"Why else would anybody buy batteries in a place like this?" she grinned.

I gave Ms. Know-It-All a $20 bill. "Can I just have my stuff?"

She handed me my batteries in a brown paper bag. "Here you go."

"Thank you."

"You know," she said, handing me my change, her hand touching mine, "those batteries you got won't last long."

"Is that so, young lady?" I was right—she was flirting. "What kind do you suggest I use?" Why not play along?

"We have some of those extra-long-lasting kind." she said. "They're in the back. Come on, I'll get them for you."

"What about the store?" I followed her into the back.

"Please, you're the first person to come in all week." She opened the door that said EMPLOYEES ONLY.

"Here we are."

"I'm not an employee."

"You want your batteries, don't you?" she asked, sauntering by me. She smelled peachy. I felt that familiar throbbing between my legs as I watched her from behind. Her round ass fit snugly inside the short-short cutoffs she wore. From the rows of lockers, I guessed it was a changing room. It reminded me of the locker room of my high school years. It was the same dull gray and had that bench that went from one end of the locker room to the other.

"You have a name, young lady?" I asked, sitting down on the bench. She was working on the combination to one of the lockers.

"Do you want me to have a name?" she asked getting the locker open.

"It would be nice to know who's trying to seduce me," I said as she sat next to me on the bench.

"Serena—and you're not wearin' a bra," she said. "I noticed when you walked in. Or should I say bounced in."

A hot flash washed over me. Maybe it was menopause and not my period that was coming.

"I'd like to see them if you don't mind," Serena said as she began to unbutton my blouse.

If there's one thing about the youth of today, they say what's on their minds.

"Let me help you with that," I said unbuttoning the last button. I tossed my blouse onto the floor.

"You got gorgeous breasts." Serena squeezed my large brown boobs. "They're so soft." She kissed my nipples.

"Oh, God," I sucked in my breath. Her warm mouth felt so good next to my skin. The throbbing between my thighs intensified. I just hoped I wouldn't leave a wet stain on my skirt.

Serena must have been reading my mind. "Lie down." I reclined on the bench, the wood cold against my back. Serena pushed my skirt up, leaving it bunched up around my waist. She licked her lips hungrily as she got a look at my goodies.

"Hold on." Serena climbed off the bench and went to the locker. From a black backpack she took two white latex gloves, a thin dental dam, condoms, and a lavender dildo already in its harness.

"Do you always carry a strap-on around?" I asked as she pulled the harness up over her shorts.

"Do you always leave the house not wearin' panties?"

I shook my head.

"I didn't think so."

Serena pulled her shirt over her head. Her breasts were small and perky, just like the tennis players' had been. Her skin was a dark creamy chocolate. I licked my lips. She slid on the gloves.

"Let's just say I'm borrowing this from the store," Serena said.

"Borrowing it?" That was a nicer way of saying "stealing." "You're gonna fuck me with a stolen purple dildo." I said.

There was cream between my thighs as I thought about the idea of getting fucked in the back room of a store by a woman I had known for only 15 minutes. It was turning me the fuck on. "I like it."

"I knew you would," Serena said, placing the dental dam over my wet cunt. I felt the warmth of her lips as she kissed my inner thighs. "I wish I could taste you," she said as her mouth moved closer to the patch of thick dark hair between my legs. "'Cause I bet you taste like heaven."

Her tongue was like a feather as she entered me. Light and soft. If I hadn't seen the dam myself, I would have sworn there was nothing between her lips and my lips. My nipples were like rocks as I rolled them between my fingers. Serena's tongue was working magic on me. In and out like a snake, her quick tongue fucked my wanting, oozing pussy. I could just imagine how my clit must have looked to her. I knew it was bursting from beneath its hood and had now taken on a deep scarlet color. Sometimes I would kneel in front of the mirror and fuck myself with my vibrator so I'd know what was happening between my thighs.

"Yes, that's it." I moaned when she started circling her tongue around my hard sex. "Fuck my cunt," I panted.

"I intend to," Serena said, bringing her head up from between my legs. "But not with my mouth," She tossed the used dam to the floor. Serena put a condom on her dildo. She rubbed its head against my slit. Her mouth found mine. She whispered in my ear. "I'm gonna fuck it good. Real good, baby."

With one quick thrust, Serena's "dick" was inside, filling me. I wrapped my legs around her waist. Serena's hands were mashing my breast, the nipples growing more erect by the second. I took one of her small tits, almost covering it with my entire mouth. I grazed the nipple gently with my teeth, sucking on the chocolate bud like a baby. I licked her, tasting the saltiness of her ebony skin.

"Oh, yeah," I moaned as she fucked my cunt, "give it to me."

"You like that, baby?" Serena asked, her hands left my breast and squeezed my ass. She raised my hips higher, allowing her purple cock to fuck me deeper. I was beyond wet; I was like a fucking swimming pool, and she was diving in.

"I think I coming," I said, my hips gyrating faster.

"Not yet baby. You're not gettin' off that easy," she said. I gasped when she pulled out with no warning. "Sit up," she ordered. I sat up, my face right in her crotch. Her dildo shined with my juice. "Lick it off."

I took the dildo in my mouth, sucking on it as if it were real (not that I know anything about sucking a real one). I licked my sweetness—I did taste good—from Serena's piece until it was wet only with my saliva.

"Good girl," Serena said stroking my head. "Now put a new rubber on me." I bent down and picked up a condom from the floor. I carefully opened the package and took it out. I dropped the used one to the floor. When she was dressed, Serena ordered me onto my hands and knees.

"Ever been fucked in the ass, baby?" She pinched my butt.

"No," I said, hoping she wouldn't hear the quiver in my voice. My knees felt wobbly under me as I steadied myself for what was to come.

"You poor, deprived woman." Her fingers were in my cunt circling my clit. "You're in for a real treat."

Serena placed her hands on my back as she slid the dildo

into my snatch, the head hitting my clit dead on. "Why bother getting the lube when you can lubricate me the natural
way?" she said as she rammed into my clit over and over.

"Jesus," I said as my arms gave out and I propped myself on
my elbows. "Serena, I have to come now, please." I begged. I
rocked back and forth as my orgasm came. Serena pulled out
of me roughly.

"I told you not to come." Serena swatted me on my ass.
"Now I'm gonna have to fuck you twice as hard."

I held my breath when I felt her hands spreading my cheeks
and the lavender dildo circling my asshole. Ms. Serena wasn't
lying when she said she was going to fuck me hard. I felt my
ass expand as she entered my previously virgin hole. I bit
down on my lip to stop the scream that was trying to escape
my throat. I spread my thighs to allow Serena to enter me
deeper. My ass was burning as she pumped it without mercy.

"You like that, baby?" Serena hissed in my ear. I could feel
her small breasts mashed against my back as she squeezed my
nipples. When I didn't answer, Serena grabbed a handful of
my hair and yanked my head back.

"Answer me." Her voice was low and dangerously sexy.

"Yes," I whimpered.

"I didn't hear you." Serena slapped my ass. "Say it's good,
baby. Loud."

"It's good!" I panted. I pushed and ground my butt on the
dildo. It was damn good! I sucked in my breath as Serena
slid one, then another, and then another finger into my
cream-filled cunt. Her fingers roughly played with my
throbbing clit.

"Fuck me harder," I begged.

"Harder?" Serena's voice was teasing. "You like me fucking

your juicy ass, don't you? Yeah, you do, 'cause you're a nasty little girl. A nasty little girl who needs to punished." My ear was dripping with her saliva as she sucked on the earlobe, telling me what a naughty girl I was. I was a nasty girl who needed her round, jiggly ass spanked."Only nasty girls leave the house with no panties."

Whap.

"Nasty girls walk down the street with their big titties bouncin' around."

Whap.

"Only a bad, nasty whore girl would be on her knees getting her ass and wet pussy fucked by a stranger."

Whap. Whap. Whap.

I came then. "Shit!" I cried out as my cunt exploded and my ass contracted around Serena's lavender dick. I felt like a wild stallion as I bucked and she pounded and slapped my sore butt. My tongue hung out of my mouth like a thirsty dog's as my back arched and Serena squeezed my breasts as she came. My knees gave out, and I collapsed onto the floor with my young seductress on top of me.

We lay there listening to each other's breathing. After a while, I felt Serena rise from me. I rolled onto my back and watched her slip out of the lavender dildo and harness. She tossed the toy in her locker. I pulled her small frame back on top of me. My mouth moved around across her full lips. I sucked on her tongue, my own tongue running over the small stud in her mouth. I ground my snatch against her short shorts. I was so wet I knew I would leave a wet spot on her cutoffs. I pulled my lips away from hers.

"Damn, girl. Who taught you to fuck like that?"

"The first woman I slept with," Serena nuzzled her head at

my breast. "She was around your age."

I squeezed that tight, round butt of hers and laughed.

So here I am now, hormones still rushing, butt-naked on my bed, and Cherrie's doing over time. I push Cherrie farther up my hole when I think of Serena and her stolen lavender dildo.

God Blessed Eva

Randi Oklevik Solberg

Eve gave Adam the apple!

As Eva walked up the hill, she could almost hear the voice of the old minister from her confirmation service 15 years ago. He had talked about sin and temptation. Eva had never gone back to that church.

She heard the bells ringing—*come, come, come*—with a heavy rhythm. She turned around and looked out at Oslo. From where she was standing, she could see the harbor of the Oslo fjord. White sails went in and out of the bay, boats taking people out to the many islands to swim and sunbathe. The right-angled U-shaped town hall overlooked the boat traffic. On one side of the bay stood a long wharf with a wild mixture of red bricks and glass buildings. Straight across from it was the fortress of Akershus. The thick castle walls had been there for centuries to protect the city from enemies. Eva loved to climb these walls, move close to the edges, and look down on the people passing by underneath.

It was a sunny, clear Sunday morning in early autumn, and Eva felt a chilly breeze coming in from the fjord. She got goose bumps on her arms, and she remembered where she was going. She pulled the jacket tighter around her.

Eve tempted Adam to eat!

The organ was already playing the prelude as she opened the heavy door to the red-brick church. A man smiled and nodded at her. He handed her a psalm book as she slid down on a bench in the back. In front of her were at least ten unoccupied benches. Here and there groups of old women sat with their hats and coats. A man and a woman were hushing their two giggling children who were pointing at an old man with a stick walking up to the second bench. It was just as Eva had remembered it. Nothing had changed. Only she had. The next moment the old minister would come out of the sacristy and repeat his words about fighting the lust of the flesh and keeping your path clean. Eva wondered why she had come. She didn't know; she had just felt like it. Maybe it had been a bad idea. Maybe it would have been better to go for a long hike in the woods around Oslo, maybe have a cup of tea and a piece of homemade bread at the Skjennung cottage. It was well-known for their bakery. Eva felt the taste of brown cheese melting on her tongue.

She stood up and was about to sneak out when she heard a voice through the microphone. It was a female voice with smile and laughter in it, but it had a comfortable dark tone. Eva turned around and saw a young woman wearing a black robe. She had not expected this. She grew curious. As the organist began the first psalm, she walked along the outside of the benches and found a place closer to the pulpit.

Eva looked around while the congregation sang and proceeded in the liturgy. The window paintings were new—bits of glass in red, blue, yellow, green, and purple. She recognized some of the Bible stories they illustrated; one was from the garden of Eden. She remembered the old minister's words: *And Adam ate the apple Eve had given to him!*

If only the minister had known, Eva thought. She was able to smile a secret little queer smile.

Eva saw the woman enter the pulpit. Dark brown hair, tucked behind her ears, reached halfway down her shoulders.

The woman's voice went straight into Eva's head, dancing inside. Eva could not catch the words, even though the minister spoke very clearly. Her tall, slim figure could be seen through her wide black robe. Eva watched her, saw how her lips moved, how she tilted her head a little to the left when she was speaking and then straightened it when she made a point. Her hands moved along on the edge of the pulpit, but Eva couldn't see them clearly. She wondered what it would be like to touch them. The woman was fully present, looking at each face as she spoke. Eva grew warm as the minister's eyes rested on her. The gaze stayed on her throughout the sermon.

"Church coffee in the congregation house," she had said. They were all invited. The house connected to the church room via a side door. Eva followed two women. She helped one of them up the one step into the room. The old woman smiled at Eva and asked her to sit with them. "It's so nice to see young people in the church," she said. "Do you come from this area?"

They sat at a table, and Eva told them about the years she had been away, how she had studied and worked in Bergen on the west coast of Norway, how she had come back from the beautiful harbor city surrounded by mountains. She spoke about the old part of Bergen with all the small, wooden houses, about the wharf, and about skiing in the mountains above the city. There was a lot she didn't tell.

While they were talking, she saw the minister move from one little group to another, sharing a word here and there. She got closer. Eva's hands grew sweaty. She hoped the minister would not shake her hand. The minister was carrying a basket, offering the churchgoers a taste of the first autumn fruit from the garden. She smiled as she gave Eva a big red apple. Eva looked into her dark brown eyes, and she recognized the unmistakable shivering. She felt the apple in her hand and couldn't help biting into it. It was as if the minister had picked it just for her. *God bless you, Adam. I really know how you felt,* Eva said to herself, as the sweet taste lingered on her tongue. The minister sat down at Eva's table and began making conversation with the women. Her eyes kept coming back to Eva, who felt her blood moving up and down throughout her body, uncontrollably, out of order. Holy mother, she was getting vibes in a totally wrong place this time.

Eva studied the minister's hand as it rested on the table: long, slim fingers but with visible strength. Looking at them made her dizzy. She had to stop thinking.

"Would you?"

Eva stared emptily as she realized the question was meant for her. The minister was looking directly at her; she had asked Eva something. She stood up and followed the minister into the church. The huge room was empty, but they both could hear the organist rehearsing. The minister explained that he was preparing for a concert. They walked to one of the church wings where two huge candles, taller than Eva, stood on holders.

"They are supposed to be in the sacristy," the minister said. "I'm really happy you can help me," she smiled and lifted one of the candles. Then she put it down again. "It's impossible to do anything with this big robe on. Will you help me loosen the collar so I can take it off?" She moved closer to Eva. Eva

swallowed and closed her eyes for a second before the minister
lifted her arms. The music sounded distant.

Eva looked into the minister's eyes as her hands were about
to touch the collar. Suddenly she heard a voice. The minister
turned around and saw an old man coming to say good-bye to
her. He gave her the psalm book he was carrying. He had
taken it with him by mistake, and now the rest of the psalm
books were taken away, he explained. The minister smiled at
him. They shook hands, and then the two women were left
alone. They looked at each other, neither of them saying a
word. The organ played on. Eva moved closer. The collar button was not visible, so she fumbled a little. She felt the woman
stiffen as her fingers accidentally touched the skin of her
throat. Eva saw her swallow. Eva lifted her eyes. They stood
still for a few moments, the air between them still. Eva could-
n't help it—she had to touch her cheek. With one finger she
followed the line of the woman's cheekbone and then moved
up to her eyebrows. The short hair tickled her finger. The
minister stared at her but didn't move. Eva followed the line
of her nose. She moved her finger along the woman's upper
lip. She felt the minister's warm breath on her finger and saw
the tip of the woman's tongue move slightly. Eva let her finger slide a little farther into the lip so that it touched the end
of her tongue. She felt it move toward her finger. A warm feeling swept through her, straight down her stomach. Their faces
were close now. She let her nose slide slowly against the
woman's nose and farther down. The minister turned her head
just a tiny bit, so that their cheeks moved toward each other.
They circled one another. Warm, soft, intense. Eva turned her
head back again, and this time her tongue hit the woman's
lips. She let it follow the outer rim of the lips before she

nipped them softly with her own. The minister's mouth opened slightly, and Eva seized the opportunity. Her tongue felt the wetness, and her knees grew weak. *God, what is happening? I am kissing the minister in the church!*

The thought flung through her, but she couldn't stop. Their bodies moved together. Eva started to undo the buttons at the top of the black robe when she remembered the organ music. Slowly she led the other woman farther back into the church, where she was sure they could not be seen. The minister was still holding on to the psalm book, her fingers white from the tight grip. Eva opened the robe. A short skirt showed tanned skin from high above the knees, and the skintight T-shirt had no chance of hiding the hard nipples that faced her. She looked at them. They were full and mature, ready to be taken. Carefully she touched one of the breasts, circling the darker area that pushed through the thin material. The minister closed her eyes and bent her head slightly backward. Eva kissed her revealed throat and let her finger touch the nipple. The minister gave a sound and pressed herself toward Eva's hand. Eva kissed her, and this time it was fully answered. Their tongues played eagerly, and Eva felt pressure on her hips. She spread the woman's legs with her own as their centers met. The music had risen. She heard a sound of something falling before she slowly pushed the other woman to the floor behind the last bench.

The organist had finished rehearsing and was about to close and lock the door to the side entrance. Before he reached the door, however, he slowly bent down and picked up a psalm book that lay half open on the floor. His face looked puzzled. He was so sure he had collected all of them before he had begun playing....

The Perfect Gift

Rhonda Jackson

I made a dreadful mistake a year ago. There it was, complete with ribbons, lying within easy reach of the birthday cake. My true love's wish list fulfilled. Within the wrappings was a blue box, which she opened with awe and amazement. She lifted the contents, tears rolling down her cheeks as she inserted the battery and felt its full vibrating throb. Her hands moved down to the hard shaft. Feeling its tapered tip, her eyes closed in ecstasy.

"Finally," she sighed, holding it close to her body. "A Makita drill of my own."

It was love at first sight. She became addicted to the erection of buildings. The hot throbbing of her drill screwing wood together, the joints tightly interlocked, gave her more pleasure than I ever could. Torquing screws became her life. I became a construction widow.

After building she would paint. Gently inserting the stirring stick into the paint can, she would sit, stirring, brushing the sides of the can softly until the paint became white and creamy. But it was the day that she slathered the cement for the basketball court in strong, rhythmic strokes, in ever smaller circles and whorls, that I realized just how much competition construction had become to my sex life. Her eyes glazed in pleasure as she licked her slightly opened lips, her body moving with the strokes of her evening stick.

She needs a new hobby, I thought. *I need her to have a new hobby.*

So I began to search for the perfect gift to launch her new creative endeavors and lead her back to me by the back route. What could it be? I didn't want something strenuous that would tire her out or something that would tax her patience or nerves. It had to fun but not sexy. Sexy was going to be me this time, not any damned old drill.

I thought of sewing, but that was too domestic, and it required inserting phallic instruments into soft, luxurious fabrics like velvet and satin. She would feel the smooth texture with her fingers. No, too erotic.

A bicycle! But days of riding and sliding on and off that lambskin seat...nope. We were not riding off into the sunset on bikes. I could tell that in advance. What to do? What to do?

Then I saw it. The perfect gift. A computer. She could write. That would take care of the creative energy, and I could come back to being her sex object again. Yes! Yes!

There it lay, complete with wrappings and ribbons in easy reach of the cake. She opened it and took the little laptop into her own lap. She threw the switch and felt its throbbing power. Her hands felt the smooth texture of the computer and the soft, clear mouse pad. Her eyes began to glaze over, and her breath came in little pants.

Damn! I chose the wrong gift again.

Love Child

Karen X. Tulchinsky

A blaring soft-drink commercial wakes me from deep sleep. I flail one arm out, searching for the snooze button. I pound it mercilessly. In the early morning quiet I fall back asleep.

"Nomi," my lover's voice calls out faintly in the distance as I struggle to consciousness. "Come on, babe. We have to get up."

I open one eye. Julie is sitting up in bed beside me. Her long black hair is loose, covering her breasts. I turn over, lay my head in her lap, and snuggle into her warmth.

"Come on, babe," she says. "I'm going to shower. You make tea."

"I've got a better idea." I reach up and cup one of her breasts. She moans softly, then pushes my hand away.

"We don't have time. Come on. We'll be late." She tosses the covers off both of us, gently pushes me off her lap, and crawls over me. I glance at the clock: 6:30. We're supposed to be at the clinic before 8, and it's a half-hour drive across town. I watch Julie leave the warmth of our bedroom, naked except for tiny black-lace panties that barely cover her beautiful ass.

Awake now, I get up and head for the kitchen. I make strong tea for both of us and take it into the bathroom. Julie is stepping out of the shower. Little beads of water glisten on her skin. I balance the tea on the edge of the sink and take her in my arms and kiss her. She throws her warm, wet arms around my neck, soaking my bathrobe. I move my hands down her back to her ass, which I cup. She sucks on my neck hard, pain mixing with pleasure. One of my hands finds its way around to her breasts. I rub one nipple, then the other. I pull her forward a few inches and attempt to push her to the floor. She breaks free of my mouth and pushes me away.

"Nomi," she says breathlessly, "we don't have time."

"Oh, right." I sigh, kiss her once more lightly, then release her, strip out of my damp robe, and jump into the shower. Back in the bedroom I throw on black jeans and a clean shirt. We are out of the house by 7:30. The sun has risen, but the cloud cover is so thick it is completely gray outside. A light rain falls.

In the car I reach over the stick shift and take Julie's hand. Our route is thankfully against morning rush-hour traffic, which is starting to build. Her hand is soft and small in mine. Three and a half years together, and I still feel like it's our first date. I raise her hand to my lips and kiss it.

"Hey, keep your eyes on the road, buster," she says, snatching her hand away.

I sulk, then reach over and lay my hand on her thigh. She is wearing a short black dress that exposes most of her legs. I stroke the inside of her thigh, glance at the clock on the dashboard, and silently wonder if there's enough time to pull over onto a side street and jump into the back seat.

"Forget it," she says.

"What?" I feign innocence.

"I know what you were thinking."

"What?" I repeat, glancing sideways, catching her eye.

She shakes her head. "I know you."

Oh, boy, does she ever. I keep my hand on her leg for the rest of the trip, only moving it off to shift gears and adjust the windshield wipers.

We arrive at the clinic on time, wave to the receptionist (who knows us by name), and take a seat in the waiting room, side by side on a tasteful green leather couch. As soon as we sit, my fierce desire for Julie rises again. It happens every time we come here.

Something about the fertility clinic waiting room makes me wildly horny. I suppose in a way it's fitting. We are here to make a baby. If we were heterosexual, making a baby would involve sex, even if it wasn't wild. The experience should feel clinical to me, given the process. But it doesn't. Sitting here beside Julie waiting for our appointment feels sexual. Without fail, every time we are here I get turned on. I inch my leg closer to Julie's and take her hand in mine. Desire floods through my body. I squeeze her hand harder. I imagine throwing her to the carpet, ripping off her clothes, and making love to her on the waiting-room floor while the lab technician defrosts the sperm we will use to inseminate Julie. Right in front of the other clients who sit patiently flipping though child-rearing magazines and infertility pamphlets, I would take my lover. In my fantasy Julie comes just as the technician hands me the syringe full of sperm, and I use it to penetrate Julie. I want to create our baby in love. My deepest regret is that we have to come here at all, that we can't just stay home and make love to get pregnant.

Julie and I are famous at the fertility clinic. We are the first lesbian couple to use the newly opened facility. The waiting room is filled with heterosexuals with fertility problems. Our only fertility problem is lack of sperm. Some of the heterosexuals openly stare at us. Others glance surreptitiously over their *People* magazines. I wave. Sometimes I stand, hold out my hand, and introduce myself. Other times I strike up a conversation.

"So, you have a low sperm count?" I once said to a balding, middle-aged man.

"What?" he sputtered.

"Isn't that why you're here?"

All eyes in the waiting room were on him. He cursed me under his breath, covered his reddened face with a brochure titled "Infertility in Men," and stayed behind the leaflet until his name was called.

I don't do it to be mean. It's just hard to be stared at constantly. As if we don't have as much right to be here.

The clinic staff have been kind to us. Even though we are a novelty, most of the nurses understand to treat us like a couple. Our favorite nurse, Wendy, has gone out of her way to make us feel welcome, always making sure there is a chair for me in the room, looking us both in the eye, calling us "dear" and "sweetheart." When being here is the most difficult, I take a deep breath and remember it's a means to a goal.

In the waiting room, Julie grabs a magazine and sits beside me on the love seat. We glance at an article together, holding hands as we usually do. Fifteen minutes later we are still waiting. I knew we had time for a quickie by the side of the road. I go over the fantasy in my mind: I hang a quick left, and we duck out of rush-hour traffic down a tree-lined residential street, find a dead end, and park under a large oak tree. Rain pounds on the roof. I park the car, reach over, and pull Julie onto my lap. I can feel the heat from her already wet cunt on my thighs. I run my fingers through her long black hair. She bends forward and plants her full, lipstick-red lips on mine. Hungrily, as if we had been apart for months, we kiss, and her tongue explores the inside of my mouth. She moans softly. The windows fog up. Her hands caress the sides of my face. I put my hands around her waist and slowly slide them up to her breasts. She is wearing her black lace bra. My favorite. It's a push-up bra that lifts her perfect breasts up so that they spill out over the top of the fabric. I unbutton the front of her dress and bury my face in her cleavage. I can smell her perfume. I suck on one nipple right through the material. I feel it harden. She moans. I slide my tongue underneath the bra and take her nipple in my mouth. My hands around the small of her back, I pull her closer. She rocks slowly on top of me. My other hand creeps silently under her skirt, up her thigh.

"Julie Sakamoto." Someone calls out my lover's name, breaking into my daydream. It's Wendy, the nurse we like. Julie squeezes my hand. We stand and follow Wendy down the long hallway and into the insemination room.

"The technician is preparing the sperm. Why don't you get changed. I'll be back in ten minutes."

She leaves us alone in the small room. There is an examination table, the kind with stirrups, a nurse's desk with plastic syringes, tubing, paper smocks, and other medical equipment. On the wall is a diagram of a woman's reproductive system, beside it is a poster explaining contraceptive techniques, and beside that a notice about the clinic's "insufficient funds" check policy. On the ceiling above the examination table is a picture of an extremely cute kitten to relax the patient. There is no chair for me, only the stool for the nurse. Julie reaches for a paper smock and begins to undress. I grab her around the waist and kiss her, turned-on from my fantasy, from the drive over, from imagining her luscious body half naked. She responds, throwing her arms around my neck and kissing me back. I ease her toward the table, with every intention of throwing her down, jumping on top, and fucking her right there in the insemination room. What the heck? The nurse said she'd be ten minutes. Plenty of time, considering our lustful state. Julie pulls back and puts a hand on my chest.

"Nomi, stop," she is laughing. "We can't."

I move forward, pull her close again. "Sure we can. Just a quickie." I attempt to push her onto the table.

"No," she says firmly.

"But, babe. Maybe it would help you get pregnant. If you're relaxed in a postorgasmic state, maybe the sperm would find its way to your egg easier."

"Nice try," she turns her back to me and slips out of her dress. It falls to the floor in a heap, giving me a front-row view of her luscious ass, her curvaceous hips. She gets into the gown and ties the paper belt around her waist. Even this looks sexy on Julie. I help her onto the table, where she lies back. I adjust the small pillow behind her head, hold her hand. I bend forward and kiss her gently on the lips. She kisses me back. I straighten up, behaving myself, hold her hand, and we wait.

A few minutes later there is a light knock at the door as it swings open.

"All ready?" Wendy, enters the room with a clipboard and a small vial.

Julie glares at me. *See?* she is saying with her eyes. *We didn't have time.* I shrug sheepishly.

"OK, Julie," Wendy says, "can you scoot down a bit…a bit more…just a bit more…good. And your feet…that's right." Julie moves down, puts her feet in the stirrups. I stand in my position, beside the table, squeezing her hand. Her almond-brown eyes sparkle at me, love flowing. This is our fifth try. I have a good feeling, like this is going to be it.

"This should be warm," Wendy pulls a stainless steel speculum from a heated drawer beneath the table and holds it up. "OK?"

Julie nods. Wendy expertly slips the speculum in place. She reaches for the small vial of sperm and asks me to check the number to make sure it is the right one. Number 9326L. Correct. We picked 9326L out of a huge binder of potential donors. There are five pages on each guy, numbered only, no names or other identifying notes. We wanted a Jewish donor, short, with brown hair and brown eyes. It wasn't hard to narrow down. In Vancouver's sperm bank, out of 100 donors, seven were Jewish.

"I want the donor to be like you," Julie had insisted. I thought she would want a Japanese donor so the baby would be like her. "We're doing this together," she persisted.

Wendy injects the sperm into a plastic syringe and inserts it into Julie. When it is ready, she moves out of position so I can push the plunger. I stand in place and look my lover deeply in the eye. She nods. Slowly I push the sperm inside her, concentrating on fielding all my love and desire out through my thumb. I pause for a moment. Julie's eyes are locked on mine. Love child. This will be a love child. Even though it is conceived in the cold medical atmosphere of a clinic, our love will be the power to bring the baby's spirit to us. I feel it deep in my belly and send it out into my lover's womb through my thumb. Julie shivers. I think she feels it. I hold her eye for a moment longer, then move out of the way. Wendy removes the syringe, puts everything away, and pats Julie on the leg.

"Good luck. I'll leave you two alone here for a while. No hurry. There's no one scheduled in this room until 9:30."

I glance at my watch as Wendy leaves the room: 9 o'clock. We have half an hour. I give Julie a lusty look.

She matches it with a lusty look of her own.

I pull a step stool from under the table and climb to the second step and onto the edge of the table beside Julie.

"Nomi…" she warns.

I cover her mouth with mine before she can say too much or think too much. I kiss her passionately. She throws her arms around my neck and kisses me back. I lean over her and stretch my legs out so that I am lying on top of her on the examination table. The full length of my body is against hers. She pulls away.

"Do you think this is OK? I mean, what if the sperm falls out…."

"I don't think it can just fall out. Remember what Wendy said. The long syringe shoots it right past your cervix into your uterus."

"Oh, yeah."

"So shut up and kiss me."

"What if she comes back?"

"She won't. Not for 20 minutes at least." I put my lips back onto Julie's. We kiss feverishly. She runs her fingers through my short hair. I tear at the paper gown, exposing her breasts, and bury my face in them. In my fantasy about fucking in the car, this is where we had left off. Her fingers in my hair. My face in her cleavage. The memory floods me; desire pumps through my body. I move my hands onto Julie's breasts. Her nipples are hard. She pulls me tighter to her. I tear the paper gown more and take her nipple in my mouth, sucking greedily. She moans underneath me, takes my face in her hands, pulls me closer. I stroke her other nipple with one hand. She moves her hips, thrusting her cunt into my body.

"Oh, god. Touch me, babe," she begs.

And I do. There on the examination table, I plunge my fingers deep inside my lover's cunt. She is wet and ready for me. Above us on the wall the woman's reproductive organs diagram looms. I thrust my fingers in and out, jostling the table. The drawer full of stainless steel speculums clatters underneath us. The paper on the table rips. I push my thumb against her swollen clit. She pushes against my hand.

"Uh-huh," she says, "that's good. Oh."

The scent of her sex is in the air. I breathe deeply as I move in and out, pushing and sliding. Fully clothed, I pump my crotch against her leg. Her hands around my ass, she pulls me to her tighter. I imagine we are calling forth our baby from the spirit world, through the power of our love, our desire. I move faster. I tear the gown apart with my teeth to get at her nipple and take it in my mouth as Julie begins to come. Loudly. I move back up and plant my lips on hers to muffle her sounds—my lover has an awesome set of lungs, and we're famous enough at the clinic as it is. Her clit throbs against my thumb as I rub myself harder against her thigh. My orgasm threatens to rival hers. As I come I stifle the urge to cry out. The door opens a crack. I am face to face with Wendy, her eyes wide. We stare at each other for a heartbeat. Then she looks down at the floor and closes the door quietly. I say nothing, close my eyes, collapse on top of Julie, and lie still while we catch our breath. Gently she runs her fingers through my hair.

"Come on, babe." She nudges me a minute later. "Get up. Wendy will be back."

"Oh, right." I kiss her one more time, slide off, and hop down, adjusting my clothes, just as we hear a knock on the door. This time it does not immediately swing open. Julie pulls the ripped gown closed, trying to hide the torn parts.

"Come in," I say.

The door opens slowly, cautiously. Wendy enters, clipboard tight against her chest. A strained smile is plastered tightly on her face.

"How's everything going in here?" She stares at her clipboard.

"Coming along nicely," I answer.

Julie gives me a look. "I'll just get dressed," she says.

"I've scheduled you in for a blood test in ten days. OK? Let's cross our fingers." Wendy fiddles with some mysterious fertility equipment on the nurse's desk, then turns and leaves the room.

"Were we loud? Did she hear us?" Julie asks.

"I don't think so, babe," I lie. "Come on, let's get out of here. I want you in my bed."

Julie hits me playfully on the chest. "Don't you ever get enough?"

"Of you, babe? Never."

Minutes later, Julie and I walk down the hall hand in hand, past the waiting room full of other anxious couples, past the pregnancy pamphlets and the racks of parenting magazines, and out into the wet morning.

With some jazz

Juliet Crichton

the sensibility of the first time
I know another's smell, another's
fingertips, another's weight centered

at the swells of my hips, the something in jazz about not guessing
the next note, the next key change,

the next time, the unrehearsed, the
same something in sex that eludes
the inevitable when the music wraps

your legs within mine, my breasts go
flat against your chest & breathless
I palm the loud floor of being.

About the Contributors

Sonia Abel is a 28-year-old writer and visual artist of Scotch-Irish and Native-American descent living in Asheville, N.C. She has contributed poetry to literary anthologies and a story to the lesbian anthology *Beginnings*.

Wendy Caster, a Jewish author living in Brooklyn, wrote *The Lesbian Sex Book*. Her stories have appeared in *Bushfire, Heatwave, Lesbian Bedtime Stories, Cats (and Their Dykes),* and *Silver-tongued Sapphistry*. She has published more than 300 opinion columns in the lesbian and gay press.

Juliet Crichton, a native Virginian, teaches English and creative writing at Old Dominion University and Tidewater Community College, where she coedits *BlackWater Review*. A two-time recipient of George Mason University's Klappert/Ai Poetry Prize, she has published poetry in *Sequoia, Hayden's Ferry Review, Hampden-Sydney Poetry Review, The Higginsville Reader, Argestes, The Amaranth Review,* and *The Prose Poem*. She is seeking a publisher for her manuscript of poems, *The Rain Shapes*.

Ouida Crozier, a Southerner by birth and acculturation, has lived in Minnesota since 1981. She is the author of published poetry, essays, and fiction.

M. Damian lives in Staten Island, N.Y. She has finally found her one true love, Amy, and they are busy planning their future together. She has been fortunate enough to have had one of her stories mentioned in *Diva,* a lesbian magazine published in England.

MR Daniel is an African-American spoken-word performer living in Northern California. She is finishing her doctorate in independent film and video studies.

Carla Díaz, a 28-year-old Puerto-Rican lesbian, resides in Miami, where she is an editorial administrator for the *New Times* newspaper as well as a freelance journalist.

Kate Dominic has a story included in *Herotica* 6 and received honorable mention in *Libido* magazine's third annual fiction contest.

Amie M. Evans is a white girl, confirmed femme bottom, postmodern slut who lives life as a spontaneous, choreographed piece of performance art.

Nancy Ferreyra is a disabled lesbian who lives in Berkeley, Calif. To date, she has had one erotic short story published, "After Amelia," in *Herotica* 6.

Connie Fox is the author of nine volumes and a play, including *Blood Cocoon, The Dream of the Black Topaze Chamber,* and *Entre Nous.*

Rhonda Jackson, a cream-colored librarian-historian, milks cows for a living. She lives with her jill-of-all-trades partner, Rabbit, in a house perennially under construction.

Myra E. LaVenue writes multimedia training and Web pages in Portland, Ore. She has published poems in *Los Angeles Girl Guide* and short stories in the Alyson Publications anthologies *Early Embraces* and *Awakening the Virgin.*

Catherine Lundoff is a 35-year-old Euro-American who lives in Minneapolis with her girlfriend. Her writings have appeared in various places, including *Pillow Talk* and *XOddity.*

Nilaja Montgomery-Akalu is an African-American lesbian who is over 18 but under 25. Currently an English and film student, she lives in the San Francisco Bay Area.

Merril Mushroom is an old, myopic, arthritic, Ashkenazi Jewish butch who has relocated to the rural South.

Nyondo Nadi, an African-American woman, lives the tarantula life in San Francisco with two wives, five cats, and way too many computers. This is her first published piece.

Lana Pacheco is a Puerto-Rican writer who has until very recently never made an attempt at being published. She resides in Brooklyn, N.Y.

Caitlyn Marie Poland was born in Liverpool, England, and has a degree in sociology-psychology. She is currently a qualified social worker and enjoys playing guitar and writing songs.

Danya Ruttenberg is a nice Jewish girl living in frisky San Francisco. She writes about sex, art, and religion and hopes someday to start a minor cult in Bora Bora.

Robin St. John has two children and a cat. **Sandra Hayes** also has a cat and three grandchildren.

M.N. Schoeman, 34, comes from South Africa, where she works as an adult educator. As a lesbian activist, she was the convener of the KwaZulu-Natal Coalition for Gay and Lesbian Equality. She has worked in townships and rural areas and is currently living in Nelspruit.

Anne Seale creates lesbian songs, stories and plays. Her stories have appeared in *Pillow Talk, Love Shook My Heart, Hot and Bothered, Ex-lover Weird Shit,* and *The Ghost of Carmen Miranda and Other Spooky Gay and Lesbian Tales.* She shares her time between New York and Arizona and is of German heritage.

Ginger Simon reads for pleasure and survival. "Finally, I'm freeing myself to write for the same reasons," she says.

Randi Oklevik Solberg, born in Norway, has a master's degree in international management as well as eight years' experience in management and marketing at a Norwegian life insurance company. A journalist, she is on sabbatical in New York doing creative writing.

Isadora Stern is a power-femme Jewish dyke as well as a writer, performer, and visual artist. She is getting her master's degree in art therapy.

Jeannie Sullivan lives in central California with her partner, their family, and a menagerie of pets. Her loves include writing lesbian fiction and erotica.

Renette Toliver, an African-American woman, has been writing for 10 years. She lives in Dallas, Tex.

Karen X. Tulchinsky is the award-winning author of the novel *Love Ruins Everything* and *In Her Nature,* a collection of short stories. She has edited eight anthologies, including *Hot & Bothered: Short Short Fiction on Lesbian Desire, To Be Continued,* and *Friday the Rabbit Wore Lace: Jewish Lesbian Erotica.* She lives in Vancouver.

Sarah Van Arsdale's first novel, *Toward Amnesia*, was published by Riverhead Books/Putnam. She is finishing a third novel and writes frequently for *San Francisco Magazine.* She teaches at the University of Vermont and Vermont College.